# BOARDING WITH MURDER

# BOARDING WITH MURDER

A Sierra Pines B&B Mystery

Kathryn Long

Kenmore, WA

CAMEL
PRESS

A Camel Press book published by Epicenter Press

Epicenter Press
6524 NE 181st St.
Suite 2
Kenmore, WA 98028

For more information go to:
www.Camelpress.com
www.Coffeetownpress.com
www.Epicenterpress.com
www.kathrynlongauthor.com



Cover design by Scott Book
Design by Melissa Vail Coffman



ISBN: 978-1-60381-730-1 (Trade Paper)
ISBN: 978-1-60381-733-2 (eBook)

Printed in the United States of America

*To my mom, Mary Schake,*
*who nurtured my love of classic movies.*

# ACKNOWLEDGMENTS

MY FAVORITE STAR FROM THE CLASSICS is Cary Grant. *Arsenic and Old Lace* is one of my absolute favorite movies where Grant shines with both comedic and romantic talent. The Bellwether siblings in my book were inspired by the Brewster sisters from the movie with all their eccentric behavior and devotion to one another. The movie definitely contributed to my ideas.

If you research prop design and the women in them, you might not find very much information. However, interestingly enough, property-woman, as the role was termed in stage theater, goes back a couple of centuries—early nineteenth to the first part of the twentieth century. As tribute to the under-represented females in the film industry, I chose to make both Julia and Alexis prop designers, rather than giving them more gender-traditional roles.

The vast of amount of movie references, facts about the Tahoe region, and other details came from research online and from books. However, I want to give a special thanks to a dear fan, Theresa Atashkar from Folsom, California. She helped me tremendously with so many details about this area of Northern California that I couldn't possibly find in books. Thank you.

Without the patience and encouragement of my family and friends I could never write a single page. And my author pals—Julie, Jane, Cari, Wendy, and Shellie, you inspire me.

Of course, none of this journey would have been possible without my fantastic agent, Dawn Dowdle. You are my rock through all this. Thank you for believing in my work. And my editor at Camel Press, Jennifer

McCord, you put me on the right path and gave me very helpful advice to make this a great series. Thank you for your guidance and patience.

Finally, to all the wonderful cozy mystery readers! Your love of this genre helps keep writers inspired. Thank you.

# CHAPTER ONE

When interoffice mail delivered my pink slip, I cried and remained an emotional wreck for days. My parents smothered me with "there-theres" and useless but well-intended advice, while my go-to person, Great-Aunt Julia, repeated one of her maxims. "Count the signs, sweetie. If you get to three, bad luck might be in the cards."

I wasn't a superstitious person. Not at all, but it was understandable why people in my family were. We were a history of theater people. Actors, prop designers, costume designers, screenwriters, playwriters, makeup crew, cameramen—it was a very long list. Theater people were typically dramatic, imaginative, and superstitious. Some might consider these traits as a stereotype. However, my view was to take each situation in life as it came. Sometimes, the signs weren't signs, and sometimes, well, let's leave it at that.

At the top of the next grade, the dense woods cleared a bit. I smiled as rooftops of stores on Sierra Pine's Main Street came into view. While cruising through the first intersection, I considered my career options for the umpteenth time—how life was so unfair, and what did I do to deserve this—when a dark, blurry blob sprang into the street. I stomped on the brake pedal of my SUV rental, tires screeching, and barely missed the cat as it sauntered across the road. A black cat. My hands gripped the steering wheel as I leaned closer to the windshield and squinted. Not completely black. It had white paws and a white chest. Maybe this was one of those nothing-to-worry-about moments. Then again, if I was to believe such a thing . . . I shook my head as one black tail swished in the air and the jay-walking kitty stepped into Lucinda's Beauty Parlor.

I rubbed to soothe the knots in my neck. After leaving New York's LaGuardia Airport this morning and flying for hours to reach Sacramento International Airport, I was exhausted. Adding to that was the hour-long drive to town. I struggled to keep my eyes open. In another block, I'd reach my destination, Sierra Pines B&B and a much-needed visit with Aunt Julia and the Bellwethers. I chuckled. If I told them about the cat, they'd fuss and might want to do something hokey like hold a séance or perform an exorcism to banish any bad omens. Maybe I'd not mention it. Why ruin a perfectly fine reunion? It had been a year since my last visit. We had a ton to catch up on, and, right now, I ached for any conversation that didn't include the words pink slip.

Sunlight burst from behind a cloud and played its beam across the pavement. Fallen autumn leaves in rustic colors splashed along the sidewalk, giving the scene a warm glow. In the distance, the snow-capped peaks of the Sierra Nevada mountains outlined a majestic background. I loved the town and the quaint shops, with their scalloped canopies and clever names like Bagels and Buns and Meeka's Mementos, all nestled together in three short blocks. The people were kind here. They always had nice things to say. This slow-paced, easygoing atmosphere gave me peace.

In the next block, at the top of Englewood Boulevard, sat the Victorian house Julia called home. Built in the late nineteenth century, the architectural structure was one of only a handful left standing between Placerville and Sierra Pines and had been designated as a historical sight. Robin's egg blue siding and yellow shudders gave the structure a cheery, welcoming appearance. It was quaint. It was cozy. It was the perfect house for a B&B with three stories and numerous bedrooms to accommodate guests. However, as I inched up the drive, I blinked and, after a second, rubbed the windshield glass as if it wasn't already clear. "What in the world?" The window shades were drawn partway, like flags at half-mast, which was unusual for midday. However, more disconcerting to me was the person who stood on the porch. Gladys Bellwether, Julia's nearest and dearest friend, was covered head to toe in black, from the lacey veil resting on top of her head down to the stockings covering her legs. I chewed on my bottom lip while I digested what was wrong with this picture. The pink slip, the black cat, and now this. What could it mean? Yeah, bad luck might be in the cards.

I pulled my suitcase out of the trunk, slung my purse over one shoulder, and marched down the sidewalk. Only one way to find out.

I reached the porch and gazed at Gladys's face. Her eyes were welled with tears.

"Gladys?"

"Oh, Alexis. It's horrible, just horrible. I'm struggling to accept it." Her head shook. "I'm so very sorry. There's no other way to tell you, but your aunt is no longer with us."

I blinked. I stared at Gladys's black dress and the veil draped across her head. My heartbeat quickened. "What do you mean?" Julia knew I was coming. Leaving made no sense. Right?

"What I mean is, Julia is gone. She's passed on, dear." Gladys sniffed as her chin trembled. "Our sweet Julia has left us forever."

My knees weakened. I dropped the suitcase and sat on the wicker settee, forcing air into my lungs.

Gladys nestled alongside me. Her hand covered mine and squeezed. "It's a bit chilly. Why don't we go inside? I'll put on another pot of coffee. Then I need to make more phone calls. There's much left to prepare before the funeral."

I followed her through the doorway and into the foyer, all thoughts about a pleasant reunion forgotten.

I weaved my way through the crowded B&B parlor to reach Gladys and Ollie, who stood near the fireplace. Rather than use the church reception hall for Julia's wake, everyone was invited to Sierra Pines B&B. My memory of the morning and the funeral service were a total blur. I'd barely had any time to adjust to the tragic news the Bellwethers gave me when I arrived. Hard to believe that was only two days ago. However, I'd kept busy, latching onto any household task—preparing welcome baskets filled with soaps, shampoo, lotion, and packets of cocoa mix for each guest, assisting Gladys with breakfast, dusting, and sweeping. Still, Julia's sweet laughter echoed in my head, along with her soft attentive voice.

I gave the Bellwethers hugs and kisses. Leaning back, I attempted to smile. These siblings couldn't be more different in appearance. Gladys was tiny, but she had such a big heart. I stood at barely five feet four inches, but the top of her head could easily fit under my chin, and one of my thighs had to be bigger around than her waist. Ollie, on the other hand, reached nearly six feet and an obvious paunch expanded his midriff. Brown liver spots and wrinkles textured his skin and bald head.

Gladys's finger twirled as she wound a lose thread from her sleeve around it. The dark dress she wore contrasted with her ghostly pale skin. My attention wavered as I gazed beyond her at the crowd of mourners with their somber faces. They nodded and talked in soft voices. Somehow, this entire scene felt surreal. I turned back to her. "How are you holding up?"

Gladys let go of the thread, and smoothed the untidy wisps of gray hair curling at the sides as she nodded and smiled. Her faded blue eyes were rimmed with sadness. "I still can't believe it. My dearest friend in the world is dead, and I didn't get the chance to say goodbye." Her shoulders heaved with one sob after another.

Ollie brushed cookie crumbs off his suit and wrapped his arm around his sister's shoulders. "I'm sure she knew how much all of us loved her."

Gladys dabbed her eyes with a hanky. "Alexis, I'm so very sorry. Her passing happened so quickly, soon after you and Julia spoke. I was about to call you, but Ollie said you'd already be on your way here. They don't allow you to take calls while in flight, do they? Oh, my. I've handled the situation completely wrong. It's just . . . finding her that way, we were in shock, you know."

I squeezed her hand. "Don't worry. I'm here, now. And I'm helping in any way I can." These were Julia's people. Kind, gracious, and devoted friends, her dearest friends, who'd let me down gently as they told me the tragic news. I didn't have the heart to ask for details, not in this moment, but the words *finding her that way* puzzled me.

"Oh! There's Sheriff Sterling. We should speak with him, Ollie." Gladys shrugged off his arm and stepped into the crowd when someone blocked her path.

"Gladys, sweetheart. How are you doing? This is such a tragedy. I still can't believe she's gone." Florence Greeley pulled Gladys into a hug, crushing her face into her ample bosom.

"Perfect." Ollie mumbled between bites of another cookie.

I pressed my lips together. Ollie's opinion of Florence was never a secret. He tolerated her, at best. However, I knew Ollie was a softy. Despite his gripes, he considered her a friend.

Florence Greeley was the president of the Sierra Pines Alliance of Cultural Activities, otherwise known as SPACA, and the town's most worthy Samaritan, which gave her a bit of an inflated ego and a large dose of self-importance, but underneath there lay a good heart. She carried a convoluted mixture of personalities with her at all times. She was kind and friendly but nosy and dramatic. She entered a room with the intensity of a thunderstorm, and no one could escape her.

"The service was so touching. I'm sure Julia loved it." Florence gave Gladys a final squeeze and then took me in her grasp. "My poor Ali. So sad to lose a family member. Speaking of family, where are Willa and Robert?"

"Mom and Dad wanted to come, but they have a television appearance this evening, you see. National coverage for their play. It's been planned for weeks." I tugged to release myself from her grasp.

"Oh? How wonderful for them. Broadway couldn't find two greater talents." Florence finally let go. She paused to stare at me. "And what about you? How is New York treating you?"

"I, you know, New York is a busy place, always something to keep me on the go." I shrugged and smiled. The topic of job loss didn't seem suited for a funeral wake.

"Well, if you get homesick for some of those on-the-go moments, you should come visit the movie set while you're here."

"Maybe I will. Not sure how long I'll be—"

"You know, the service was so touching. I'm sure Julia would have loved it." Gladys cut me off.

"Yes, indeed. Pastor Bob always delivers." Ollie snatched a bacon roll-up off his plate and popped it in his mouth.

Florence nodded. "Everything was perfect. I don't know how you managed with so little time."

"Julia made arrangements for her funeral long ago. It's what we older folks do," Gladys said.

"Yes, we do. Isn't that right, Florence?" Ollie glimpsed at me and winked.

Florence arrowed her penciled brows skyward. "Humph. Don't include me in your little geriatric club. I'm barely in my fifties."

"Uh, huh. Sure," Ollie mumbled through bites of pasta. "Been singing that tune for years."

"The buffet is certainly a hit." Shifting the conversation to a safer topic, I chuckled while eying Ollie's heaping plate.

Delicious aromas wafted from the kitchen. Warming pans filled with roast beef, ham, Italian pasta dishes, and a medley of vegetable casseroles were lined up on the counters, along with so many desserts I'd lost count. A steady queue of guests with their plates filled kept streaming into the parlor.

Ollie tapped Gladys on the shoulder. "Well, well. Look who decided to attend."

"Oh, I see all right, but we couldn't stop him from coming, could we? No matter what we think of the man, he has a right to be here. He was Julia's friend." Gladys clenched her jaw as she fixed her gaze on the doorway, along with Ollie's and Florence's.

I turned my head to follow. An elderly gentleman with receding gray hair and a pencil-thin frame shook hands with Pastor Bob and then worked his way through the crowd, shaking hands and talking to several guests. He made eye contact with us for a brief moment, nodded, and smiled but then circled around the parlor in the opposite direction from where we stood.

"All I can say is he has some nerve, after all that has happened." Gladys pursed her lips.

"Let's not start up again." Ollie muffled words between bites of pasta. "The walls have too many ears."

"Too many ears? What are you babbling about?" Florence's forehead wrinkled with concern.

"It's nothing." Gladys patted her arm. "Ollie hates to hear me talk. That's all."

"That's not it, but like I said, let's leave it be for now." He swiped his lips with a napkin.

"Now that I'm completely confused, I think I'll go mingle with the guests. I see our movie director, Mr. O'Neil, coming out of the kitchen. Talk to you all, later." Florence waved an arm and clip-clopped on her heels across the room.

I shifted my gaze to the Bellwethers. "So, who is this man you're unhappy to see?"

"Thaddeus Beale, a scoundrel and a shady Don Juan who flirted with our sweet Julia." Ollie's ample chin jiggled as he wagged his head.

"He's an old associate of ours and fellow actor, who always boasts about his career, which is nothing special, in my opinion. A small part in O'Neil's movie is the reason he's in Sierra Pines," Gladys added.

I searched my memory for the name Thaddeus but didn't recall Julia mentioning him. She'd spoken of Cary and Errol and William, who were stars from her glamor days, Lenny Taylor, her friend from Bagels and Buns, and a few other residents and business owners from Sierra Pines. Never a Thaddeus.

"He's terribly sure of his talent, though, and quite the ladies' man." Gladys nodded.

"Ladies' man?" Ollie snorted. "More of a scalawag. Can't be trusted, that one."

"Which is hardly the issue." Gladys tapped my arm. "You see, Alexis, Ollie and I think Thaddeus might have—"

Her words cut off as a taller than average man with broad shoulders and a receding hairline approached. "Quite a wonderful turnout, wouldn't you say?" A generous smile stretched his lips to display perfectly straight teeth. He nodded at Gladys and Ollie then extended a hand to me. "Sorry, we haven't had the chance to meet until now. I've been on a short business trip the past two days. Ralph Emory. Squaw Valley. Co-owner of Emory and Treadwater Winter Apparel Boutique. And you must be Julia's great-niece, Alexis." He cleared his throat. "My deepest sympathy for your loss."

"Yes. Thank you, but please call me Ali. Gladys told me you'd be returning to the B&B today. Winter apparel, huh? Squaw Valley must give you plenty of business."

"Indeed, it is a popular hub for skiing, snowboarding, tobogganing, and bobsledding. My husband and I opened the business ten years ago. We have the one shop and are ready to open a second. Sierra Pines would attract plenty of customers. I've been spending lots of my time here canvassing the area and talking to folks. Very friendly. Very busy." Ralph dropped my hand and blushed. "Excuse me. I tend to get over enthused when talking shop. Do you ski, Ali?"

I shook my head. "I've never tried. Blame it on my fear of heights. Ski lifts are scary places."

"If you ever decide to visit Squaw Valley, I promise to help you cure that fear."

"Ralph, we were telling Alexis about Mr. Beale," Gladys said.

"The actor friend who comes to visit several times a week." Ralph nodded. "That man certainly knows his theater. No matter which Shakespeare play I mention, he can recite lines for it. He acts out the scene, too. His King Lear is perfect."

"Where is your plate, Ralph?" Gladys smiled sweetly.

"I had a late breakfast with a potential client. You've put together a wonderful spread and it's very tempting, but I need to watch my figure." He patted his stomach and winked at me. "So, you're from New York? I hear it's the place to visit."

"If you like theater, restaurants, and smothering crowds, it's the perfect place." My smile wavered. Thinking of home made me anxious.

I'd lost my job. Twice. First, as a screenwriter, and then a few years later, as an assistant researcher for a TV show that, according to the network, needed a boost in ratings. Their solution? Become trendy with the younger audience. They hired a team of fresh-out-of-college grads to write the scripts, which left room in their budget for one researcher. Number one stayed, and I cleared my desk. Now, at twenty-eight, I was back on the street and in need of a do-over.

The job loss, followed by listening to well-meaning advice from my parents on how to fix my problems, had set me on edge. As they said, nothing to lose and everything to gain. After hearing Julia's invitation, it took only a New York minute to decide my next move. I bought a ticket and packed my bag, longing for the peace and quiet in Sierra Pines.

My attention strayed away from them to the wall, where a map of the town hung, an oil painting presented to Julia's mother by the city council in 1920 for her contributions to the arts. At the bottom, a caption with old-fashioned swirly black letters read: *Sierra Pines—founded in 1852.* A cozy town nestled in the California Sierra Nevada Mountains. What wasn't to love?

"If you'll excuse me, I have a business dinner with a client this evening and lots of paperwork to finish," Ralph said.

"Thank you for making an appearance. Julia would've appreciated such kindness." Gladys's voice hitched.

"My pleasure. Even though the time was brief, I enjoyed spending it with her. See you all at breakfast." Ralph nodded and walked away.

"Here you are. I've been working my way over, but so many folks wanted to talk."

"Mr. Fenworthy. We're so glad you could make it," Gladys greeted.

I studied Fenworthy as he and Gladys embraced. Fashionably dressed, he wore a navy blue, tailored three-piece suit, complete with a silk necktie. His short, dark hair was neatly cut and matched the professional look.

"You're a vision of beauty, Gladys." Mr. Fenworthy smiled at her then slapped Ollie on the back. "Bellwether, you look old and cranky as ever."

Ollie laughed. "Ali, this is Sal Fenworthy. He's Julia's lawyer. In fact, he's everyone's lawyer. Isn't that right, Sal?"

"Everyone's in Sierra Pines, yes, which is why I need to speak with you." He turned and settled his attention on me. "Especially you, Alexis. It's about your aunt's will."

My breath caught. The will. If any of us had been in denial about Julia's passing, mentioning her will put a lid on it.

Fenworthy took me aside and lowered his voice. "Let's say we meet in my office tomorrow afternoon at one, if it's convenient? I don't mean to rush, but I'd like to take care of the matter as soon as possible. The wife and I are attending a family reunion upstate. We're leaving first thing the morning after and won't be back for a couple weeks."

"I, of course. I'll be there." My voice strained.

Fenworthy turned. "Ollie and Gladys, you're invited to attend as well. Julia left specific instructions which include you."

As Fenworthy disappeared, Gladys gazed at me then at Ollie. "Well, what do you think about that?"

I shrugged. I'd enjoyed every visit with Julia. We'd gotten along well and had much in common. In fact, after shadowing her one summer during a Sierra Pines theater production, my career interests changed. I'd been mesmerized watching her create scenery props out of things as simple as Styrofoam. All because of her influence, I enrolled in a dual major—screenwriting and art design. The fact was, I had no idea what to expect from the reading of the will.

"Think about it. Julia never married, had no children of her own. You were like a daughter to her." Ollie lightly patted my hand.

"It's true, Alexis. You might not know it, but she spoke of you nearly every day." Gladys scanned the room once more. "I guess he's left already. Perhaps we can take the time to stop in tomorrow after we see Mr. Fenworthy."

"Who?" I asked.

"She's talking about Sheriff Sterling, and I don't think there's any more to say, Gladys." Ollie straightened his shoulders.

"It's my business if I want to speak with him. If you'll excuse me, I see Nina Sayer across the room. I want to have a word with her, if that's okay with you?" She gave Ollie a steely-eyed stare.

He shrugged. "Why should I care? She's not the sheriff, is she?"

As she turned her back on him, Gladys threw up both arms and skirted around the guests to reach the other side of the room.

"Nina Sayer?" I questioned Ollie with raised brows.

"She's in prop production for O'Neil's movie. Julia volunteered with her. Well, I'm going to take one last stroll around the room and thank anyone I missed." Ollie tipped his hand and walked away.

The crowd of mourners soon dwindled to the Bellwethers, a few of the church members, and me. I helped gather empty plates and cups and carried them to the kitchen. The size of the room never failed to amaze me. My entire New York apartment could fit inside. The Victorian architecture contrasted with modern stainless-steel appliances, including two double ovens and an upright freezer that Julia had added when she opened the B&B. Copper cookware dangled from hooks above the center island, while fifties-era ceramic kitsch items splashed bold colors around the room, with red rooster canisters, apple green trivets, and a yellow bird-shaped clock, to name a few.

"Thank you for helping, but we can take it from here." Gladys hugged each of the church ladies in turn. "And don't forget your items. There are too many leftovers for us to keep."

"I'll just see everyone to the door." Ollie stacked as many food containers in his arms as he could carry and followed behind the trail of women.

After they left, Gladys plopped down in a chair. "I don't know about you, but I'm exhausted."

The dark circles under her eyes and the way her hands trembled reminded me we all needed a break from this tragedy. I grabbed the whistling teakettle off the stove and poured water into two mugs. After adding honey, whiskey, a couple squirts of lemon juice, and some cinnamon, I carried the mugs to the table and sat across from her. "Hot toddy?"

She wrapped her fingers around the mug and took a few sips. Her chest heaved. "I've been meaning to tell you how glad we are you're here. In some ways, it helps ease the pain. I mean, when I look at you, I picture Julia in her twenties. You have her eyes and smile."

I reached across the table and squeezed her arm. "Please. If it wasn't for your friendship and the stories you tell about the old days to cheer me up, I wouldn't be holding it together either. We need each other, I guess." I sent her a warm smile.

Gladys raised her chin. "That's why I must tell you. As Julia's niece, you have a right to know."

Footsteps grew louder as Ollie returned. "That Minnie Short is quite a talker. I had to practically shove her out the door just to get away."

"Yes, she does like to gab, especially to you." Gladys leaned back. "Ollie, why don't you see what needs tidying in the parlor? Alexis and I can finish up in here."

"Whatever you say, sister dear." Ollie waved an arm and limped toward the foyer.

A tumble during his stuntman days had left him with a bum leg. I recalled Julia's story. As a double on the set of a swashbuckler starring Errol Flynn, Ollie leaped from the balcony and missed his mark. He stayed in traction for a month.

"Now, where was I?" Gladys tapped her lip.

I opened my mouth to remind her of the statement left hanging like a question mark when the shrill sound of wind gusted and a door slammed. I smiled. "Something you must tell me because I have a right to know?"

"Yes." Gladys poked the table with a gnarled finger. "I refuse to let him get away with it. It's not fair. Julia's death needs closure."

I scratched the back of my ear. "Who can't get away with what? And what's this have to do with Aunt Julia's death?"

Gladys leaned over the table to whisper. The muscles in her face stiffened and molded it into a taut, birdlike image with sharp lines. "Thaddeus Beale, the man I pointed out to you at the wake. I tell you, he's a veritable Svengali who will charm women into doing anything he wants. I promise you. He did something to Julia."

I leaned back. Gladys was a charming, gentle soul. The person sitting across from me appeared angry, almost malicious.

"What are you saying?"

She tapped her knuckles on the table. "I know there's something suspicious about Julia's death." She cupped one hand around the side of her mouth. "Maybe murder."

"Murder? But how? Why?" I gripped the edge of the table. She was talking nonsense. Julia died because, well, she turned ninety-three in the spring. Wouldn't it be reasonable to think it was a natural death?

Gladys shook her head. "You don't understand. You couldn't because you weren't here. He came by every day and filled her head with memories and romance. He carries a torch for the old days, which no longer exist. He did everything to convince Julia to leave with him, and I warned her, but she refused to listen."

"You're right. I don't understand. Maybe we're all too exhausted and not thinking clearly right now." I massaged my forehead to relieve a pounding ache.

Gladys stood. Her face paled and shoulders sagged. "I'm sorry. You're right. I am rather tired, and this isn't the time." She finished her toddy, slid the cup away from her, and moved toward the doorway. "Let's finish cleanup tomorrow. Good night, Alexis."

"We can talk about this later, okay?" I received a nod of silence as her steps lumbered in a defeated motion. *Nice, Ali. Handled that one with the finesse of a lumberjack.* I hadn't meant to be rude or patronizing, but, after her statement suggesting Julia was murdered, how could I react? I reflected on the comments about Thaddeus. Ollie considered him a cad, Gladys accused him of murder, and Ralph commented he was entertaining. What would my opinion be?

I felt sure of one thing. Murder was a ridiculous notion. Too worried to sleep, I grabbed a dishrag and a plate from the tall stack. As they said in the theater world, the show must go on. Well, as long as murder exited the stage and would never be a thought or suggestion in anyone's mind again, I'd be okay with that performance.

# CHAPTER TWO

I SNUGGLED DEEPER UNDER THE COVERS and pulled the comforter over my face as light shined through the curtains and bathed the room. Tall buildings and city smog filtered the sunrises in New York, a dull comparison to the bright, clear mountain skies of Sierra Pines.

During the night I checked my memory to decide if what happened really did happen. I'd tossed and turned in a restless sleep, which no number of meds or hot toddies could've relieved.

Great-aunt Julia was dead, and, according to Gladys Bellwether, possibly murdered. I shuddered. Regardless of how strongly she felt, I'd find a way to reason with her, if I found the right words this time. Not like the mess of insensitivity I blurted out last night.

The house creaked with the patter of footsteps and the echoing murmur of conversation. The residents of Sierra Pines B&B had started their day. Rather than attempting more sleep, I tossed the covers aside, slid out of bed, and threw on my pants and a hoodie then sank onto the bed once more. The sadness of losing someone close to me had finally delivered its emotional impact.

"Alexis, breakfast is ready," Gladys shouted from downstairs.

"I'll be down in a minute." I lifted a gold heart necklace from my overnight case. My eyes teared as I read the engraving. *May your star always shine. Love, Julia.* I fastened it around my neck then tucked the pennant inside my hoodie. After a brief glance in the mirror, I descended from the third-floor private quarters to join everyone in the kitchen. The B&B accommodated guests on the second floor with six rooms. Julia and the Bellwethers stayed on the third floor, leaving one spare room in the attic for emergencies. If the ski lodge and area motels were booked, Julia and her kind heart couldn't turn away a guest in need of a place to stay. Fortunately, every bedroom in the house had a private bath. Julia had insisted on the extravagant expense by adding them when she took over the B&B.

Gladys stood at the stove, while Ollie and Ralph sat at the table shoveling eggs and bacon into their mouths. She turned and smiled. "Thank you for cleaning up, Alexis, but you shouldn't have."

"Of course I should. I want to help." I took a seat and frowned at the empty chairs. "Where are the other guests? They haven't all checked out, have they?"

The B&B usually kept a full house, especially this time of year. Late fall through early spring was the busy season in Sierra Pines because the ski slopes were covered and ready. If Mother Nature didn't cooperate, snow cannons filled with precise amounts of air and water sprayed the ground, though the temperature had to be cool enough for the process to work.

"Oh, let's see." Gladys tapped her chin. "According to Ollie, Dean Thornton, our soap opera star, had a difficult time yesterday and is sleeping in. I'd rather not know the details. Marianne Lane is busy with research for her Atlanta travel magazine article. As a camera technician and part of the visiting movie crew, Brooke Seale is always on set and hardly ever here. With Sierra Pines becoming a favorite spot for producers to film, our tourism has hit a new high."

She flipped eggs onto two plates, carried them to the table, and set one in front of me. "Anyway, Miss Seale left for the movie set at five, and Miss Lane spent the night at our Tahoe Pine Ski Resort. Sebastian Tubble, he owns the resort and has been an active member of SPACA these past few months, invited her to stay and do research for her article. Though hotels and B&Bs have little in common, so I don't understand what the point is if you're writing an article on B&Bs."

I held my fork midair as she rambled on about the characteristic comparisons of hotels and B&Bs. "Maybe I'll get the chance to meet them before I leave."

"Leave? Don't be silly. You've only been here a couple of days. Hardly time for a proper visit and . . ." Gladys sniffed. She lowered her eyes to study her plate.

"I believe what my sister is trying to say is we'd very much like for you to stay as you planned, even longer if you'd consider," Ollie said.

"Of course. I didn't mean to sound like I was leaving soon. I only thought—you know what? I'd love to stay and visit." I smiled. I didn't know what I wanted to do next, but staying here felt comfortable for the moment.

"That's wonderful. Julia insisted the room next to hers be kept vacant these past several days. It's as if she knew you'd be coming before you even planned it. Strange how things work out." Gladys stared blankly.

Was she thinking about last night's conversation? "I'm free, with no obligations in the immediate future. Maybe Aunt Julia mentioned I lost my job?" Might as well get the news out.

"Oh my. How awful." Gladys laid down her fork and touched my hand.

"Not a happy place to be. We've had our share of lean years, haven't we, Sister?"

"I remember when Owen and I opened our store in two thousand five. We lived on tuna and saltine crackers for a year. It wasn't easy. However, those challenges made us resilient. I'm sure you'll pull through and figure things out." Ralph finished his coffee and stood. "Breakfast was delicious, Miss Bellwether."

"Thank you, Ralph. I've plenty more, if you like."

"But I'm handling the situation," I interjected. "I have money put aside and I'm making plans." What those plans were, I hadn't a clue yet. I emptied my orange juice glass and placed it on my empty plate. Besides, maybe getting fired was an opportunity to do something different.

"I better pass on seconds, Miss Bellwether. I'm taking a tour through the town, but I'll be back this afternoon."

"Hold on, Ralph. I have a question about business you might be able to answer." Ollie limped in double time to catch up to him. They walked side by side down the hall.

Gladys gathered dishes and utensils from the table, while I carried the juice glasses. "Look, dear, I'm sorry the way I handled talking about your aunt's death."

"You?" I set the glasses into the sink. "I'd say it was me who bungled the conversation. It was such a, well, it came as a surprise." I couldn't repeat her words. Maybe I'd misunderstood.

"It's not easy to accept." She shook her head. "However, an autopsy would've proved us right, if the sheriff had agreed to it. I have proof, and we must get justice for your aunt.

"Oh, I know what you're thinking. People die of old age, but Julia was happy, healthy, and excited for the future. Only last month, the movie director personally invited her to help with prop design. There's no one better for the job. She had so much left to do." Gladys smoothed the dish towel over the sink divider.

I studied her weathered face that showed every detail of her eighty-some years—exactly how many I wasn't sure since she refused to admit her age to me. The reminders of one's mortality must be hard to accept. "Whether Julia had much left to do didn't matter. Life doesn't play fair."

Turning, Gladys fixed her gaze on me and waited, as if deciding what to say next. "But this was different."

"How?"

"We should have stayed home that evening."

"The evening Julia died?" I leaned against the counter with arms crossed.

"Ollie and I went to the town hall for bingo night. Julia declined, though I tried to persuade her. I even offered to stay home and keep her company." Gladys picked up the dish towel once again and twisted it in her hands. "It worried me, for some reason. All the guests had plans to see a movie at Sierra Pines Theater. It was half price admission that day. Julia would be left all alone in the house. I didn't feel right about it. Anyway, she insisted I go out.

"We argued for a bit until she confessed Thaddeus was stopping by later. I had the impression she didn't look forward to the meeting. Her exact words were 'Thaddeus and I need to have a serious discussion,' but she refused to tell me what it was about." Gladys shook her head. "I should've stayed home. I figured it out too late."

"Figured out what?" My mind raced to digest everything she was telling me.

"I'd warned her. If she planned to leave with him and go back to Hollywood, I told her she should at least make sure it was safe. I mean, to travel with someone alone? A lady has to protect herself. Why, he could have taken advantage of her." Gladys laid the towel down once more and drew a tissue from her pocket to dab her eyes.

She'd lost me. "How does your warning lead to thinking he killed Julia?"

"I assume she followed my advice. At least that's what the note implied."

"What note?" I scratched behind one ear. "Gladys, I want to understand, but . . ."

"Please. I'm trying. Give me time." Gladys motioned to the table, and we sat once more. She rummaged through her sweater pocket and pulled out a folded piece of paper. "I found this on Julia. If you read it, maybe you'll understand what I mean." Slowly, she slid the note to me.

"You say this explains everything?" I unfolded the paper and read the words aloud. "'Hollywood scandal in nineteen eighty-four. Embezzling. Fraud. Checked sources. Contacts in the industry verify.'" I looked up. "What does this mean?"

"Don't you see? Julia followed through on my suggestion. She checked his background and found out he's a fraud and a criminal."

"Oh, Gladys." I struggled to wrap my head around what she implied.

"No. Now listen to me. The discussion she intended to have with Thaddeus was serious because she planned to confront him with this information. And, and she did, but she never . . ." She covered her face with both hands.

"Did you tell Sheriff Sterling and show him the note?"

Gladys nodded. "I did. The night she died he was here at the house. I showed him then. He said the note could've referred to her research for a movie project or possibly for the book she often spoke about writing. Still, he promised to speak with Thaddeus."

"And did he?"

Gladys waved an arm. "Yes. He got back to me the next morning. Thaddeus denied having any plans with Julia, and he had an alibi. Now, why would Julia lie to me, her closest friend? She never did before. Thaddeus was here that night. He's hiding the truth because he's guilty."

"Yes, but if there was no appearance of foul play, how can you think it's murder?"

"Maybe she was poisoned. Quite easily done and to hide. Alexis, I'm certain Julia was murdered, and Thaddeus Beale is right in the thick of it."

"Oh, Gladys," I repeated. I didn't want to argue. The sheriff would be the first to act if anything was suspicious.

Her damp hand touched mine. "Don't worry, Alexis. Ollie and I will take care of it. After we find more substantial proof, Sheriff Sterling will have to listen."

My jaw slackened. I could find no words. I was familiar with her eccentric behavior, but this ventured to the extreme. Not to mention, two octogenarian siblings becoming sleuths sounded dangerous.

"He came here most every day since arriving in Sierra Pines three weeks ago. He tried to convince Julia to leave with him and return to acting. He filled her head with those stories about the old days. Why, the affair with Cary nearly killed her. I can never forget. If she stayed in Hollywood, well, I don't know if she could've survived. When she called to ask for our help, we packed our things and came the next day. Her idea was the perfect do-over. Turn this house into a B&B. It was the best decision for all of us." Gladys stepped into the hall, and I followed.

I knew how Viola Winston, Julia's mother, died of pneumonia in 1947, which was soon after Julia had returned to Sierra Pines. "Aunt Julia never told me the whole story about the affair."

"It was painful to talk about, if you want my opinion. Thaddeus had no right to remind her. All that nonsense. 'Come to Hollywood. We'll be the golden couple, like Astaire and Rogers or Burton and Taylor.' Can you imagine? Poor Julia."

"Did she consider his suggestion?"

"She did. Talk about walking into the lion's den. Hollywood would've eaten her alive." Gladys hung her head. "Instead, it was Thaddeus, not Hollywood, who took our sweet Julia."

Her theory was weak, with no hint of proof other than Julia's note. To be honest, that little detail gave me pause. Even if Thaddeus had come to visit Julia that evening, it didn't mean he was guilty of anything other than being a friend who wanted to chat. Bottom line? It would be of no use telling her not to worry or that her theory was flawed. She wouldn't listen to reason.

Gladys stopped at the library room doorway. She smiled and touched my cheek. "You don't have to decide right away about the B&B. We'll understand if this isn't what you want."

I swallowed hard. Too much had happened in the past several days. Losing my job and Aunt Julia and then learning I was included in her will—not your typical week. Certainly not mine.

Gladys appeared to be waiting for a response. She fussed with the buttons on her dress.

"I'll need a few days to think about it."

"Of course." She glanced at her watch. "I should go. When I spoke with Nina Sayer last night, she asked that I come to the movie set and pick up Julia's belongings." Her jaw tensed, and the dark shadows beneath her eyes became more pronounced. "And I know I should go through Julia's room and her things, but I can't find the courage."

I patted her arm. "Of course, I understand. We'll do that together, maybe in a day or two or when you're ready. There's no hurry. In the meantime, why don't I go to the set in your place? It will give me a chance to get a closer look at where Julia worked. Besides, I could use the exercise."

"If you really don't mind." Gladys raised her brow. "According to Nina, it's only a small box with a few of Julia's personal items."

"I can handle that. The set is off the main drag, right? I think I caught a glimpse of the trailers and camera equipment when I passed through town the other day."

"Yes. You can't possibly miss it. Scenery production is actually in the building our local theater uses for storage since the old warehouse fell apart. Anyway, it's located close to the parking lot, on the right as you enter." Gladys nodded. "Barn-sized with brick red exterior."

"Got it. While I'm there, I might check out the set and see what's being filmed."

"Take your time, dear. We don't need to meet with Mr. Fenworthy until one. The cast is wonderful. You might run into Brooke Seale. Oh, and, of course, Florence. She spends lots of time on the set. SPACA has a trailer for members to use when they're volunteering. Which reminds me, you should attend the meeting tomorrow evening."

"Ah, do you think that's a good idea? I mean, doesn't Florence make those decisions?" I bit down on my lip. "I wouldn't want to intrude."

Gladys lifted her chin. "Nonsense. Julia would want you to attend. I'm a member, so I insist."

"Okay, then. Tomorrow evening it is." I grinned.

She patted my arm. "And thank you, Alexis. This will give me the morning to sort my thoughts about Thaddeus. Maybe I'm missing a clue." Gladys disappeared into the library.

I shook my head. There was no stopping her, and any argument I presented would fall on deaf ears.

On foot, I took a direct path toward the center of town and the movie set. Yesterday, I'd listened to the local news station on my way into Sierra Pines. The movie, *The Sierra Winds,* was an Indie production, which meant the producer had to stretch the dollar as far as he could manage to stay within budget. Filming outside of Hollywood and casting little-known actors, ones who hoped to make it big and become stars one day, cut costs drastically.

Being a big star wasn't for everyone, though. Julia had walked away from a leading role. She'd started acting in her early teens as my great-great-aunt dragged her from audition to audition. No wonder Julia needed a change. She found her passion behind the scenes doing what she loved: prop design. It was quiet and satisfying, with no directors shouting to do a scene over or critics bashing your performance and confidence.

I rounded the corner and reached Main Street. Posters advertising the annual play were plastered on several store windows. After my first few visits to Sierra Pines, I learned October was a special month for the theater committee and SPACA. They put on a new production each year to raise funds for the holiday season. The week before Christmas, gift baskets and toys for tots filled the community center, ready to be delivered to needy families. The winter event was Sierra Pines' biggest and most appreciated and sponsored by SPACA.

"Good afternoon, Miss Winston."

The greeting brought me out of my daydream. I twisted around to find the same slender, balding man who attended Aunt Julia's memorial. I grinned. "Mr. Beale, isn't it?"

His brows peeked. "My reputation must be either very bad or very good if you've already heard about me."

I laughed. "I guess I could say the same, since you recognized me without an introduction. Gladys pointed you out yesterday at Aunt Julia's wake. I take it you and my aunt were friends."

"Yes, Julia, the Bellwethers, and I met decades ago. I'm sure you've heard stories about me, especially from Gladys or Ollie, but don't believe a word." He shook his finger and grinned. "I'm much worse."

"Everyone has an opinion about everything, don't they?" I chuckled, while studying his face.

His eyes shown bright and warm, with tiny lines feathering the outside corners. Laugh lines. Someone who smiled or laughed most of the time couldn't be all bad.

"You're absolutely right. Say, do you mind if I walk with you? I haven't the slightest notion where you're headed, but it's a gorgeous day and perfect to enjoy the fresh air and sunshine." He breathed deeply and his chest expanded.

"Sure. I'm going to the movie set to pick up Julia's things." We walked together, from one block and into the next. "I hear you have a role in this movie?"

"Yes, I do." Thaddeus's smile widened. "An elderly grandfather, which is fitting, who is ill and on his death bed, hopefully not so fitting." His chuckle quickly grew silent. "Your aunt was a special lady. I enjoyed spending time with her." Creases in his face had deepened and his eyes glistened.

I rushed to comment. "I wish I'd had more time. Visiting once a year wasn't enough."

"All the same, Julia cherished you. From what she told me, you two are alike in many ways." He heaved his shoulders, and a frown pruned his lips. "Such a tragedy. She had plenty of life left in her, and she enjoyed living it to the fullest."

"She did, didn't she?" His words were convincing and repeated Gladys's sentiment. Either Thaddeus was the master con of deception, or he had no more to do with Julia's death than I did.

"Well, here's my stop." Thaddeus waved his arm.

I panned the scene before me. Both actors and crew hurried about from one place to another. Makeup artists blotted and brushed to touch up faces. Someone with a megaphone shouted orders, which appeared to annoy one of the actors whose lips curled.

"Jax Westworth. Arrogant and spoiled, but also a superb actor, which is why directors tolerate his temper tantrums," Thaddeus explained.

"I know the type." I'd dated one but gave him the boot after a few months.

"Oh, and there's little Janie Spencer. She's a director's dream. That child has more maturity and discipline in her than most adults. Obviously more than Jax Westworth possesses."

I chewed on my bottom lip, mulling over my take on Thaddeus Beale. "With such a small part in the movie, what do you do between scenes to keep from getting bored?"

"Oh, I take walks several times each day, past the movie trailers and through the crowd of spectators on set. I love getting to know the people around me." He leaned closer and winked. "I learn all sorts of things that way. Well, looks like I'm being called to work." He pointed at the woman who waved her arms in our direction. "Have a wonderful visit, Miss Winston. Prop design is in that large building." He pointed before nodding goodbye.

Backtracking, I hastened toward the red barn structure. I reached the entrance and found the expansive doors fully open, leaving me a clear view. Industrial-sized fans blew air in my face as I stepped into the storage area. A woman with tightly curled, flaming-orange hair sat behind a worktable. A turquoise blue peasant blouse and bandana matched her jeweled bracelets. She held an airbrush in one hand and a rock-shaped object in the other. A mask covered her nose and mouth.

I cleared my throat. "Hello, there. You must be Nina."

The hum from the airbrush grew silent, and she pulled the mask down. Her sun-weathered face formed deep lines as she wiped her brow. "You found me. Now what?"

"I'm Ali Winston. You spoke to Gladys about collecting my aunt's things?" I stepped nearer to the table. Up close, the streaks of gray in her hair were visible.

Her stern look softened into a smile. "Thought you looked sort of familiar. Julia kept a photo of you and your parents at her workstation. Anyway, sorry. You made a trip for nothing. I had one of the crew deliver your aunt's things to the B&B a few minutes ago."

I pointed. "That's a model two hundred, isn't it? Don't you love the adjustable spray? I use mine for almost every medium. Paints, oils, ceramic stains. It sure does the job."

Nina's brow arched. "It's simple enough in a quick fix. I turn to my Iwata dual gravity airbrush, though, when I'm using enamels or watercolors."

I nodded. "Great for smaller more detailed jobs."

"Huh. I thought your aunt told me you were a research assistant for some TV show."

"I am. Or *was*. I lost my job a few days ago. Television. It's never steady or dependable."

Nina snorted. "Neither is the movie business. But neither of those facts explain how you know so much about this." She held up the airbrush.

"Let's call it a hobby. It keeps me sane." I grinned.

Nina chewed her bottom lip and suddenly smacked the table. "Say, I don't suppose you'd like to take Julia's place?" She gestured around her. "Maybe to keep your sanity intact?"

I opened my mouth then shut it. It was a tempting offer but, how could I? "There must be others. I mean, people more qualified who'd help you."

Nina shook her head. "Nada. Not around here. Prop design takes experience. I won't let just anyone in my shop." She fanned her arm across the stacks of materials. "If any of these items get butchered, it's costly to replace them, and that stingy bag of bones who runs this show won't fork out an extra penny. So, will you help?"

"Um, well, I won't be here long, I don't think. This is temporary." All the what-ifs which came into my life recently hindered any decision-making.

"Yeah, temporary as in after the shoot, which won't take more than a couple weeks, we'll be on our way back to Hollywood. Before long, I'll be looking for the next gig."

I shifted my gaze around me and took inventory of the room. Design equipment, everything from airbrushes to band saws, paints which covered the entire color spectrum, glitter, enamels, stains, materials of all shapes and sizes made of wood, Styrofoam, metal, and more filled the storage building. I'd never had the money for expensive equipment. This place looked like a holiday scene with never-ending presents under the Christmas tree. "Sure. I'll do it, but I'm leaving in a week or so."

"That works. We can't pay you, though. Your aunt volunteered. I hope that's okay with you." Nina took my hand in a hardy grip to shake on it.

I winced. "Not a problem. Is tomorrow morning okay? I have plans for the rest of the day."

"Sure, but let's try for early morning. Like around seven, if you can manage. We have a heavy order. They'll be filming the scene staged in a park. See the wood over there? And those boxes of wax flowers? A flowered pergola is one of the many projects we need to build. So, the earlier we get started, the better. Okay?"

"I'll be here." I scratched behind one ear then pointed at her. "I was talking to Thaddeus Beale a short while ago. He tells me he and Julia are old friends. Do you know him?"

Nina coughed. "That man. He sure can talk a blue streak. Builds on my nerves, but your aunt didn't appear to mind. Whenever Beale came around, he grabbed her attention by talking about the good old days. Not sure what was so good about them. The Great Depression, WWII, the McCarthy witch hunt, and, all the while, Hollywood was filling people with pipe dreams on the silver screen. Anyway, he talked and talked. Never stopped."

"Did my aunt ever mention she wanted to return with him to Hollywood?"

"Seemed interested. Never exactly said the words, but then I don't think she would have. She loved Sierra Pines and the people, especially those friends of hers, the Bellwethers. At least that's my take on it."

"One more question. What's your opinion of Thaddeus? I mean, do you think he's as nice as he puts on?"

Nina shook her head. "I'm sixty-plus years old. I don't trust most men. I've been around that barn more than a few times and never once did the relationship end happily ever after like in the movies. Thaddeus Beale is a smooth talker, says what you want to hear. I let my guard down with him once, but I was young and dumb. He was much older but a glamorous star and classy. The man oozed classy, like he invented the word. Handsome. Wavy blond hair and—oh, what the heck. That's all I'm saying. See you tomorrow." Nina walked back to her station, shoved the mask over her face, and powered up the airbrush.

I blinked and stood there before moving on. "Huh." I dismissed my plan to tour the movie set. Instead, I mulled over what I'd learned. I counted three people who considered Thaddeus Beale unpleasant, one of whom suspected he was a killer. I refused to go there. Not yet. Maybe never. Gladys spun a convincing argument, and she had a note with curious details, but she tended to be eccentric and imaginative. In any case, it was best not to jump to anyone's conclusion before gathering the facts.

Stepping outside, I glanced at my watch. I had plenty of time to take a casual walk through town and meet the Bellwethers and Mr. Fenworthy at one o'clock.

The sidewalks in Sierra Pines were lined with post lamps and Western Redbud trees with decorative light strands woven through their branches that twinkled when night came. The scene was picturesque and romantic. Colorful gourdes and candles with spicy pumpkin and caramel scents covered wooden benches in front of the shops. Artsy craft items were displayed in windows, like painted jewelry, native pottery, and homemade soaps carved into apple shapes. I loved the smells and sights of autumn in Sierra Pines.

I rounded the corner and spotted Gladys and Ollie standing underneath a hanging sign with Sal Fenworthy's name engraved in huge gold-colored letters.

"Here you are and with plenty of time to spare," Gladys gave me a hug. "How was your visit on set?"

"Nice. I like Nina. She offered me a job to take Aunt Julia's place, which should be fun."

"Oh, how wonderful. I'm sure—"

"For the love of Saint Genesius." Ollie puffed his cheeks. "We're here for a meeting, not a gabfest."

My eyes widened. "Genes who?"

"Genesius is the patron saint of actors and other artistic people. My brother has decided recently it's classy to use it." Gladys lifted her chin. "No need to get huffy, Ollie Bellwether."

We shook hands with Fenworthy before seating ourselves. His office reminded me of a Tudor or Georgian style library. Black walnut furnishings and wall paneling darkened the space, while accents of gold, from picture frames to bookends, enriched the atmosphere.

Fenworthy motioned for us to sit as he opened a folder with a document inside. He slid his glasses to rest on the bridge of his nose. "Now, let's see."

My breath hitched. Whatever Julia had decided, I'd be satisfied because I hadn't expected any of this in the first place.

"I'm sure you all are anxious, so I'll get straight to the heart of it. The will and testament of Julia Louise Winston states that you, Alexis Winston, inherit Sierra Pines Bed and Breakfast, as well as Julia's sports convertible. She claimed Ollie would wreck it and Gladys doesn't drive, so you're the best choice." He chuckled then cleared his throat. "However, with the B&B there's one caveat. You must agree to continue the employ of Gladys and Ollie Bellwether as long as they wish to remain." Fenworthy took off his glasses and set them on the desk. "Ali, she also wanted you to have her movie collectables. They're actually quite valuable. Our financial assistant researched to assess each item's worth. Everything is listed. I made you a copy to keep for your records, along with a copy of the will."

He shifted his attention. "Gladys, she wanted you to have her award plaque and photo albums from your Hollywood days together."

Gladys nodded and dabbed her eyes with a tissue.

"Ollie? She'd like you to care for her parrot, Blackbeard. He belongs to you, as well as the musket from her collection. She says it will mean more to you than anyone."

Ollie smacked his leg and grinned. "Errol Flynn and his swashbuckler flicks. I never managed those leaps from the balcony without a tumble or two. Bless Julia's heart."

"Everything else in the house belongs to you, Ali." Fenworthy stood. "I'll have the paperwork drawn up for you to sign the deed, which will complete the transfer of ownership of the B&B. If you'll place your signature on this line, stating you agree to the terms as I've explained them to you?"

I stared at the pen he handed me. The tightness in my chest threatened to cut off any air. This was too much. Owner of a B&B? Sure, I needed a do-over and career change, but running a B&B?

"Maybe I should take some time to think about it? I mean, this is such a huge surprise." I swallowed hard and shifted my gaze from one face to the other.

The Bellwethers grew quiet. Gladys ran her tongue over her bottom lip, while Ollie rubbed the back of his hand across the stubble covering his jaw.

Fenworthy, thank goodness, simply nodded and smiled. "Absolutely. I totally understand. You should give it some time, consider your options, maybe talk it over with the Bellwethers and your parents. After I return from my family reunion, we'll get together. Or take longer, if you like. I don't mean to rush you." Fenworthy closed the folder and dropped the pen into a drawer.

My chest relaxed, and I breathed in huge gulps of air. "Thank you. I'll be in touch."

Gladys stood. "We should be getting back to the house. I need to start preparations for dinner."

"Of course." Fenworthy stood and accompanied us to the door.

Gladys turned to me as we stepped outside. "I hope you aren't too overwhelmed. Sal shouldn't have pushed. There's no call for being in such a hurry."

"Please, Gladys. He didn't push. He's only doing his job, and I'm not offended. I'm, well, at least I have time to . . ." Who was I kidding? I couldn't run a B&B. I picked up my pace and gained distance ahead of the Bellwethers. My thoughts swerved and bounced in my head like a pinball as I whipped around the next corner and straight into the arms of a stranger in uniform.

"Oh!" I jumped back. "Oh, I'm so sorry." My face heated, and I stared at his tall, well-built profile.

Jet-black hair peeked beneath the brim of his hat. He studied me with dark blue eyes, deep like a midnight blue sky. He steadied my wobbling form and chuckled. "If you were driving, ma'am, I'd be inclined to give you a speeding ticket."

"Sheriff Sterling." Gladys beamed with a smile as she caught up to us. "What a surprise."

Sterling volleyed his attention between Gladys and me. "Miss Bellwether, it's good to see you. Thank you for the invitation to the wake. Such a large turnout. Shows how Julia was well-liked. She was a wonderful and kind lady."

"She certainly was, and, speaking of Julia, I'd like to discuss the details of her death. I think there's a possibility you might have—" Gladys started.

"Quint, how's the family?" Ollie leaned around Gladys to shake Quint's hand.

"Mom's recuperating after hip surgery, and Violet is doing a fantastic job nursing her, despite all Mom's gripes. I don't know where Violet gets her patience."

"Well, you're lucky to have her. Women like Violet are gems, I tell you," Ollie added.

Gladys let out an exasperated sigh. "As I was saying, I believe there is more—"

"Where are my manners? Quint, this is Ali Winston, Julia's great-niece. Ali, this is Quint Sterling. He's the new sheriff of Placerville."

I covered my mouth. If Gladys scowled any deeper, her face would fold in on itself and disappear.

Quint smiled. "Nice to meet you. Julia spoke of you several times. I'm sorry for your loss. It must be difficult."

"Yes. I was shocked to hear the news. I only arrived a couple of days ago, you see."

"Are you planning to stay awhile?" Quint asked.

"Maybe awhile. I haven't really made plans." An awkward silence took over, and every inch of me grew self-conscious. "Yes, well, it's nice meeting you, but we should go. I'm sure you're busy with sheriff duties. Anyway, Gladys wants to start dinner and Ollie has Blackbeard to care for and I have . . . things." When awkward moments happened, I rambled. And boy, was I rambling. My face burned with embarrassment as Quint Sterling frowned with what must have been confusion. *Take care of Blackbeard? I have things? Talk about first impressions.*

"I should let you go then." He tipped his hat.

"Wait. Sheriff, if you're free, why don't you join us Friday evening for our game night and snacks? There's something important we need to discuss." Gladys spoke while Ollie rolled his eyes.

Julia and the Bellwethers had started the tradition years ago. Once a week, when guests were willing to participate, they provided guests snacks and arranged a board game or some other form of entertainment. On occasion, the Bellwethers were thrilled to act out scenes from their favorite play. Julia just loved the company and conversation.

Quint widened his eyes. "Yes, I'd love to come, but let me check with Violet. If she can't watch Mom because of work, I'll need to pitch in. It's how we manage."

"Perfect. We'll hope to see you Friday. Let's say around seven? Have a wonderful day." Gladys pulled Ollie down the sidewalk before he had a chance to comment.

I tagged along behind them, listening to Ollie's argument about there being a proper time and place for delicate conversations. I failed to resist the urge to glimpse over my shoulder. Sheriff Quint Sterling hadn't moved. In fact, he was staring directly at me. I gulped and snapped my head around to face forward.

What was it about small town male authority figures? Like a character in one of those romance novels, this guy fit the profile perfectly. Tall, handsome, caring, and devoted family man. But there was a Violet in the picture. I shook my head. It didn't matter. I had quite enough to think about, and Quint Sterling shouldn't be included in my agenda.

# CHAPTER THREE

By six thirty, I'd showered and dressed. I had plenty to keep me busy today on prop production, and I didn't want to be late. I made a quick stop in the kitchen for one of the B&B breakfast specialties. I craved those lemon and poppy seed scones.

Gladys handed me a mug full of Julia's special brew and a bag. "I gave you a couple extra scones. Be sure to share some with Nina. Sweets might improve her disposition."

I pursed my lips. "I'm sure she'll be wonderful to work with. Besides, I can't back out now."

"Well, let's hope she appreciates your help."

I reached over to plant a kiss on her cheek. "You're the perfect host, Gladys."

"Employee, don't forget." She embellished her remark with a wink. "At least for the meantime."

"Who knows?" I shrugged because I truly had no idea.

"Take all the time you need." Her eyes brightened. "Oh! One more thing. I talked to Ollie and we both agree you should turn in your rental and start driving Julia's convertible. It's only fitting since whenever you visited, Julia gave you the keys to the car. Seriously, why wait to sign with the lawyer?" She tilted her chin and blinked.

"Hmm. I don't know. Sure would save me a lot of money. Those rentals aren't cheap." I chewed on my bottom lip. Julia always insisted I drive her car. Unless duties at the B&B overwhelmed her, she would pick me up at the airport so I wouldn't need a rental. I shrugged then grabbed the keys hanging from the kitchen organizer. "I'll call the rental company.

They won't charge much to come pick up the SUV. Thanks, Gladys. See you later this afternoon." I waved with my free hand and hurried toward the foyer.

"Not too late. Remember, we have our SPACA meeting this evening."

"It's on my calendar."

"Hey. Mind if I tag along to the movie set? If you're heading there, I mean."

Startled, my breath caught, and I stepped backward as Dean, the soap opera star, jumped into my path. We'd met briefly yesterday evening. His flattering comments didn't impress me, especially when he switched to boasting about himself. Maybe I was over-judgmental, but he was beyond annoying.

"You'll give somebody heart failure, popping up like that." I barely managed the words.

His orange and blue flowered Hawaiian shirt, purple wide-rimmed sunglasses, and tight tie-dyed jeans, that made his skinny legs look like toothpicks, were out of place in Sierra Pines. Stray curls of hair sprung out from underneath a Panama fedora.

He pointed at himself. "My disguise, in case I run into any fans. Listen, I'm on edge, total bonkers with boredom. I miss the cameras and lights. Anyway, I could use someone to talk to." He opened the door and waved me through. "I promise to go away if you tell me I'm getting on your nerves."

"Uh, huh." I sniffed then held my breath as I passed by him to get outside. He reeked of cologne, an overdose of some pricey number like Armani, which was only a wild guess. The men I'd dated couldn't afford pricey.

"I doubt you will, though. Women can never escape my appeal." He sighed.

"Oh, I'm sure they can't." I faced forward to hide my curled lips. Good looks lost their appeal with that attitude. "We'll ride to the movie set." I pointed at Julia's red convertible parked in the drive. Rain was in the forecast.

"Nice wheels. Anyway, as I was saying, it's the Thornton male curse."

"Is that so?" I shifted into gear and tromped on the gas. After taking several sips of fortitude from my mug, I set it in the carrier and nibbled on a scone.

"I didn't stop for breakfast. Care to share yours?" Dean with his flashy smile eyed my scone.

I moved the bag to my other side without comment.

He shrugged. "Enough about me. Are you planning to stay on in Sierra Pines and run your aunt's B&B?"

We swerved to the right at the next intersection. Tires squealed and Dean clenched the shoulder strap of his seat belt.

"I haven't decided."

"It's a nice enough town, but you can't beat the excitement of L.A. Always a party going on somewhere. I have tons of friends, most of them actors with lots of money to spend." He leaned against the headrest. "It sure is the life, and I miss it. Why, I wouldn't be stuck in this stinking town for the past two weeks if it wasn't for that lousy critic."

So much for not talking about himself. "I happen to like Sierra Pines, though running a B&B isn't in my plans for the future." I tapped the steering wheel as the car idled at the traffic light. A little more than half-way to go before we reached the movie set.

"Who cares if I popped him in the nose? He deserved it. Calling me names, claiming I'm a has-been with no talent. I've got the article. Carry it with me as a reminder." Dean pulled a folded sheet out of his pocket. "Listen to this, will you? 'Dean Thornton, the star of daytime soap *The Young and Beautiful,* is neither young nor beautiful and sadly has no talent to make up for the fact. The network might improve its ratings by firing Thornton and finding someone worthy of the role.' Can you believe it? Me, Dean Thornton, a no-talent, according to this lamebrain. How about I've been collecting a six-figure income for eight years. Well, I showed him."

I blinked but kept my focus on the road. We pulled into the parking area, and I found a spot close to the storage building. After shutting off the engine, I turned to Dean, waiting for him to exit the car. A groan rumbled under my breath when he didn't. However, my parents raised me to be polite, even in the most difficult situations. "What happened after you, ah, popped the lousy critic in the nose?"

"Everybody has a camera phone, and every rag is ready to buy juicy celeb photos. Me on the front cover with my fist in the lousy critic's face is what happened. My agent? He gave me two choices. Leave town and stay away until the story dies or get fired from the show. I can't get fired. I have a mortgage and three car payments and alimony and child support." He raked fingers through his hair.

"Then you came to Sierra Pines. Why? Of all the places you can afford to go, why this town?" My words were sharp rather than sympathetic, but an actor with a long-running gig and a six-figure income who whined about one negative review didn't deserve anyone's sympathy.

"Say! There's Jax Wentworth. I've been trying to talk to him all week. Hey, thanks for the ride." Dean threw open the car door.

"If you want a lift home, meet me at the car around one. Okay?"

"You bet." Dean jumped out and slammed the door, leaving me behind. He jogged toward the set, the flaps of his oversized Hawaiian shirt billowing like a kite.

I shook my head. "Now there's something you don't see every day."

I made my way to the production building. Peering through the doorway, I pulled up short to view a cozy scene between Nina and a hefty-built man who looked vaguely familiar. They sat in the far corner, laughing and talking. I waited in the doorway, hoping one of them would notice me, which didn't happen. I cleared my throat and coughed.

"Oh, there you are." Nina jumped out of her seat. "I was explaining to Tom how you agreed to help me out." She nodded at the man. "This is Julia's niece, Ali Winston. Ali, this is Thomas O'Neil, our director and producer."

Her face beamed like a neon sign with *I love this guy* flashing in bright red letters. *Stingy bag of bones*? Go figure. I moved forward and extended my hand. "Glad to meet you, Mr. O'Neil."

"Tom. No one on the set calls me mister. You think you know prop design, heh?" His eyes narrowed, and his tone carried a hint of cynicism.

"One of my majors in college."

"She's been designing as a hobby ever since. Knows her equipment. Anyway, I'm willing to give her a chance," Nina said.

O'Neil grunted. "Don't botch anything. We can't afford to buy more of this." He waved an arm around him. "Tight budget, you know."

"Yes. Tight budget. Everyone is keeping that in mind, Tom." Nina crooked her arm around his and coaxed him toward the door. "I'm sure you've got a full day ahead of you, and so do we. A director can't keep the crew and cast waiting, can he?"

I grinned as Nina turned to wink at me. She kept her conversation going with O'Neil until she'd led him out the door.

"Smooth and clever," I teased with a smile when she returned. "What happened to not trusting most men?"

"I have no idea what you're talking about." She pressed her lips tightly together.

I wagged a finger. "Uh, huh. Sure." I handed her the bag. "From Gladys. She makes the best lemon scones."

"I don't trust men, but it doesn't mean I won't play." She winked as an impish smile curled her lips then opened the bag to take a sniff. "Yum."

"Ha. So, tell me, what do we tackle first? The pergola, I bet." I grabbed one pair of safety goggles off the table and covered my eyes. "Ready when you are, Miss Love 'em and Leave 'em."

"Smarty pants." Nina grumbled but with a wide grin. "I'm liking you already, Ali Winston. Trust me, that's in record time. Now, grab a two-by-four and take it over to the table in the corner, the one with the band saw. I'll get you a copy of the blueprints."

The next several hours passed in a blur. The room filled with a thick veil of powdery dust while the band saws whirred and hammers pounded. I had never built a pergola or anything quite as large. A scaled replica of a stage scene and a rock structure or two made of papier-mâché filled my resume. But with a project, plenty of materials, and a tool bag at my side, I was complete, totally empowered, and energized.

"Job well done, Winston." Nina brushed the layer of sawdust off her jeans. She popped the rest of the scone in her mouth and then pulled a cooler out from behind a stack of cardboard boxes and opened the lid. "Care to join me? It's my way to celebrate finishing a project." She smiled at the pergola and its beams twined with a rainbow of flowers.

"Sure. I could use a bottled water to wash down all this grit." I ran my tongue across the ridge of my mouth.

"How about something stronger?" Nina grinned as she dug into the cooler. "Two ice cold beers coming up."

I took the bottle from her hand. "Does Mr. O'Neil know about your private stash?" I teased with a wiggle of my eyebrows.

She snorted. "Take a peek inside his trailer fridge. I'd say he's got enough booze in there to serve a party for the whole town." She swigged down half her beverage. "Tell me your life story, Ali. What makes you tick?"

I choked on beer and wiped my mouth with the towel she handed me.

"Hey, if you don't want to share, I won't press. How about I tell you some dark and wild secrets about me? Maybe it'll set your mind at ease."

My eyes widened. "It's fine. You don't have to. We can talk about weather or sports or . . . something." Who knew what dark or wild secrets she had in mind?

Nina bellowed with a full throaty laugh. "The weather is crisp and sunny as all get out. Sports aren't my deal. So, here's the something. I loved your aunt to pieces. She was the most honest, generous, and kindest person I've ever met. We had a swell friendship going, and it's a shame she's gone, but here you are."

It wasn't easy, yet somehow, I worked my way through what Nina suggested. "I'd love to hear about your secrets, dark or otherwise, and maybe I'll share some of mine." My lips drew in to suck down several swigs of beer.

"I was pulling your leg. I won't embarrass you." She tipped the bottle in my direction. "Not at first, anyway. Got to know you better to share those details."

Her grin was mischievous, and the glint in her eyes matched the mood.

"How about I ask you questions, small ones, and then you take a turn?"

"Sure. Fire away."

"What did you and my aunt talk about? You must have lots of stories." I leaned back and took another sip of beer. The liquid chill soothed my throat.

"We did talk quite a bit and shared all kinds of things. Dark and wild included." She laughed then, without warning, sobered. "Like I said, she was friendly and kind. Not a single person I spoke to ever had anything bad or mean to say about her. That's rare in this business."

I drummed my fingers on the beer bottle for a second or two. "Did she feel the same way about everyone?"

Nina leaned forward. "One time, and pretty recent, come to think of it, she commented how not everyone in Sierra Pines was trustworthy or kind. It was a peculiar day. She refused to explain. In fact, she didn't have much to say about anything. When Beale came around, she chased him off, claiming she was too busy for chitchat. It was odd since we weren't busy that day."

I stiffened. "You think she was referring to Thaddeus Beale as a person who's not trustworthy or kind?

Nina shrugged. "Maybe. Like I said, she refused to talk about it. I figured she must've had a run-in with a cranky sales clerk or one of her B&B guests. Nothing important. The comment seemed peculiar, though."

I rummaged through my memory for a conversation with Julia where she'd complained about anyone in her life. I failed to recall a single account. "You're probably right."

"My turn. Why didn't you go into acting like your parents? Oh, don't look shocked. Your aunt loved to talk about you and the family."

"Then she must've told you how much I hate being center stage. I'm more comfortable behind the scenes." I didn't see the point in going into personal or embarrassing details. Something told me Nina already knew most of them.

"Oh, you mean how in seventh grade you were cast as lead role in a play. Hmm, let me think. Yeah, in the school production of *Annie*. You played the freckle-faced, red-haired orphan." Nina smacked her leg. "Julia said you were a hit, according to the write-up in the newspaper."

I wrinkled my nose. "Okay, *that* turned into a nightmare. All the attention was suffocating. Off-Broadway producers, friends of my parents, wanted me to act in their plays."

"I'm guessing your parents pushed too hard until you grew desperate enough to do something about it. Pretty smart girl."

"I don't know how smart you'd call it, but I caved and agreed to an off-Broadway role." I cringed, remembering the play and how I did my best to make it the worst performance ever.

"Julia told me. I guess the offers ground to a halt, and you were happy with the results."

"Not my parents. The next couple weeks were pretty quiet in our house. None of us talked about it. I was an awkward thirteen-year-old girl who hoped her parents would forgive and forget without explaining the real reason I took the part of Annie in the school play. I was too embarrassed to say anything." I shook my head. "So stupid."

"A school girl crush on the leading man?" Nina reached over to pat my leg. "We've all been there. Trust me."

I shrugged and then rose from my seat. "That obvious, huh? Well, it was an experience I'll never forget. That's my dark secret."

"Hope we can talk more tomorrow after work. I enjoyed this. Meet here, same time, same place?" Nina smiled, and, on impulse, she gave me a hug.

"Sure. No problem. See you tomorrow morning." I waved and exited the building, intent on taking a quick tour of the movie set. I had enough time to spare. Besides, if I ran into Thaddeus Beale, maybe we could have a Q and A session, too.

Siding with the Bellwethers and Nina was too convenient. I liked to form my own opinions on most everything and especially wanted to about this. Gladys accused Thaddeus of murder. That was serious business. I wanted to be supportive and not dismiss her comments. I rubbed a hand across my chin. Without a doubt, I was overanalyzing the situation.

I wormed my way through a maze of trailers, occupied with my thoughts, and ran smack dab into the locomotive force of Florence Greeley. "What in the world?"

"Ali! Oh my." She clutched her throat and her eyebrows peaked. "What are you doing here? I thought you had a B&B to run."

So, the word was out. I pursed my lips. "I'm helping Nina with prop production. How about you?" An impish grin crossed my lips. Of course, I knew why she was on set, but I couldn't resist playing with her ego. Maybe Ollie's behavior was rubbing off on me.

Florence smoothed the front of her autumn-flowered dress, shifted her ample bosom, and, with a tilt of her chin, straightened to her full five-feet-something frame. Add the spiked heels she wore, and she towered over me. "I volunteer to help with the movie production. Didn't Gladys tell you about SPACA's involvement? She must have at least mentioned it. We cover all the arts and cultural activities in the community. You should really be more informed of what goes on in Sierra Pines, Ali, now that you're one of the business owners."

My jaw dropped, and I missed any opportunity to respond because Florence had twirled on her stiletto heels and marched off in the other direction within seconds. She was more like a tornado than a locomotive, zipping here, zooming there.

"Well, Florence, maybe I should."

I continued to follow a path toward the noisy chatter, bright lights, and someone shouting, "Action!"

"Miss Winston, how nice to see you, again."

My breath hitched as I faced Thaddeus Beale, the scalawag who charmed the ladies to death. I winced at thinking of the unintentional pun.

"Hi, Mr. Beale. What a surprise." I paused. "Are they filming your scene today?"

"Not until tomorrow afternoon. I hope you'll come. I love an audience." He beamed with pride. "And please, call me Thaddeus."

"Sure. I'll try to swing by after my work with Nina. Which reminds me, she mentioned you two know each other pretty well." I studied his reaction, but nothing struck me as unusual.

"Ah, yes. What a beautiful lady. Nina is full of spirit and . . ." Thaddeus blushed. "We dated once. Years ago."

"Dated?" Something told me, Nina wouldn't call it dating.

"Short, brief, during the filming of *Anderson Meets His Match*. Witty and clever."

"Nina?"

"No, no." Thaddeus laughed. "The movie. Loved the humorous lines. Fantastic script. I didn't want it to end."

"The movie." I nodded.

"No, the affair with Nina. She has passion and unending . . . well, enough of that. I should let you be on your way." He tipped his hand and moved around me.

"Wait." I stepped sideways into his path. "I was wondering, maybe we can talk more about Julia? There's so much about her life I don't know. Since she's gone, I sort of have this need to learn more. Does that make sense?" In truth, what I needed were assurances and proof that Thaddeus had nothing to do with Julia's death. I struggled to accept the idea of her dying by any means other than peacefully.

Thaddeus placed a gentle hand on my shoulder. "I'd love to. Your aunt was dear to my heart. Maybe Gladys told you I asked Julia to return to Hollywood with me. She was talented. I know she could've made a go of acting. Plenty of roles for us old folks."

"Did you convince her?" My breath hitched as I wondered if his answer would match Gladys's claim.

He shook his head. "I thought I might, but she wanted to stay here. She loved Sierra Pines more than Hollywood. Too many sad memories from her film days, I guess. You know, the one man she loved broke her heart. A true Shakespearian tragedy. Undoubtedly, Grant was no great loss, but her promising career was ruined."

"I see." I puzzled over the quick dismissal of Julia's love affair with Cary. "How about we meet tomorrow? Or the next day? We can have lunch or something."

"Tomorrow will be a busy one for me. I'm free the day after. Does breakfast sound good? I found the diner on Main Street serves delicious blueberry crepes."

"Sunrise Eatery. I love it. Let's say around seven? I'll stop by to let Nina know I won't be at work until eight thirty or so. She probably won't like it, but that gives us plenty of time to chat."

Thaddeus wagged his finger. "Don't let her push you too hard. She might be sweet and passionate, but I'd add bossy to the list. Well, I'm due on set to practice my lines. Take care."

My face split into a grin. "Good luck tomorrow. I'm sure you'll do great." I sidestepped to let him pass and then continued on my way. Contrary to the Bellwethers' opinions, I found Thaddeus pleasant and amusing. I grew excited for our breakfast meeting, no matter how worried or displeased Gladys would be if she found out.

Curious to see where the cast members stayed, I geared my steps toward the path of trailers. The SPACA trailer Gladys mentioned should be among them. If there was any truth to Gladys's story, asking questions wouldn't be a bad idea. Especially ones about Julia and Thaddeus.

Because of a tight budget, actors had to share quarters when on the road. A few trailers were provided and sat in a tightly spaced row near the storage building. Names written in black marker on whiteboards labeled each. Nina had informed me Thaddeus shared his quarters with Jax.

I kept my eyes open for SPACA's sign. I skirted around a parked service vehicle and approached the first trailer. When I passed by the third, I spotted Thaddeus's name. I rubbed the line of my jaw. The trailer door hung wide open. Without giving the situation too much thought, I leaned in to take a peek.

It was like the infamous odd couple, Felix and Oscar, inhabited these close quarters. I stared at a contrasting display of disarray and tidiness. It took one guess whose half was tidy. My fingers tapped the doorframe as I contemplated my options. Trespassing was a crime. Then again, the door was open. It wasn't like I'd be both breaking and entering.

I glanced behind me then side to side. The surroundings were empty and quiet, but for how long? Nervous adrenaline propelled me up the steps. I moved inside the trailer and took quick inventory of the area. Several items sat on a small table next to Thaddeus's bed. Photos. More hung on the trailer wall. My brow wrinkled. Photos of Julia. Lots of them. Even one with Julia and Cary, their arms wrapped around each other, while he planted a kiss on her cheek.

However, most were of Julia alone. I recognized several from a movie she'd done. Julia had similar photos in her scrapbook, an album of her last movie role before she quit acting. I gazed from one photo to the next. Not a one included Thaddeus. Why did he keep these? My heart sank. Maybe because he was in love with her after all. The sincerity in his voice when he spoke earlier about Julia was convincing. No wonder he'd begged her to return with him to Hollywood. My breath hitched as another murder motive came to mind. *Scorned lover goes berserk and murders former actress.* A chill shivered through me. Now who was overly dramatic?

I picked up on the faint murmur of conversation. My heartbeat quickened. I hurried to retrace my steps and escape the trailer. *Murders former actress? Please. You're letting Gladys rub off on you, Alexis Winston.* Unnerved and confused, I took the wrong turn and found myself facing an oversized, ostentatious spectacle with a gold-lettered plate to label its ownership. Thomas O'Neil. I guessed budgeting on a shoe string overlooked certain amenities, like ostentatious trailers.

Movement caught my eye, and I leaped sideways to hide behind the far corner of Janie Spencer's trailer as a man stormed out of O'Neil's classy lodging. My jaw dropped. Dean Thornton jerked his head to the left then right before he hurried toward the parking lot. Puzzled, I took cautious steps from my hiding place. When I reached O'Neil's trailer, I leaned against the side. Muffled sobbing broke the silence, which abruptly elevated into a high-pitched wail. I winced. Florence's caterwauling couldn't be mistaken for anyone else's. I tapped my foot, debating what to do. A soft heart for all things broken and bruised kept me moving toward the door.

I turned the handle as I peeked inside. "Florence? Are you okay?"

"Oh, oh d-d-dear." She buried her face in a crushed velvet throw pillow and sobbed.

I sat next to her on a flimsy stool and patted her shoulder. Unsteady wooden legs wobbled underneath me, and I struggled to balance my weight on the seat. "What's wrong?" I kept my voice leveled to a whisper.

"Nothing. Everything. I can't talk about it." She sniffed, pulled her face out of the pillow, and dabbed her eyes with a tissue.

As if a new thought came to her, she stiffened and tilted her chin upward. "Are you spying on me?"

My jaw went south and my eyebrows climbed north at the accusation. So much for kind and caring gestures. "I, of course not. It's just . . ." I waved my arm wildly. "I was passing by on my way to the parking lot and heard you sobbing. *Loudly.*" It was partly true. In fact, I'd be leaving right this minute if not for Dean Thornton and Florence Greeley and whatever transpired between them.

"Well, you can go now. Be on your way." She waved a hand to dismiss me.

I crossed my arms and stared, but she waved harder. "Fine. I *should* go." I stood and the stool teetered until it tipped on its side. We both stared at it for a second or two. I wanted to ask why she sat in O'Neil's trailer sobbing into his gaudy, crushed velvet pillow, but the question seemed irrelevant in this situation. "Be seeing you this evening, I suppose?"

Her forehead puckered.

"For SPACA? The meeting? There is a meeting this evening, right?"

"Oh. Yes, but plans have changed. Mr. Gaines, the play's director, dropped off a dozen free tickets to the preview performance of our town play. Incredibly generous of him, don't you think? Anyway, it's this evening, so we will all attend the play instead." She dabbed her nose.

"You sure you don't want to talk about that?" I pointed at her wet tissue. "I'm a great listener."

"See you this evening, Ali." Her chin tipped skyward as she waved the tissue at me.

I gave up and exited the trailer. Whatever had transpired between her and Dean, she planned to keep it a secret, which, considering all the weird and questionable events in the past few days, made me all the more curious to discover what they were hiding.

After a quick stop to let Nina know my plans for tomorrow, I traveled to the parking lot and spotted Dean leaning against my car door. He held the sunglasses and Panama hat in one hand, while raking fingers through his hair. I could question him about his meeting with Florence, but a thought nagged at me, like a warning. It might be wiser to avoid the topic, at least for the moment. No doubt, Dean was odd and a convoluted mix of behaviors. Besides being conceited, spoiled, and overly dramatic, he carried a hot temper. Obviously, it made him angry enough to pop somebody in the nose. Any trigger might send him flying into another out-of-control episode. I refused to be anybody's trigger.

I took a quick glance at his brooding face. Mr. Talkative with nothing to say? I guessed that was hardly normal. In any case, I wasn't about to comment. Instead, we travelled back to the B&B in silence.

I inched the convertible along the curb out front then switched off the engine. "Home, safe and sound."

Dean grumbled a dreary thank you and, without waiting for me, jogged up to the house.

"To be continued." Having no patience left to try again, I got out and slowly followed him. Barely past one. I had plenty of time to prepare for the evening. *Murder in a Small Town*. Too bad it wasn't a comedy. I could use a couple of laughs to brighten my day.

The dimmed lights signaled to everyone IN THE THEATER. Noisy chatter softened to a whisper as people rustled in their seats to get comfortable. While Gladys and Ollie chose spots near the stage for a closer view, the rest of us sat in the back row. Since some of the SPACA members declined the play invitation, there had been enough tickets to include the B&B guests. We'd all ridden to the theater in a limo, a complementary service supplied to SPACA members and their guests on such a night. The town's way of saying thanks.

Despite their best efforts, the folks of Sierra Pines were amateur actors. This was a small-town play with residents who viewed the production as a means to an end, that was, money for the Christmas event to buy toys for the children and food for the needy.

Marianne leaned closer. "Do you think this will go past nine? I want to get an early start tomorrow. I have an article deadline coming soon."

"It shouldn't. Ollie claims it's a short play," Ralph said.

Next to me, Brooke played the game Capture the Dragon on her phone. "Gotcha." She laughed and received a few critical stares from those around her.

"I'm surprised Dean bailed on us. He loves this kind of thing," Marianne added.

I shrugged. Dean had declined to attend this evening, supposedly because of a migraine. My guess was he either suffered from a bruised ego or sore-loser syndrome. Take your pick. Whatever happened in O'Neil's trailer this afternoon must've put a serious ding in his happy meter. Florence, on the other hand, appeared to have bounced back from the ordeal. According to Gladys, since the director's assistant suddenly fell ill, Florence snatched the opportunity to take her place. She barked orders at each member of the cast and crew and then settled cozily next to the director.

The curtain opened and music played in soft, eerie tones as a woman in a ragged coat shuffled onto the stage. I settled back in my seat and focused on the story, ignoring Brooke's furious finger tapping in her

Capture the Dragon quest.

By the third act, I let my mind wander. Echoing sounds from the stage faded while my inside voice grew louder and carried on with reasons to leave Sierra Pines. I had a life in New York, sort of. Plenty of jobs to choose from, I hoped. Parents who loved and supported me. That much was true. So, why was I waffling about my answer? I squirmed in my seat and came up with nada. My phone conversation earlier this afternoon hadn't helped. Both my parents put on the pressure. They wanted me to return home. If I refused, they had other ideas, like flying to California to help me. *You haven't a clue how to run a B&B, sweetie. Your dad knows people who can renovate the place. I'm sure Julia hasn't updated since the turn of the century. Do you have any idea how much income your aunt made last year? I bet no amount to brag about.* Mom's comments bruised my confidence. I was more confused than ever. The problem was, I needed to decide what I wanted to do, and soon.

"*Psst.*" Brooke nudged my shoulder. "I'm heading out front to find a vending machine with coffee. You want anything?"

I opened my mouth to comment but then shook my head. She edged her way to the end of the row and then slipped through the doorway toward the lobby. I suspected she might keep moving until she reached the B&B. The play, already into the fourth act, was somewhat drab. The murder took place early in the first act and, by this point, had fizzled into boring lines and little action.

When the final curtain drew closed and the cast made their bow, I heaved my shoulders. Ralph and Marianne rose from their seats. I stood, and my knees wobbled in protest. "Are we waiting for Gladys and Ollie?"

"Oh, they walked out ahead of us a few minutes ago. Ollie grumbled something about a kink in his rear." Ralph laughed and shook his head.

"Maybe we should hurry and catch up." I kept my gaze on Florence, who approached at breakneck speed. If she'd returned to her chatty self, we'd never get home.

Fortunately, a large group of guests blocked her path. She waved both arms to grab our attention, but we managed to escape to the front entrance before she could join us. I looked forward to a hot bath and early end to the evening.

"Where's Brooke?" Marianne asked as we stepped outside to find Gladys and Ollie waiting.

"Probably back at the B&B." I explained how she'd left her seat during the last act to find a coffee vending machine.

"But we don't have any vending machines in the theater," Gladys said.

"I know. Exactly the point." I grinned as we piled into the limo.

We took a short five-minute ride through town before pulling up to the B&B. My shoulders tensed. All the windows on the first floor were cast in darkness. "Funny. You'd think somebody would be up and about. It's still early."

Gladys and Ollie reached the porch ahead of us. I walked alongside Ralph up the sidewalk.

Ralph chuckled. "Not so strange. With that migraine, Dean probably stayed in bed. As for Brooke, the play might have bored her to sleep."

"Ha. Good point." But I wondered whether she'd come straight home from the theater. Maybe something more entertaining caught her eye. Or someone.

"I'm off to bed myself, right after I grab a bite to eat." Marianne threw her jacket on the coatrack and marched toward the kitchen.

My stomach growled as if on cue. "Not such a bad idea. Ralph? You with us?"

"I'll admit, after the dinner scene in act two, I'm craving roast beef and fried potatoes."

I gave him a playful jab with my elbow. "What a coincidence since that's what Gladys made for dinner."

We dropped our coats and bags in the foyer and took a path to the kitchen. Gladys had pulled leftovers out of the fridge and plates from the cupboard. She turned to greet us. "Now, how did I guess you'd all be wanting a bedtime snack?" She winked.

"The dinner scene in act two." We all chimed at once.

"Except for Ollie. He needs no excuse." Gladys squeezed her brother's arm. "Such a dear."

"My compliments to the chef." Ollie piled several slices of roast beef on his plate.

"Now, shall we talk about the play?" Gladys asked as everyone sat at the kitchen table.

Ollie mumbled between bites. "Let's not. Wouldn't want to add indigestion to our meal."

"Don't be rude, brother dear. The scenery was exquisite. All those props were designed by our dear Julia."

Everyone nodded and echoed words of admiration and, a few seconds later, grew quiet while eating.

At once, Gladys popped up from her chair. "Let me show you Julia's award. You know, the glass plaque she received for her production work on the film *Notorious*. Such a proud moment, it was. One of the few good ones from that time, in my opinion."

"Why don't you finish your sandwich first," I said.

"Really, I don't feel that hungry. When I think of how thoughtful Julia was to put me in her will and to give me the plaque..." She lifted her trembling chin and smiled. "Anyway, it was a kind gesture. Did I mention she kept the award on her nightstand so she could look at it every night before going to sleep? There's a tiny scratch across the front. A reminder of the ugly night when Cary told her about his engagement." Gladys shook her head. "She'd received her award earlier that evening and was anxious to show him. Well, she showed him all right. She threw the blessed plaque straight at him. Good thing he ducked." She snickered. "I'll be right back."

My gaze followed her as she made her way out of the kitchen. I threw a worried glance at Ollie, who shook his head.

"She's fine. A bit excited is all." Ollie heaped potatoes on top of his roast beef. "I say we indulge the poor woman. Julia's death took a lot out of her."

"Yes, I know, but it's—" A scream cut me off. I sprang out of my seat and turned to stare wide-eyed at Ollie. "Gladys?" I took long strides toward the hall, with Ollie close on my heels.

As I reached the foyer, Gladys staggered down the stairs and landed straight into my arms. She sobbed, her body trembling.

"It's, it's—oh my, oh my lord." She covered her mouth and forcefully shook her head.

I stroked her arm and spoke as gently as possible. "Gladys, what is it?"

Her chest heaved until her breathing evened. She nodded once and slowly removed her hand. "There is—I know this will sound like I'm a hysterical woman having a breakdown, but there's a body in Julia's bed."

# CHAPTER FOUR

"A BODY?" THE WORDS BARELY ESCAPED MY mouth.

"Yes. A body." She sank down until seated on the bottom stair and lowered her head into both hands. "A body."

"That's—for the love of Saint Genesius. Are you sure? I mean you know how . . ." said Ollie.

Without taking my eyes off Gladys, I held up a finger to stop Ollie from finishing. By now, Ralph stood at Ollie's side. Dean had rushed out of his bedroom and sprinted down the stairs.

"Ralph. Dean. Why don't you two check Julia's room?" My tone warned not to argue.

As they climbed the stairs, Ralph hurriedly explained the situation to Dean.

I motioned for Ollie to come around his sister's other side. "Gladys, let's take a walk to the kitchen. Maybe I can fix you one of your hot toddies, and I'll add a generous dose of whiskey. How's that sound?"

She stood on wobbly legs. We each took an arm and led her down the hall.

Time dragged on, as if seconds were hours, until Ralph and Dean entered the kitchen. My stomach lurched as they shook their heads. Ralph motioned for me to come into the hall. With fists clenched and my back stiffening, I followed them. Nothing good came from comments starting with "there's a body."

"She's absolutely right. There's a body," Ralph said.

"Dead as in can't get much deader." Dean wiped the back of his neck. He paced from one end of the foyer to the other. "Two bodies in one week. Sure, it happens in movies and TV, but here? Right under our noses? Crazy insane."

I chewed on a fingernail and sat on the foyer bench seat. Their words sank into my brain, word by miserable word.

I stared at Ralph. "Is it, I mean could you tell if . . ."

"Definitely foul play. There's blood on the pillow," Ralph said.

"Who? Do you know?" My voice strained as I choked on my words.

"It's Thaddeus. He's—oh, man." Dean twisted back and forth with both hands gripping the back of his head.

"Get control of yourself, will you?" I shifted my attention nervously toward the kitchen. "Gladys doesn't need for any of us to fall apart. I'm afraid she won't be able to handle it."

"She's right," Ralph said. "Besides, no time for losing our wits. We need to call the authorities."

"The authorities!" I stood and patted my pockets, searching for my phone.

"It's all right, dear. I've got it." Gladys had approached. She waved her phone then brought it to her ear. "Yes, this is Gladys Bellwether. You need to send Sheriff Sterling to Sierra Pines B&B. It's on Englewood. Seven, seven, three . . . Yes, that's it." She paused to listen. "Concerning? Oh, I do believe there's been a murder. The victim is lying in Julia's bed. Mr. Thaddeus Beale. Thank you."

She dropped the phone to her side. I shivered. She was calm once again and smiled at me in an unsettling way, but her eyes were glazed over. Shock made people calm and unresponsive to a traumatic event, didn't it? I forced myself to sit once more on the bench. Two dead in one week. Like Dean said, this scenario belonged in front of the cameras, not in the Sierra Pines B&B.

I couldn't move. I didn't trust my legs to stand. The composure and wherewithal I'd had minutes ago vanished. When the sheriff arrived, Ralph escorted him to Julia's room. As Sterling passed by me, he tipped his hat and nodded without a word.

"Are you all right, dear? I can make you a hot toddy as well. We'll drink them together." Gladys patted my hand.

I shook my head. "I should be the one consoling you."

"When you get to be my age, death isn't so traumatic. At least not when the person who dies means little to you."

"Gladys." My lips tightened. "Don't you think that's a bit cold?"

"What I mean to say is I've been accusing the poor man of murder. All along, I thought he was, well, I need time to figure this out. I need time to deal with what's happened." She covered her cheeks and gasped. "Oh dear, I forgot about the plaque. When I find it, I'll show you. There's a lovely engraved sentiment on the front." She turned and walked toward the kitchen.

I blinked, at a loss for words.

Ollie drew near and stroked my arm. "It's shock, but she'll come around. We might as well follow along and keep her company. Besides, there's nothing more we can do about Thaddeus, poor man." He tipped his chin toward the stairway. "His murder is in Sheriff Sterling's hands, now."

I stepped down the hall with Ollie on my heels as I cleared my head to analyze the possible scenario. How did Thaddeus Beale end up in Julia's bed? And murdered, which, come to think of it, shot quite a few holes in Gladys Bellwether's theory. Seldom did someone suspected of murder become the murdered, did he? In any case, the Bellwethers' fears about Thaddeus's behavior weren't a concern any longer. The accused was dead.

I scratched the back of my arms. They'd gone all goose pimply. Approaching the sink, I poured a glass of water before joining the others at the table. Thaddeus must've come to the B&B while we were at the theater. Did Dean let him in? He was the only one at home. Or Brooke might have, if she'd returned to the B&B, which I wasn't sure of since none of us had checked. Sheriff Sterling most certainly planned on speaking to everyone. Dean and Brooke included.

We sat at the table, Gladys, Ollie and I. Marianne straggled in and took her seat without uttering a word. Soon, Dean and Ralph joined us.

"Has anyone checked for Brooke?" I peered over Ralph's shoulder to stare at the empty hallway.

All except for Ralph shook their heads. "I peeked inside her room. She's not there."

I turned to Dean. "Did you see or hear her return?"

"No, but I was in my room with headphones on, watching episodes of *The Young and Beautiful*." He grew quiet and his mouth curved into a frown.

"Meaning, you aren't aware of Thaddeus arriving at the house, either?" To my way of thinking, his excuse was too convenient and not such a reliable alibi.

He shook his head, again. "Sorry. No help." With that, he turned to strike up a conversation with Marianne.

I opened my mouth to comment, but the doorbell rang.

"Excuse me. That might be the coroner Quint is expecting." Ollie limped to the front door as fast as his bum leg allowed him.

When Sterling entered the kitchen, we all straightened in our seats and grew quiet. Ollie followed behind him and took his place beside Gladys.

"Okay, everyone, bear with me. A few quick questions, and then I'll let you go."

I studied Quint Sterling's face. He remained stoic. Expressionless. Even indifferent, like he'd constructed a wall to hide behind, which offered me no hint as to what he'd found or was thinking.

He turned to Dean. "Let's start with you, Mr. Thornton. You were the only one home this evening?" Quint set a pad and pen on the table as he sat in the remaining empty chair, next to me.

Dean shrugged. "I guess. I mean, everyone else wanted to see the play. Me? I wasn't feeling hot so I stayed here." He leaned back in his chair. "I watched videos of *The Young and Beautiful* all evening. I wore headphones and didn't hear a thing."

"*The Young and Beautiful*?" Quint threw him a clueless stare.

Drew's lips thinned into a tight line. "It's the popular daytime soap I happen to star in."

"Hmm. Okay. I guess that'll do."

I hid my grin with one hand. The sheriff of Placerville had dismissed the boastful blathering with an ever-so-appropriate "this isn't Hollywood, bud." And Dean's pained expression told me Sterling had scored a bulls-eye by deflating the soap star's ego.

After he scribbled a few lines in his notepad, Quint looked at Ralph. "You went to the theater along with the others?"

Ralph nodded. "I did and remained until the final curtain then rode back with the others in the limo to get here."

Quint's attention shifted to everyone around the table. "I guess this goes for the rest of you? You went to the theater, sat and watched the play, and rode home together in the limo, which got you here by . . ." He checked his notes. "At nine forty-five or thereabouts, from what you told me earlier."

"Except for Brooke. She left during the last act. But she never returned to her seat and wasn't out front of the theater when we left," I said.

Ollie spoke up. "She got into a cab about twenty minutes before the play ended." Ollie released a nervous chuckle. "I can't hold the plumbing for long. When I came out of the restroom, she was waving down the cab and left a minute later."

"I see." Quint twisted his head around. "Did anyone check if she's here?"

"She's not. I looked in her room after walking you to Julia's," Ralph said.

I waited until Sterling finished scribbling a few more lines on the pad. "She said something about needing coffee or a snack. Maybe she stopped at a café in town."

Marianne shifted in her seat and cleared her throat. "I need to mention something. It might not be important, but I should mention it all the same."

Quint pulled his attention from the notepad to study Marianne while she fidgeted and twisted the rings on her fingers. "Now is a good time," he urged.

She nodded, shot the Bellwethers a nervous glance, and then spoke. "During intermission, Ollie left his seat. A couple minutes later, Gladys did the same."

"I told you, weak plumbing. I had to use the facilities," Ollie explained.

"What about you, Gladys? Did you also need to use the facilities?" Quint asked.

Gladys wiggled in her seat, avoiding eye contact.

Marianne wagged a finger. "Neither one of you returned to your seats until after the third act started."

Marianne's lips tightened as she lifted her chin, no longer nervous or uncomfortable. It was as if she'd grown bolder with her observation.

"I see. That's a long restroom break, wouldn't you say?" Quint turned from one Bellwether to the other. "Do you have something else to add?"

Gladys twisted and rolled the edge of her sweater. She hummed nervously for a second or two.

"Gladys, don't." Ollie touched her arm.

It wasn't clear to me whether his words meant she should still her fidgety fingers or stop talking.

"I have to tell him, Ollie." She wagged her head then steadied her gaze on Quint. "You see, my phone buzzed. I turned the ringer off, but it still buzzes if I get a call or message, and I got a message. From Thaddeus." Her shoulders quaked, and Ollie leaned over to hug her.

"From Thaddeus?" Quint's brow arched. He set the pen next to the notepad and folded his hands together in front of him.

"Yes. Thaddeus messaged me."

"About?" Quint leaned forward.

"He wanted to meet. He believed Julia's death was suspicious. It was urgent, he said. A matter of life and death." Her voice faded to a whisper, and her eyes widened with fear. "Those were his words. A matter of life and death."

"What time was this?" He picked up his pen and pad, once more.

"I think it was right before the end of act two." Gladys fidgeted and hummed. "Which must've been close to seven thirty."

"Does this have anything to do with you and Ollie disappearing from the theater during the play?" Quint asked.

Gladys nodded and Ollie took over. "He wanted to meet, at once. He suggested Bagels and Buns. Since it's a short distance from the theater, Gladys and I agreed we could meet with him and be back in plenty of time to see the rest of the play."

"But he wasn't there," Gladys added.

"No sign of Thaddeus. We waited no longer than a few minutes." Ollie squeezed his sister's hand.

"I tried calling him but got no answer." Gladys fidgeted with her sleeve again.

"Then we came right back to the theater." Ollie gave his head a firm nod.

"Not at all suspicious, you see." Gladys rested her gaze on Marianne with a sad smile.

My heartbeat quickened. Not suspicious? The whole story reeked of suspicion and foul play with the Bellwethers at center stage. Without anyone or anything to confirm their account of the evening's events, they were left with a vulnerable moment in their alibi. I snapped my fingers. "Did you save the message?"

"It would help to back up your story," Quint added.

"Oh, dear. I didn't." She resumed her fidgeting. "This looks bad, doesn't it, Ollie?"

"It's fine, Gladys. You didn't mean to do it." Ollie rubbed his stubbled chin and glanced at Quint. "She meant to save the message, just in case, but she panicked then hit the wrong button. You can find the information on Beale's phone, can't you?"

Quint nodded. "As soon as we check it into evidence."

"But I did call him. You can see, right here." Gladys handed Quint the phone.

He tapped the screen several times. "Seven fifty-five." He wrote in his notepad. "You returned to the theater at what time, would you say?"

Gladys and Ollie shrugged. "I didn't check my watch, but the third act had begun," Ollie said.

"That's right." Marianne nodded. "They returned to their seats. It must've been around eight fifteen."

"If your account is accurate, and Thaddeus did indeed text you, he would have been alive at seven thirty." Quint tapped out several more beats on his notepad, intermittent like Morse code.

"This means he died between seven thirty and nine forty-five." I finished the thought for him.

Quint remained quiet for a moment while he chewed on his pen tip. "The problem is I can't confirm your whereabouts from the time you left the theater until you returned, other than taking your word on it."

An inward grown vibrated through me when another idea suddenly came to mind. "What about witnesses?" I pressed my lips together.

My outburst earned me stern disapproval from the man in charge. However, he quickly returned his attention to the Bellwethers as if I hadn't tried to hijack his interrogation.

"Did you run into anyone at Bagels and Buns who might verify you were there this evening?"

Gladys shook her head slowly and her eyes teared as if to convey total defeat.

"Bagels and Buns closed by six. It's Lenny's birthday today. He and his wife go to the ski lodge for dinner on his birthday. Every year," she said.

"Roast beef, potatoes, and gravy with those tiny peas," Ollie added.

Gladys sniffed. "Emily loves those tiny peas."

Quint heaved a sigh. "I see. Well, then, I—"

"Hello, everyone. What's going on?" Brooke stormed into the kitchen, her face flushed and hair windblown. "The sheriff's cruiser is parked outside and . . ." She pulled up short in front of Quint and, with a stiff smile, she nodded. "Sheriff Sterling."

No one answered for an uncomfortably long moment. When she opened her mouth to speak again, Quint interrupted. "Why don't you take a seat and join us? We were discussing Thaddeus Beale. You haven't spoken to him recently, have you?"

Brooke pulled up another chair and sat between Dean and Marianne, her flushed coloring had paled. "I, no, not since this afternoon when he rehearsed his scene. Why? What's this all about?" Her gaze shifted to each of us in turn.

"Thaddeus Beale is dead," I said, which earned me another scowl from Sheriff Sterling.

"Can you tell me where you've been since leaving the movie theater?" Quint cleared his throat, and his jaw muscles flexed as he nodded at the rest of us. "They've told me you left during the fourth act, and Ollie claims you drove away in a cab."

Brooke stared at the pen in Quint's hand before her head snapped up to meet his gaze. She smiled brightly. "I went directly to the movie set. I had to work on edits of the film we shot today. I finished about twenty minutes ago then came straight here."

I sipped my drink and peered at her over the rim of my mug. Funny how she'd never mentioned to me that was her plan.

"Did you work alone?" Quint asked as he scribbled.

"No, the director was with me. The whole time."

Quint stopped writing and glanced up at her. "O'Neil, right? I'll need him to corroborate your story."

Her tongue ran across her bottom lip. "Sure. No problem."

"Good enough."

"Look, we all know who has hard feelings for Beale. It's not like she's ever kept her opinion of the guy a secret." Dean's gaze landed on Gladys.

"I'm not drawing any conclusions about anyone, yet," Quint said.

Marianne cut him off. "Still, the both of them disappeared for over a half hour during the play. That alone is suspicious."

"They explained why they left." I narrowed my eyes at her.

"Which nothing or no one can confirm." Dean stared defiantly.

The Bellwethers' situation reeled out of control.

I scrambled for another idea. Any idea. "Say! How about contacting the phone carrier? Gladys, who's your plan with? We'll call. I'm sure someone there can retrieve the deleted text message." My tone begged Sterling to listen.

Ralph chimed in. "Great idea, Ali."

His smile warmed and encouraged me.

"If you check the phone records then you'll have the proof to confirm the Bellwethers' story."

Quint shook his head. "It's a start, but maybe not enough." He stood and pocketed his notepad and pen. "Well, folks, I'll need you to stick around Sierra Pines for a while. Also, as a matter of procedure, each of you need to stop by the office for fingerprinting."

"Fingerprints? Seriously?" Dean straightened in his seat. "Is that really necessary?"

Quint narrowed his eyes. "Absolutely necessary, Mr. Thornton. Do you have something to hide?"

Dean swallowed and paused for several seconds. "No. I guess not."

"Great. Then we don't have a problem," Quint said.

"This doesn't look good, does it, Ollie?" Gladys trembled and remained in her seat as her chin tilted upward. "How could I have gotten it so wrong? Julia, I'm sorry. I misunderstood, but I'll keep trying. You shouldn't worry."

My eyes widened while everyone around the table fell into an awkward silence. Conversing with the dead couldn't reflect well on her behavior. "You can see she's distraught and exhausted. How about I take you upstairs, Gladys." I stepped around the table and gave Ollie a warning glance. He nodded and gripped one of his sister's arms to help her stand. This time, she didn't resist.

I dared a glimpse of Sterling's face and held my breath. His muscles grew taut while deep creases furrowed his brow. Doubt had crept into the room and taken over. The stage was set and the Bellwethers were doomed if we didn't find proof to clear them.

Ollie, Gladys, and I had taken no more than a couple steps when a deputy charged into the room. I stiffened as he whispered to Sterling, whose expression grew sterner. This wasn't a good sign, not if what he had to say added more to the growing mass of evidence.

Quint returned to his seat. "Sorry, but it seems we're not finished."

I sank back into my chair and kept a concerned eye on Gladys. Her face paled and jaw slacked in a haggard expression. "Maybe this can wait until tomorrow? I don't think she can handle much more." I gave Sterling a cautious stare, but he shook his head.

"This can't wait. My deputy tells me there's a freshly dug hole in the backyard. Care to explain? Anyone?" He crossed his arms and rested his back on the chair.

"That would be us," Ollie answered.

Of course it would. I slouched in my seat. Why not pull out the handcuffs and take them away this very minute? Save us time, and then everyone else can go off to bed.

"Wow. This reminds me of the old black and white movie, *Arsenic and Old Lace*." Dean shrugged as everyone stared. "What can I say? I binge on the classics. Helps me fall asleep."

"I remember. It's a Cary Grant movie. He starred with whatshername, ah, Priscilla Lane. The Brewster sisters poison lonely old men, and their cousin Teddy buries them in the basement. It was a play before a movie, and . . . um, yeah." Brooke's voice dwindled into silence as I glared at her.

"The hole?" Quint redirected the conversation back to the Bellwethers.

"We wanted to create a memorial, something for Julia. Some of you might have heard me mention it the other day at the wake. Anyway, Ollie and I decided to plant a dogwood tree. The rosy teacup. Julia loves those pink blossoms in the spring. So, we dug the hole this morning. That's what it's for, you see." Gladys squeezed her eyes shut as she swayed back and forth.

"Seriously, she's ready to pass out." I leaned in to whisper so only Sterling heard me. "Unless you want another casualty on your hands, I suggest you stop and call it a night."

He nodded. "One more question. Did you purchase a tree? Maybe you have a receipt? That would be helpful." His voice and demeanor had softened.

"It was on our to-do list to call the nursery tomorrow morning, which doesn't help us, does it?" Gladys reached for Ollie's hand.

"My sister doesn't have a mean bone in her body. Sure, she talks. Certainly, she didn't care for Thaddeus. Neither of us did. But murder?" He shook his head forcefully.

"What about you, Ollie?" Quint asked.

"Me? I suppose in the moment, if I were defending someone I cared about, I'd step in and do what's necessary."

"But not murder."

"No. Not if I could help it." Ollie's voice grew solemn. "Sheriff, I know it looks bad, but do you seriously think Gladys or me capable of murder?"

"I don't know, Ollie. Too often my job shows me the flaws in human nature." He glanced at each of us. "Until it's proven otherwise, each of you is a suspect in this case. My team searched the bedroom, scanned it for prints, and collected evidence. The coroner is doing his part and will examine the body when he gets back to the lab. My opinion, Ollie, will have to wait until I get those results."

He stood and walked toward the doorway. "Even though we've done a thorough sweep, Julia's room is off limits for the next few days. I'll be in touch when and if I have other questions. You folks try and get some rest." He turned to me. "Ali, may I speak with you privately?"

"Excuse me for a minute. Ollie, wait here. I'll help you take Gladys upstairs when I get back." I hurried along to catch up with Sterling, who stood by the front door.

He removed his hat and raked fingers through his hair. "I'm sorry. I know this has been stressful, but I'm trying to do a thorough job."

"I get that. I shot off my mouth because I worry about Gladys's health. She hasn't been herself lately." In truth, none of us had been the same.

"Understandable." The back of his hand scraped the day-old stubble on his chin.

I glanced behind me and toward the empty hall. With one hand, I motioned for us to go outside then closed the door. "Can you tell me anything about Thaddeus? It's murder, but how was it done?" I shivered and crossed both arms tightly over my chest.

"It's murder. That much is certain."

I pushed. "With what?"

"I can't tell you yet."

"Okay, how about evidence? Did your team and the coroner find any to suggest who might have done this? I mean, other than the Bellwethers. Dean was here alone with the body. And what about Brooke? She disappeared during the play, too. Or maybe it's too much bother to investigate anyone else. You've already got the Bellwethers." I winced at the accusatory comments and pursed my lips. "Sorry, Sheriff Sterling. I know you're doing your job."

His chest rose and fell for several breaths. "Ali, I can't tell you anything the coroner or my team found. It's an investigation. I'll examine all possible suspects. Like you said, I'm doing my job. And please, call me Quint. Something tells me we'll be seeing quite a bit of each other."

"Hopefully not about the case. Well, I guess you need to be going. Quint." I stepped away and wrapped my fingers around the doorknob.

Placing his hat on his head, Quint nodded. "I'll be in touch."

He jogged down the driveway. I peered out of the window as he caught up to his deputies and the county coroner, who were huddled outside the ambulance. Men loaded the stretcher carrying the body bag through the rear doors.

After the last vehicle drove away from the house, I returned to the kitchen. Everyone sat in their chairs. The tense atmosphere had subdued their mood and left them quiet. "Ollie, let's get Gladys up to bed. You both need a break from all this." I took one arm while he supported the other, and we walked out of the kitchen. I called to the guests over my shoulder, "Can everyone please wait here for me? I'd like to run an idea by you." I was thankful not to hear any protests.

When I returned to the kitchen, I rushed to speak before I lost my nerve. "Okay. I'm about to ask a big favor, and please, at least hear me out." I went on to voice my support of the Bellwethers' innocence.

Marianne pursed her lips and Brooke lowered her head to stare at her drink.

"I know it's hard when plenty of evidence weighs against them, but try and put yourselves in their place. What if you were the Bellwethers and no one came forward to help prove your innocence?" I leaned forward. "How would you feel?"

"What are you suggesting we do that the authorities can't?" Brooke asked.

"Lots, if we put our minds to it." I made the suggestion but got nothing in return from Brooke, other than silence.

"So, we'd do what exactly?" Marianne chimed in.

"We return to Bagels and Buns and ask merchants close by if any of them happened to spot the Bellwethers waiting outside this evening. Maybe even question shoppers. Never know who might have seen Gladys and Ollie."

Marianne was quick to argue. "I'm sure Sterling can handle it. He has to check out the phone carrier's records, too. No one but a judge can authorize such a thing."

"True. But we might learn information the sheriff and his two deputies can't. You know how some folks are. They clam up at the sight of a badge and uniform." I stared defiantly at Marianne. My hunch? She and possibly Brooke would bail on my intended mission, which left Ralph and Dean Thornton.

"I think it's a great idea, Ali," Ralph spoke up. "We can scout around to ask questions and cover more territory in a short amount of time. Even stop by the movie set and talk to the cast and crew."

"Good point." I smiled. "And maybe our efforts will uncover evidence about who else had a grudge against Thaddeus, if we ask the right questions. You never know."

Dean waved an arm. "Count me in. I'm always willing to help a fellow actor."

I blinked. Wasn't he the one who raised suspicions with his remark about Gladys's dislike of Thaddeus? "Thank you, Dean. I appreciate your offer."

He shrugged and grabbed an apple out of the fruit bowl. "Anytime. Well, people, I've gotta get my beauty sleep. Let me know the deets of our agenda tomorrow, okay?" He strolled out of the kitchen and tromped up the stairs.

I turned to Brooke. "Are you with us?"

She shook her head. "My work has piled sky-high, and O'Neil will be ready to fire me if I don't measure up." She stood. "Night, all."

Marianne stepped away from the table to follow. "I think I've made it clear how I feel. Besides, I have an article deadline. The best I can do is promise I won't mention the murder when I write about Sierra Pines B&B. That kind of detail will kill business. Good luck."

Both of them disappeared down the hall. "Well, at least we won't be front page news in Atlanta. Thanks, Ralph. We can talk more tomorrow."

"Yes, I think I'll turn in for the night, too." Ralph tipped his hand and left me alone in the kitchen.

I stood, bracing both arms on the table as my legs protested the effort. Every fiber of my body protested. It shocked me how, in a matter of days, more had happened than in my entire past year. Sad and tragic events had rained on Sierra Pines, hardly the cheery, sunlit atmosphere of the autumn I'd come to know.

I kneaded my temples with fingertips to diffuse a pounding headache. If I expected to be any help in this situation, I had to keep my brain sharp and my emotions in check. Things could go downhill quickly. Somebody murdered Thaddeus Beale—no point in thinking it was anything but murder—and unfortunately Julia's lovely B&B was the crime scene.

Gladys's harsh words and accusatory tone echoed in my head. Dean was right. She let anyone who would listen know her opinion of Thaddeus. What were we supposed to think now? Revenge was a common motive to kill, but I had to believe the Bellwethers had a solid alibi. I had to believe Thaddeus was murdered while Gladys and Ollie were in the theater with us, watching the premier of *Murder in a Small Town*. How ironic. When art imitated life. My drama teacher had called it mimesis. In this case, I'd call the situation plain creepy.

I pushed myself to climb the stairs to the third floor. The soft cackle of Gladys laughing and the sliver of light shining from underneath her door steered me to her bedroom. I raised my hand to knock.

"You know Sheriff Sterling is an honorable man. He will find the killer."

The rustle of bedcovers broke the next measure of silence before Gladys spoke again. I pulled away and lowered my fist.

"Everyone is being so kind. To help Ollie and me when there's so much evidence against us touches my heart. It's such a nice gesture. Don't you agree, Julia?"

*Julia?* I blinked. My fingers tightened and gripped my thighs. Peculiar behavior didn't cover this instance by a mile.

"What do you think? Nightlight on or off? It's no matter to me, unless I need to use the bathroom at night."

I swallowed to ease the tension in my throat, and my stomach bunched into knots. She'd gone completely bonkers.

"Tell you what. I'll turn the light off and take my chances. If I need to get up, and I stumble on my way to the bathroom, it's on me. Good night, Julia. I wish you could answer me."

I waited another few seconds, but she said nothing more. Shuddering at the sight of yellow crime tape stretched across Julia's bedroom door, I quickly tiptoed across the hall then slipped inside my room. I snuggled into bed, pulled the covers up to my chin, and closed my eyes. I couldn't erase the disturbing images of psych wards and doctors in white coats and my worries about Gladys with her peculiar behavior. No use in fighting it. I was in for another restless night of sleep.

# CHAPTER FIVE

I PEEKED THROUGH THE BEDROOM WINDOW CURTAIN to view the glimmer of early morning sunlight topping the Sierras. Bright yellow beams fanned in a wide arc to bathe the ground. It proved a fine morning for a walk, which was what I needed to clear my mind of troubling thoughts. Besides, I had lots on my agenda today. After my work with Nina in production and dinner at the B&B, I was meeting with our newly formed sleuthing team to discuss strategies on how to help the Bellwethers. I hadn't forgotten my plan to call Florence and beg for SPACA members to help. I didn't know all of them, but she and senior member, Minnie Short would surely come on board with the idea.

"Good morning, everyone," I greeted the guests gathered in the kitchen, minus Dean who'd probably slept in.

Warming pans with scrambled eggs, bacon, sausage, and waffles were lined up on the counter. Gladys flipped blueberry pancakes—they were Ralph's request—onto a plate and handed it to him.

"Good morning to you, too, Ali." Ralph nodded as he passed by on his way to the table.

Brooke held up one finger as she swallowed a bite of waffle. "Heading to the movie lot?"

"Yep. You?" I spread cream cheese on a bagel.

"Not until later this morning. If you happen to run into O'Neil on your way in, could you let him know I'll be late? I have some errands to do. I tried calling but his phone is turned off."

"Sure thing." I took the coffee mug Gladys handed me.

"You have a good morning, dear. Tell Nina we said hello." She nodded.

I bagged my bagel and raised my mug. "Later, all."

I was out the door with a shopping bag hanging over my shoulder. Buying souvenirs for my parents felt like the right thing to do. I'd rejected their advice on my unemployed status and my future. I was worried how they might try to take over running the B&B, if I chose that path. But they were good people and had heartfelt intentions.

I had a hunch Aunt Julia meant the B&B to be more than just an inheritance. She always listened when I commented how my life never seemed to settle comfortably in one place for long, neither professionally nor personally. Maybe she intended for the B&B to give me that comfort and a place to call home. Now, if only I could explain that to my parents and make them understand I needed to cut those ties of parental advice and make decisions for myself.

Arriving in town, I spotted Meeka's gift shop and made a mental note to visit. The front window displayed plenty of California vintage glassware for Mom and local history books for Dad. These items fit their tastes perfectly.

I shifted my gaze away from the sidewalk to study the display and gasped, as, with my next step, one toe stubbed the uneven cobblestone. My arms circled like windmills to gain balance. Instead, I fell forward and right into the firm, broad chest of Sheriff Quint Sterling. My face burned and most likely blushed to the deep red of a ripe tomato. "Oh boy. I am so sorry." I winced. "Again." What was it about this guy that made me trip over my tongue and feet? This counted the second time in a matter of days I'd face-planted into him.

Quint's eyes twinkled while his grin spread ear to ear. "Here to serve and protect. Even when you stumble and I break your fall, Miss Winston." He tipped his hat.

"Sheriff." I stepped back a comfortable distance and adjusted the shopping bag on my shoulder. The reminder prompted me to point at the gift shop and comment about anything but the murder, unless he brought it up, which was a remote chance. I'd written enough scripts for cop shows. You couldn't pry details from their lips. Not about open cases. "I was checking out gift items for my parents when, well, you know."

"Meeka's Mementos. Great choice. Meeka has everything and anything you need, and merchandise is never overpriced."

"Does she pay you for advertising?" When he drew a serious face, I sobered and cleared my throat. "Yes. I've been inside, once or twice. She has a great selection."

"Folks around here like to help each other out. Besides, my sister, Violet, works part-time for Meeka. One good turn deserves another." He leaned in to whisper. "Be sure to tell Meeka if you speak with her, though. I can't miss out on a good turn or two." He winked.

I bit down on my lower lip, and a smile slowly simmered. "Gotcha. Well, I should be moving along. I have a job to do." My insides glowed. *Violet is his sister.*

"Oh? How's that?'

"I'm taking Aunt Julia's place as assistant to Nina, the prop designer on the movie set. Have you met her?" I slung my shopping bag over the other shoulder.

"Once or twice, when I visited the set to check out security. She's curt but polite. Says what's on her mind. I like that in people." He crossed arms over his chest and leaned back. "You know about prop design, I take it?"

"A dual major in college. Art design and screenwriting. Let's say I'm keeping arts in the family. Though, I've never had the opportunity to work prop design." I shrugged. I didn't want to dive into a conversation about my personal life, which was where this might lead, if I kept talking.

"Really. What's been keeping you busy back in New York? Workwise, I mean."

"Fact checking as a television researcher."

"Interesting. How's that work?"

I chewed on my bottom lip. "Okay, you know when you do a profile on a suspect, collect all the information, study his background, and other things important to you? That's sort of what it's like for a researcher. For instance, if the show's writer decides to put a bomb disposal diver in the script, I'm the go-to person who finds out about that occupation, how it's done, the equipment used, and other stuff." Or at least I *was* that person, but I refused to mention that detail. No way did I want a pity party from this guy.

His brow hitched. "Bomb disposal diver?"

I squirmed. "That's one example, but they're not all so intense. One time I did research on people who taste-test dog food for a living." I shuddered. "Disgusting."

Quint laughed. "Still, the job sounds challenging."

"It has its moments. I collect tons of information, even if the only benefit is to better my chances at winning a game of trivia. Look, I'm sorry, but I need to scoot. Nina is expecting me. You have a great day, Sheriff."

"Quint. Remember? Maybe we can continue our conversation during the game tomorrow evening." He smiled.

"Oh, is that tomorrow? Yeah. See you then." I kept my gaze on him and backstepped, careful of the uneven pavement.

I pressed my lips together. *Is that tomorrow?* Being coy wasn't something I did well. The grin on his face told me as much. I pivoted on my heel to face away from him and escape his amused expression. Still, my insides warmed. He didn't laugh out loud or make some snide remark. He was polite and mildly teasing, his smile divine. Besides that, Violet was his sister. With a grin still plastered on my face, I reached the storage building. What was I doing? Maybe there was no harm including Quint in my thoughts. He was a pleasant distraction and this was innocent flirtation. Nothing more.

The morning shifted to afternoon. I stood back to admire the foam snow caps in various sizes and shapes. "Nice work, right?" I wiped off my jeans with a damp towel.

"Yep. Perfection. You've got skills, kiddo. Wish you could stick around to help me start those pillars." She pouted and batted her eyelashes.

I chuckled. "That face won't work on me. Besides, I have some errands to run before dinner, then a meeting this evening."

"Fine. I can manage but promise me I'll get a full day's work out of you tomorrow." Her finger pointed in my direction.

"Promise." I grabbed my bag and skipped out the door. "Bright and early."

We'd covered the uncomfortable topic of Thaddeus's murder when I arrived. I chose a brief version of the horrible event. Fortunately, Nina pushed her bold and outspoken self to the background and let the matter drop when I switched the conversation to a safer topic.

The afternoon foot traffic had dwindled as folks hurried home, most likely to carry on their evening ritual. I looked forward to dinner, as long as the conversation remained pleasant. Gladys had invited the guests, her way of saying thank you and sorry for ruining their stay at the B&B. I figured it was more of a distraction, anything to keep thoughts of murder out of her head. I doubted it would work.

I covered the last few yards to my destination. My eyes widened as I stepped inside Meeka's Mementos. Ralph Emory leaned against the counter with arms crossed over his chest while he talked to a tall, broad-shouldered, middle-aged man.

"Hi, Ralph. Surprise running into you here," I said.

Ralph unfolded his arms and grinned. "Ali. Good to see you. Hey, maybe you can give us your opinion. I was telling Sebastian how I can't make up my mind which location my husband would agree on. You know, for our new store? He's pitching the ski resort, but I'm thinking downtown seems an ideal choice. Plenty of foot traffic, which would mean loads of customers. What do you think?" He drummed his fingers on the counter.

My brows lifted. "Well, I . . ."

"But the ski lodge attracts the sort of people looking for your products. It's like filtering to narrow down your search and get the best results. Don't you agree, em, Ali?"

Sebastian's brow creased and his eyes grew somewhat unfocused for a second as if he tried to figure out something puzzling.

I studied his expression and responded with my own wrinkle of confusion. Sebastian. There couldn't be more than one in this small town with such an uncommon name.

"I'd say it depends on what Ralph's objective is, Mr. Tubble."

His creased brow deepened.

"You are Sebastian Tubble, owner of Tahoe Pine Ski Resort, right? Gladys informed me."

"Ah, yes. Ali as in Alexis Winston, Julia's great-niece." He sobered and clutched my hand. "We didn't get a chance to meet at the wake. I'm awfully sorry for your loss. Julia was a special lady. It's such a tragedy." He patted my hand then released his hold. "And then to have a murder happen last night, right inside the B&B. Too, too much."

"Yes, it is." I gave Ralph an apologetic glance. "Sorry for hijacking your conversation. Sounds like you were doing business."

"Not a problem. I always discuss these decisions with Owen. He's my equal partner, both at work and at home." Ralph winked at me.

"I wholeheartedly agree, but I insist you come up to the resort. I'll give you the grand tour. You'll see. Nothing can top the locale." Sebastian nodded firmly.

Ralph fussed with his collar. "After I talk to Owen, I'll be in touch."

"I won't take no for an answer. You know, great business deals don't come along often. Act fast or you'll lose out. Ralph, I promise to make you an offer you can't refuse. How about next Monday for the tour? That should give you plenty of time to speak with your partner."

Sebastian's eyes gleamed as he leaned closer to Ralph, whose coloring blanched.

I tugged at my shirt. It billowed up and down to let in air. How hot and stuffy was it in here? In a flash, my hand flew sideways and collided with a pyramid stack of air freshener. Cans toppled and clattered on the floor. I scrambled to retrieve the mess. "Sorry. Clumsy me." From the corner of my eye, I caught Sebastian's reaction as he screwed his face into a pointed glare. I bit my bottom lip to avoid comment.

Ralph stepped over to catch the last can as it rolled. He set it on the counter and grinned at me before turning to extend a hand to Sebastian. "We'll see, after I speak with Owen. Thank you, Mr. Tubble. You've made a generous offer."

Ralph stepped toward the exit, while Sebastian's face morphed into a full-blown pout.

It was almost comical, if not childish. Sebastian must be a barrel of laughs to work with on the SPACA committee. Instinct told me it wouldn't be healthy to spend a great deal of time with him. I feared this man's intimidation could be suffocating.

"I'll walk back to the B&B with you, if you're heading there." Ralph took a step closer to me.

The gift search could wait another day. I linked my arm through his and stepped lightly out the door. "I can't think of better company at the moment, Ralph."

As we passed the display window, I caught a glimpse of Sebastian. He stared, or more like glared at us. I was taking an immediate dislike to this guy.

Ralph nudged my shoulder. "You pushed those cans off the counter on purpose."

"Did not."

"I don't believe you." He snickered and gave me an affectionate squeeze.

"And you shouldn't."

I grinned with a delectable taste of satisfaction. My gut told me Sebastian Tubble was a bit of a bully, whose aggression took him over the line. Bullies should never be allowed to ruin anyone's day. I learned to be on guard with his type and avoid showing my vulnerable side. The Sebastian Tubbles of the world were always waiting, ready to gobble you up.

"New York is exciting, isn't it? I travel there several times a year for expos and writers' conventions, and I fight for every assignment that takes me to the Big Apple." Marianne Lane scooped more layered salad onto her plate.

I nodded as I eyed the various dishes on the table. "It has its perks. I enjoy coming here to unwind, though."

"Yes, but don't you find this boring after a week or two? No offense, Gladys and Ollie. I'm from Atlanta, and we have plenty of entertainment, lots to do and see. Sierra Pines?" She shrugged her shoulders and raised her hands, palm side up.

"I'll admit, our town isn't L.A., New York, *or* Atlanta, but we find it perfect for our lifestyle." Gladys scooped a huge spoonful of alfredo pasta and plopped it on my plate. "You must try this dish, Alexis. I got the recipe from our new neighbor, Agnes Benning." Gladys glanced at Marianne. "She's a gourmet chef, one of the many talented people living in Sierra Pines."

"Eh, em. Speaking of exciting things to do, how's the movie coming along, Brooke?" I switched topics before Gladys dove into a lengthy argument on big city versus small town lifestyles.

"It's been a real struggle. I mean, I love camera work, but if I'm to be honest, this movie belongs in a trash bin. I'd be surprised if the production breaks even at the box office, and we're filming on a low budget. Makes O'Neil, the director and producer, real tight-fisted with money. It stinks for the rest of us."

"I've read a lot of positive press in the news about it, though." I picked at the huge helping of pasta and added calories in my head.

Brooke rolled her eyes. "No surprise there. The critics haven't seen anything yet."

What made a producer sink money into something that promised little profit? "Well, let's hope it surprises everyone." I turned to Gladys. "In other news, I'm enjoying my work with Nina. She's teaching me a lot about prop production. Makes me rethink my goals about work."

She clasped her hands together. "How wonderful. Julia would be proud."

"Let me warn you. Nina Sayer is a grump and not to be trusted." Brooke pointed her fork at me. "Keep your guard up."

I narrowed my eyes. "What do you mean, not to be trusted? She's abrupt and forward with her words. I'll admit that."

"Let's say she cozies up to O'Neil whenever it benefits her."

I pursed my lips. Brooke spoke like a chronic complainer on a mission to trash everybody and everything. I'd keep my guard up when around *her*.

"I think it's time for dessert, don't you?" Gladys popped out of her chair. "Alexis, will you help me?"

We left the guests and Ollie to chat and made our way to the kitchen.

I lifted a serving tray off the top shelf and set it on the counter next to the plates. Despite the humor in our talk, the serious topic about Thaddeus and murder refused to leave my mind. My hunch was everyone at the table experienced the same problem.

"How are you doing, Gladys?" I asked.

She shrugged. "Oh, as well as can be expected. It's difficult to put murder out of your head, isn't it? I'm sure Sheriff Sterling will figure out things."

"We're going to help in every way we can. You know all of us believe in you and Ollie." I patted her shoulder.

"Of course, dear. Of course. Now, let's get this dessert out to our guests. If I know Ollie, he'll be shouting with impatience any second now. That man and his appetite." She clucked her tongue.

Marianne carried on the conversation as I set the tray down on the sideboard and distributed dessert around the table.

"I know exactly what you mean, Ralph. After spending the night at his resort and listening nonstop to all his bragging, I couldn't wait to leave," she said.

"Did you get enough information for your article, though?" I asked.

"I have two more B&B's to visit this evening. I just wish I hadn't wasted time at Sebastian Tubble's ski resort." Her tone grew agitated.

A thought came to me at the mention of his name. "I met Sebastian today at Meeka's Mementos. He and Ralph were chatting." I glanced at Ralph and smiled. "I don't recall seeing him before. Has he been in Sierra Pines very long?"

"Actually, he moved here more than thirty years ago. Since you visit in the fall, it makes sense you've never met him. Sebastian travels to North Lake Tahoe for the annual sports expo during October. This is the first year he missed going. Very odd, come to think of it. But then again, with everything that's happened this month, we're all out of sorts. Anyway, he joined SPACA a couple of years ago. There'd never been any occasion for us to associate much before then. We don't ski," Gladys explained.

My brows lifted as I pictured the elderly Bellwethers dressed in parkas, strapped into skis, and slaloming down the slope.

"I had no idea this place has such history. So many of Julia's ancestors carved out quite a reputation for themselves back in the pioneer days of California. Gold miners. Saloon owners. Even a gunslinger or two. Why didn't you tell me?" Marianne shot the Bellwethers a reproachful stare.

Gladys lifted her chin. "Julia never was one to toot a horn or hang out the dirty laundry when it came to family. I don't think it's my place to do so."

"Still, it's fascinating stuff. Did you know, Ali? I mean, it's your family, after all." Marianne broke off a piece of cake with her fork.

I shook my head. "Skeletons in the closet. The family rule was you hide them and never talk about them. Especially stories about the saloon owner and gunslinger." I laughed.

Gladys stuffed the end of a napkin inside Ollie's collar. "You're such a slob." Her eyes twinkled.

"I love you too, sister dear. Why don't we all forget about skeletons and eat this delicious cake Gladys baked?" Ollie shoved a generous bite into his mouth, while crumbs sprinkled the napkin on his chest.

"See what I mean?" Gladys sat next to him. "What would he ever do without me?"

"Let's hope I never find out." Ollie quickly added, "Enjoy, everyone!"

By seven o'clock, we gathered in the breakroom inside the city building, which wasn't much of a room. The mere twenty-by-twenty-foot area contained several fold-out chairs surrounding a long, narrow table with enough nicks and scrapes to show its age. The walls were painted a drab gray. Not even a single colorful decoration adorned the room to infuse some life into it.

Few attended. I hadn't had much luck convincing others to aid the cause, namely, to save the Bellwethers from a murder charge. Besides me, Ralph and Dean came, as promised. Adding to the three of us were Florence, Gladys, Ollie and Minnie Short, the oldest member of SPACA. In truth, probably the oldest citizen in Sierra Pines, and, according to Florence, she was the dreamy-eyed spinster who had been crushing on Ollie since the Bellwethers arrived in town many decades ago. She was cute as a button and small enough to fit into my suitcase. But her energy and spunk could rival Superman's. I could count on Minnie to go the extra mile.

Even Sebastian scheduled an appearance, which came as a surprise to me. According to Florence, when she spoke with him on the phone this afternoon, she got nothing but excuses. Absolutely, he'd love to help but must keep a low profile. Being associated with a murder case could damage his standing in the community and destroy business for the ski resort.

Even Florence revealed her reluctance when she offered her support with a list of conditions. The Bellwethers must agree to distance themselves from SPACA until the ugly mess was resolved. They weren't to attend any meetings or volunteer for any functions the alliance represented and refrain from posting on the official website, which was ridiculous since the Bellwethers didn't know how to use a computer or the internet. Florence insisted residents in this fair community wouldn't stand for anyone but those with the highest moral character to be a part of their organization. Those were her words, her opinion. To show my opinion, I told the Bellwethers it was in their best interest to attend the meeting. It gave me the utmost satisfaction witnessing Florence with a sour expression as the three of us entered.

While waiting for the SPACA president to finish her long-winded speech, I wiped down the utility sink and scraped off the scummy layer inside the microwave. When she finally paused, I dropped the sudsy sponge into the sink and turned to face the front.

"Not that I'm pointing fingers, mind you." Florence tipped her chin and ended her running commentary. Her eyes narrowed to give us the don't-mess-with-me stare.

I returned to my seat. "Is that all, Florence?" A syrupy sweetness flavored my tone. She opened her mouth as if winding up for round two, but I rushed to stop her. "I think everyone in this room came here this evening for one reason. I was sure you felt the same way."

"Well, I only mention . . ." Florence's words sputtered into silence.

"We all believe Gladys and Ollie are innocent. Someone killed Thaddeus, and we aren't here to point fingers at them." I dismissed whatever reasoning she intended to use.

Gladys raised her hand.

"You don't have to do that, Gladys. Just say what you want." I smiled.

"Yes, well, I believe we should include Julia in our investigation."

Ollie leaned closer to whisper. "Julia is gone, Gladys."

"What I mean is I might have been wrong about Thaddeus, but there's no reason to dismiss the notion of foul play in Julia's death as well."

Everyone, including me, groaned. "How about we make a list?" I hurried with the suggestion before someone pounced on Gladys's comment.

"What sort of list?" Dean asked.

"Places we can go, people we can question, and any other ideas of how to help with the investigation," I said.

"We are hardly investigators." Florence adjusted the cuff of her jacket.

"I imagine you'd be a perfect investigator." Ollie hugged his arms to his chest.

"Oh? And why do you say that?" The spoon clinked loudly as Florence stirred creamer in her coffee.

"Because you seem to know every little detail about everyone in Sierra Pines, that's why."

Ollie's words sparked and caused everyone in the room to squirm in their seats.

I pressed my lips together. Without too much of a delay, Ollie had taken a jab at Florence. He was smart enough to guess she had objected to the Bellwethers being here.

"Well, of all the—" Florence huffed. "What about this list? Shouldn't we get started? I have things to do and certainly can't spend all evening arguing with you."

I walked to the whiteboard. "Give me your best ideas, people." Within minutes, black marker filled the space with our suggestions of people and places to visit and tasks to complete. I drew arrows to connect the first few items and wrote names next to them. "Dean, Ralph, and Ollie, why don't you cover the movie set? Florence, would you mind putting out a post on the SPACA Facebook page? Ask folks to come forward with any information that might help." I turned to face Gladys. She rubbed the rim of her coffee mug with one thumb, around and around in a mindless gesture. I cleared my throat. "Gladys? Why don't you and I visit the business owners near Bagels and Buns? Somebody must've seen you and Ollie last evening."

She glanced up and nodded. "That's fine."

"Okay, then. That leaves Sebastian and Minnie." I searched the room, but Sebastian had disappeared. Minnie busied herself with refilling the napkin holder. "Or just Minnie. Do you still volunteer on Fridays at the sheriff's office?" With funds having been reduced in recent years, the budget was typically lean, and the Placerville station depended on the generous nature of folks willing to volunteer their time to help.

"Every Friday morning for the last five years. Never miss." Minnie beamed.

Minnie Short matched her name. A tiny woman, she was even shorter than Gladys, but her sparkly personality made up for the lack in height. Unlike most her age, she dressed in a youthful, trendy style with a haircut to match. You couldn't help admiring her flair and energy.

"Great. Keep your eyes and ears sharp to pick up on any details about the case. Can you do that?"

Quint had been tight-lipped when I asked for any information. Understandable, but frustrating to me.

"Absolutely. Anything to help the Bellwethers." However, Minnie kept her attention on Ollie alone and giggled.

Ollie's cheeks blushed beet red.

"I'd say that about covers it. Let's regroup sometime tomorrow and go over what we find." I hung the strap of my bag over one shoulder.

Once we stepped outside, the Bellwethers, Ralph, Dean and I headed on foot toward the B&B. A gentle breeze scattered leaves across the walk. The evening air was crisp and cool. I slipped on my jacket and zipped it closed. As we drew near Bagels and Buns, loud voices echoed from inside. I slowed my pace, and the rest of the group followed suit. In the next few steps, I had a clear view through the window front. Sebastian Tubble was having a conversation with Lenny Taylor, or more like an argument.

"I don't appreciate the innuendo, Taylor," Sebastian shouted.

"Then take your business elsewhere." Lenny shoved a finger at his chest.

"Perhaps I should. I came to you first, trying to do you a favor, but you insult me with this pathetic offer." Sebastian leaned forward to tower over Lenny's small build. "I should've known."

"Oh dear. Maybe we should turn around or cross the street. I don't feel comfortable eavesdropping like this," Gladys whispered.

"Nonsense. This is a public sidewalk, and we have every right to walk where we please," Ollie spouted.

Lenny waved a bag of bagels in Sebastian's face. "You saying I'm a skinflint? Well, looky here. I don't do business with people like you. She warned me, and I should've listened. Now, we're done."

"The feeling's mutual. And I'd be careful throwing around accusations about me, if I were you." Sebastian grabbed the bagel bag out of Lenny's hand and tossed it on the floor. "*Now*, we're done." He stomped out of the store and nearly collided with Gladys. "Watch where you're going, why don't you?" With those words, he marched up the street.

"How about that? Seems Sierra Pines isn't such a happy place for everyone." Dean chuckled then skirted around us to jog ahead. "Might as well get my exercise. Gotta keep in shape for the job."

I rolled my eyes then paused to gaze inside the bakery.

Lenny bent over to pick up the scattered bagels.

"I wonder what that was all about?" A sudden gust of wind caused me to shiver.

"Oh, probably just a silly squabble. You know how people get sometimes." Gladys's eyes brightened. "My, what a beautiful fall evening. Cool and comfortable. I should bake pumpkin pies to celebrate."

I scratched underneath my chin, replaying the conversation between the two men. Sebastian's behavior wasn't flattering. He'd been aggressive and pushy with Ralph earlier this afternoon. And now, I'd add quick-tempered to the list.

"Alexis, are you listening to me?" Gladys tugged at my sleeve.

"Hmm? Oh, yes. Pumpkin pie. Sounds delicious." I gave Lenny a final glance before moving on. "Canned pumpkin or fresh?"

"Always fresh. You know that. Right from our garden, mind you." Gladys laughed. "I'll add the spices, don't worry."

"I'm not worried." My eyebrows pulled together.

Gladys patted my arm. "I wasn't speaking to you, dear."

My mouth opened, but only a sigh escaped.

"I'm thinking out loud. It's what we old folks do on occasion." Gladys tossed me a smile of reassurance.

"I'd like to help, if you don't mind."

"With baking pies? Certainly. It's your aunt's recipe. You know, this entire predicament with the murder investigation reminds me of Phillip Marlowe in *The Big Sleep*."

"How's that? And who is Marlowe?" My body relaxed as we moved ahead to comfortable ground.

"Oh, he's a character in Raymond Chandler's novel, which became a movie back in, let me think, nineteen thirty-three or was it thirty-four?

It doesn't matter. Anyway, Marlowe was a private eye who never, ever gave up, no matter how difficult the case. Such a strong man. Bogart was perfect for the role."

"Did you or Julia work on the film?"

Gladys giggled. "Goodness no. Think, Alexis. In thirty-four we weren't even in our teens. Though, if I remember correctly, Julia's first acting part came when she was quite young. Fourteen, I think? Anyway, Julia met Bogie at a party, years later." Gladys pointed at me. "Then there's Sam Spade. He had a tall order figuring out who killed whom, no matter how hard he tried. It's not easy when a femme fatale like Brigid O'Shaughnessy is involved."

I rubbed my wrinkled forehead. "Sam Spade. Didn't Bogart play him in the movies, too?"

"Yes. *The Maltese Falcon*. Excellent camera shots. We were new to the business, still in our teens, believe it or not. Ollie did the stunt work. Julia was working on another film, her third or fourth, I believe. I became a companion of sorts to actress Mary Astor, who was battling addiction. Poor woman. She'd lost her third husband in a plane crash." Gladys rambled on as we climbed the stairs to the B&B.

Ollie trailed close behind us. "Gladys, Ali isn't interested in all those details."

"Certainly, she is. She's told me as much. Haven't you, Alexis?"

"When it involves Aunt Julia, I'm curious. Right now, I'm more interested in baking pies." I threw the comment over my shoulder then turned to face the house.

Dean waited on the front porch. He was bent over with both hands locked on his knees. His chest moved with each breathy burst.

I grinned. "Great run, Dean?"

He held up one arm and nodded. "Yeah, great."

"Why don't we go inside for some cold lemonade?" Gladys winked at me.

"Excellent idea." I linked my arm through Gladys's, and we all stepped into the house.

"Good evening, everybody."

I rocked on my heels and came to a halt. Sheriff Quint Sterling sat on the foyer bench seat. He smiled, but his jaw muscles stretched in taut lines. My stomach quivered. This wasn't a good sign. Not at all.

# CHAPTER SIX

"WHY, SHERIFF STERLING. WHAT A PLEASANT surprise." Gladys smiled, but the quiver in her voice marred the enthusiasm.

Quint slowly stood and clenched his hat in both hands. "I hope you don't mind. One of your guests let me inside."

"Of course we don't mind. You're always welcome." Ollie moved to stand next to his sister.

I kept a tight grip on Gladys's arm. Why couldn't we have one day without bad news? Not that this was bad news, but the anxious look on Quint's face didn't shout the words happy or great.

"I'm sorry to disturb your evening, but I'm here on official business." Quint nodded at each of us. "Do you think Brooke and Marianne would join us? I think all of you should hear what I have to say."

"They both have plans this evening. Miss Lane is visiting a few more B&Bs to gather information for her article, and Miss Seale told me she's working late at the movie set," Gladys explained.

Ollie waved an arm. "How about we go into the parlor?"

The walk across the foyer felt like the death march, each step slow and anxious. I sat next to Gladys on the sofa, with my back straight and rigid as a board. Official business. Hope lingered in the back of mind, but I wouldn't wager any bets. My gut told me this was about to trail south and sink the Bellwethers' chances even further.

Quint cleared his throat. "First off, I need to clarify these results are merely preliminary."

"What results?" I asked.

"From the dirt sample my team found with the victim."

"Dirt? You mean like you'd find on the bottom of shoes?"

Quint shook his head. "Dirt as in what we found in Julia's bed. Anyway, to get a quick analysis—like I said, this is preliminary and not conclusive—I took a sample to the local nursery."

"Justin Digmoore's nursery." Ollie nodded.

"Yes."

"And you found out what?" My nerves sparked as I grew impatient.

"Color, texture, and pH level of the sample matches the dirt in the backyard where Gladys and Ollie were digging." He tugged at the collar of his shirt.

"That's hardly conclusive. Why anyone, even Thaddeus, could've been in the backyard and snooped around. It doesn't mean . . ." I broke off.

"I'd agree with you, but then there's the other evidence." He paused a second, and his attention shifted to the Bellwethers. "The other day? When we first searched the house, we found a towel with dirt stains in Gladys's clothes hamper. Didn't raise my suspicions since the Bellwethers admitted they'd been digging in the backyard."

I opened my mouth to say more, but Quint raised his hand.

"I'm not finished. We also found blood stains on the towel." He grew quiet. His gaze fixed on Gladys.

"A splinter from the shovel gouged my finger. I grabbed the towel to stop the bleeding, didn't I, Ollie?" Gladys's response ended with an anxious glance at her brother.

He nodded.

"I'll have the lab in Placerville check it out, of course. In the meantime, can you explain how dirt got on the bed?" Quint asked.

"Well, I, no, I can't say."

Ollie straightened in his seat. "She's telling you the truth, Quint. Why can't we wait and let the lab people do their job before answering more questions?"

I considered the implication of Quint's words in silence. His news buried the Bellwethers' chances in their freshly dug hole. No telling how they'd climb out.

Dean let out a whistle as he stared at Gladys. "*Arsenic and Old Lace*, part two. Crazy nephew Teddy buries a body in the backyard." He chuckled but fell silent when Quint clenched his jaw.

"This isn't a movie script. This is real, and it's serious business. I'm going by the evidence, which does appear to lead in one direction." He turned to Gladys and Ollie. "So, I'll ask you once again, do you have any idea why dirt, apparently from your backyard, was found in Julia's bed?"

Gladys stood and shook off Ollie's hand when he gripped her arm to stay. She paced the room, glanced upward once or twice, and murmured to herself. She finally slowed and came to a halt in front of Quint.

"This will sound like I'm crazy, but I assure you I'm not. You see, I miss Julia." She wrung her hands before they dropped to her sides. "I find comfort when I'm near her, well, near what belonged to her. It's why I spend so much time in her room." She turned to face all of us. "That's why I lay in her bed. But only once, after we dug the hole. The idea of planting a tree, her favorite tree, is so overwhelming." She paused and bit down on her bottom lip as her chin quivered. "In that moment, it struck me. Julia's gone. It was peaceful, somehow comforting, to lie in her bed."

I blinked. Whether pretense or sincerity, I couldn't guess. Her peculiar behavior in the past few days had been a real eye-opener.

Quint raked fingers through his hair. "Miss Bellwether, Gladys, I'm not sure—"

"Maybe we should take a break." I sprang up from my seat.

"I don't need a break. I, *we* need answers, Alexis. Sheriff Sterling is being very helpful, and you shouldn't interrupt him. It's rude." Gladys admonished me with both her words and grim stare.

Yeah, he'd help her, all right. Straight into a jail cell. I sank back in the chair and kept quiet.

Quint cleared his throat. "As I was about to say, Gladys, I'm not sure where this investigation will go or what the evidence will tell me, but I'll keep digging until I find the killer. That's a promise."

I shivered, hearing his comment. What he dug up might lead right to the Bellwethers.

"Thank you, Sheriff. And the invitation to game night tomorrow evening still stands." Gladys stood and smoothed the wrinkles from her dress.

Innocence expressed itself in her bright eyes and gentle smile. I blinked away the tears welling in my eyes. How could she be guilty of anything more murderous than baking desserts scrumptious enough to die for? No pun intended.

Ollie raised his brows. "Under the circumstances, maybe we should put that off until next week?"

"Nonsense. Julia would want us to carry on the tradition. Doesn't the B&B brochure say we promise to entertain our guests? It's part of our charm." She shook her head fiercely and her voice hitched. "Don't you ruin things for me, Ollie. I won't have it."

Everyone grew quiet until Ollie laughed. "Well, then, I guess we're having a game night this weekend."

"It's settled." Gladys gave a firm nod. "Who's up for movie trivia? I don't mean to brag, but Ollie and I are hard to beat. We do love a challenge, though. What do you say, Dean? Ralph?"

While the four of them chatted, I casually walked over to Quint. "May I have a word?" I jerked my head to the side and headed to the foyer, hoping he'd follow.

We came to a stop at the front door.

"I hope this isn't to prod me for more information about the case." Quint's legs spread and rested in a firm stance while his arms crossed snuggly against his chest.

I raised my eyebrows at his posture. Whether he meant to intimidate or defend, I wasn't sure. "Not at all. See, I know this looks bad for the Bellwethers. Really, really bad." I clenched my jaw. "There's something you should know. Something that might sway you in another direction."

At once, he let his arms drop then reached to open the door. "Outside?"

I nodded and grabbed my jacket off the coat rack before stepping through the doorway. The gray cloud-covered sky released a fine mist that glistened as it landed on the grass and leaves. We sat on the wicker settee, sheltered by the overhang. I glanced sideways, opened my mouth, then closed it. I puzzled over how to explain or whether to keep what I wanted to share to myself. Weighing the pros and cons, I sighed.

"Ali, why are we out here?" His soft tone carried no judgment, no impatience.

I chewed on a thumbnail then pulled it away from my mouth and spoke. "Don't take them into custody."

"I hadn't planned on it. There's not enough substantiated proof yet to arrest either one of them."

"I guess you noticed from the things she's been saying, Gladys acts rather odd. I'm not sure, but I'd say she's depressed and lonely over losing Julia." I rested both hands in my lap and willed them to remain still.

"Yes, I'd expect that." Gently, he reached for one of my hands and wrapped his fingers around it.

I trembled slightly.

"Ali, I'm trying to do my job in the best way possible. Getting answers to my questions helps me solve cases. I'm not accusing the Bellwethers of anything, just collecting information."

"Sure. I know." I nodded and fixed my attention on our intertwined hands.

He must've caught me staring because, in the next instant, he pulled away.

I traced my tongue across dry lips. "I'll keep an eye on them. Don't worry."

"I'm not worried."

"What I'm trying to say is they're old, and Gladys seems so very weak and not at all herself. To be spending time in jail . . ." My voice trailed off into subdued silence.

"I agree. I'm not arresting them, Ali." Quint patted my arm and then stood. "You worry, but there's no reason for it. Trust me. The Bellwethers will be fine."

"Will they?" I lifted my gaze to search his face. I found no sign of concern or hint of insincerity. This time, he didn't answer. "If you need to go, that's fine. I'd like to be alone for a bit, maybe to digest everything that's happened."

"Yeah, I guess I've asked enough questions for one day." His chest moved in and out for several breaths as he stared at me. "I realize it doesn't make a difference, but I'll say again . . ."

"I know. They'll be fine." I smiled. "Now, go. Have a good evening, what's left of it." I waved my arm to dismiss him.

Quint tipped his hat. "Same to you, ma'am." He sprinted down the driveway to his cruiser.

Once he was out of sight, I leaned back and closed my eyes. Dean and his movie reference. I scoffed. Quint was right. This wasn't *Arsenic and Old Lace*. No dead bodies buried on the premises. Nobody to poison. Certainly, no crazy nephew who believed he was Teddy Roosevelt hidden in the Bellwethers' family tree. And I doubted these siblings kept a decanter of wine laced with arsenic stored in the cabinet. My brows peaked. "Or at least I hope there's not."

Getting out of my seat, I brushed off the leaves stuck to my bottom then stepped inside the house. I wandered into the kitchen but found it empty. Most likely, everyone had escaped to the safe, quiet haven of their rooms. A plate piled high with chips and a double-decker ham and cheese sandwich sat on the counter. A note with my name on it was attached. *In case you'd like an evening snack. Love, Gladys.*

"I absolutely would." I reached for the plate, but a loud squawk stopped me and diverted my attention. My gaze followed the sound coming from the back. "Blackbeard. You finally decided to come alive, huh?" I chuckled and made my way to the atrium adjoining the screened porch. Julia's pet bird had been overly quiet and not at all himself. Everyone in the B&B hoped it was temporary.

"Ah, I see. Someone forgot to cover your cage. Can't say I'm surprised. Ollie has been preoccupied the past few days." I lifted the black cloth off the shelf. "But we can forgive him, can't we?"

Blackbeard nuzzled his beak into his feathers then tucked his head on one side to rest. Like most parrots, he loved to talk and whistle a tune now and then. According to Gladys, he'd grown much quieter since Julia's death. Everyone, including birds, had a right to mourn in his or her own way.

"No comment, huh? Yeah, I get it. Healing takes time. Maybe a good night's sleep will help. I'll try and do the same. Deal?" I draped the cloth over his cage and walked back into the kitchen.

With plate in one hand and a glass of apple cider in the other, I mounted the stairs to the third floor and headed to my own safe, quiet haven. As I passed Gladys's room, the sound of words being exchanged muffled through the door. Normally not one to eavesdrop, extenuating circumstances warranted this an exception. I held my breath and paused to listen.

"Sister, it's fine. Stop worrying. Quint has no way to prove we're guilty of anything except caring about our dear friend."

"But what if he discovers . . ." Gladys voice caught.

"*Shh*. Don't. Just trust me. He won't find any proof. Now, get some rest. You're looking pale. Did you take your pill?"

"Yes. I'm fine. Really. You can go on to bed."

I hurried to my room before Ollie reached the hallway. Setting the plate and glass on the nightstand, I sat on the edge of the bed and stared at the sandwich. My stomach lurched. This wasn't good. What Ollie had said could be taken more than one way. What if he meant there was proof to find them guilty, but he'd hidden it where no one, not even Quint, could find it?

"Stop with all the negatives. Julia would believe in her friends, and so should I." I argued aloud as I grabbed the sandwich and took a generous bite. That settled it. No more doubts. Doubts deflated my confidence and soured my attitude. Not to mention, all the wavering back and forth and the "did they or didn't they" conundrum exhausted me.

My cell phone vibrated across the nightstand to distract me. An unfamiliar number lit up the screen. Curious, I grabbed for the receiver. "Hello?"

"Hey, Winston. It's Nina Sayer."

I frowned at the clock. It was past nine, and if this was a request to come in to work for some project, I'd be tempted to hang up. "Everything okay?"

"No. Not at all. The production building was trashed this evening. I got a call from security. I ran like the dickens from my trailer. Rollers in my hair and still in my jammies. Not a pretty sight."

I paced the room. "Trashed? How? Why? Who?"

"The way anybody would trash a place, by making a total mess. Don't ask me why. And I certainly don't have a clue as to what gutter snipe would do this. Heavens to Betsy. The props are fine but the supplies and boxes of materials, my desk, your desk, and everything else are tossed and scattered. It's a real mess to clean up. O'Neil has his boxers in a twist. He says this will delay production, and he can't afford delays. The man drives me bonkers."

I chewed on my bottom lip. "Can you tell if anything's missing?"

Nina snorted. "Are you kidding? Needles in haystacks, kiddo. Look, I don't suppose you'd be willing to help with cleanup? The maintenance crew on set is taking care of the heavy lifting, which doesn't involve much."

I stared at the clock, again. "Now?"

"No. Of course not now. I'm only warning you what you're facing when you come in tomorrow. Look, if you'd rather not, I can find people here to help."

"No, I'll be there. Early tomorrow. Promise."

"Thank you. You're a standup lady. Just like Julia. Okay, get some sleep. You'll need it."

After ending the call, I made my way back to the bed, tossed the phone on the nightstand, and then sat. I lowered my chin to rest in both palms. Who would break into a building full of props? They weren't worth much to anyone but O'Neil. I considered him for a moment. Maybe someone had a grudge against him and this act was a way to punish him. I shook my head. "Lame idea."

The whole place was tossed, Nina said. Right down to the tiniest item. What if the intruder was looking for something? I couldn't think of anything in Julia's work area worth stealing. I wasn't sure about Nina's. My brows peaked. In truth, I didn't know Nina that well, especially about her past. Other than her love life, which, come to think of it, opened up another world of possibilities. Scorned lovers held grudges, too.

I picked up the sandwich when the house phone chimed the tune of "Que Sera," the one Doris Day sang in Hitchcock's *The Man Who Knew Too Much*. The famous director and producer had the phone designed and sent it to Julia on her birthday.

"Geesh. Can't a girl cut a break?" I grabbed the receiver.

"Oh, Ali. Thank goodness you answered."

My stomach curdled at the sound of Florence's voice, which was more high-pitched and shriller than usual. As if that was even possible. "Florence, what's wrong?"

"It's horrible. So horrible. The comments. I can't stop imagining what this will do to the committee, or to the town, for goodness sakes. Horrible, horrible." She broke down into a cacophony of sobs.

I gripped the phone with white-knuckled force. "Now, Florence. You need to calm yourself and start from the beginning."

She spouted and sputtered. "I'm finding comments on our website, our Facebook page, our Twitter account, even on Yelp. They keep popping up and won't stop. Heaven help us. The words are so vindictive. Everyone from here to Sacramento must've heard the rumors about his murder. It's purely slanderous. SPACA is ruined. All because of the Bellwethers."

"Florence, people are gossipmongers. They talk about one thing only until the next juicy story comes along, which will most likely be soon. That's how it works. As for Gladys and Ollie, try and have a little faith." Her remark about the Bellwethers stung. I kept my emotions in check and clamped down on my lips to stop from snapping at her.

"But . . ."

"In the meantime, we can find ways to dampen that gossip fire. Maybe some positive PR about the work you've been doing on the movie and the theater fundraiser would help. Take out an ad in the paper. I'll think of other ideas. Give me a day or two." It proved difficult to dampen Florence's hysteria once it took off.

"Well, I'm not so certain any of this will save us. We're like a sinking ship. I ran into Mayor Simpson this morning at Bagels and Buns. He practically threatened me. He warned if this ruins SPACA's reputation, it would also tarnish the town. Visitors will stop coming to Sierra Pines. Shop owners will lose business, including you and your precious B&B. Why we could become a ghost town." Her voice shrieked.

"Florence, get hold of yourself. No more talk of ghost towns. Got it?" My words passed through gritted teeth.

"Yes. Yes, you're absolutely right." A nervous chirp escaped her mouth.

"Now, I'm getting off the phone to think. I suggest you do the same. We'll strategize and come up with a solid plan. I'm sure this will blow over in a couple of days, but if not, we'll be ready." I set the receiver back in the cradle. I rolled my neck side to side, easing the tension one roll at a time. Not that I'd come to a decision yet, but there was no way I could leave Sierra Pines anytime soon. I refused to desert the Bellwethers when they needed me most, not while they were stuck in the muck, as Julia used to say. After the murder was solved, I'd think about my future plan. In the meantime, there was a barn-sized mess to put back together. I reached for my cell phone and set the alarm for six, thought for a second, then reset for five thirty. I studied the plate of sandwich and chips. My stomach rolled and I crawled into bed. Suddenly, an evening snack didn't seem so appetizing.

# CHAPTER SEVEN

THE MOOSE CUCKOO CLOCK CHIMED SIX. The sound echoed loud enough to reach my ears as I stood at the far end of the house inside the atrium. Aunt Julia discovered the oddity one summer in a clockmaker's shop, far north in upper Vancouver, Canada. She fell in love and brought it home, where she proudly displayed the clock in the foyer, despite Gladys's objection. She argued anything in the shape of a moose would scare away the guests, but it never did. Ollie, on the other hand, loved it.

I reached inside the bird cage to fill Blackbeard's feeding tray with bird seed and an apple slice for dessert. As I expected, he started with dessert. I couldn't blame him. We all needed soothing comfort food at the moment.

I'd talked to Ollie and we agreed to split caring for Blackbeard. I'd cover the mornings and he'd make sure to do everything else, which included the bedtime ritual. Of course, I'd check in on occasion. Ollie as caregiver was still a work in progress.

I smiled and stroked the top of Blackbeard's head. "I know this is rough on you, sweetie. We all miss her, but I promise you'll have a home here forever." I fed him a last bit of apple then left the atrium.

Reaching the foyer, I grabbed my jacket off the coat rack. I messaged Nina I was on my way then sprinted across the front lawn. After a morning shift cleaning the production building mess, I planned to return to the B&B and clean the house. Keeping busy was my remedy to distract myself and avoid worrying.

Traffic was nonexistent at six in the morning. The cold night left behind a layer of frost. It glistened on lawns and tree branches with their sparse covering of leaves. The streets hushed with quiet abandon. It would be a few hours before shops opened and customers filled the sidewalks. I liked the peace and quiet. It was comforting.

Moving into the next block, I flipped on the turn signal and pulled into the parking lot. At once, I spotted the cruiser parked next to Nina's car. She or O'Neil must've called Quint to investigate. I figured, for insurance purposes, the producer needed a report filed.

I jogged up to the building. The doors had been left open. Quint and Nina stood inside. Nina held up one of the sanding tools. Its severed cord dangled in her other hand. I winced. This was worse than she'd let on.

"Hey, Nina. Quint. That doesn't look so good." I nodded at the sander.

Nina snorted and laughed at once. "You think? I found this behind a stack of crates. It's an easy repair, but let's hope we don't find any more damaged goods. We can't afford to lose equipment."

Quint's mouth formed a fine line. Red etched across his pupils and dark circles shadowed underneath his eyes.

"You okay?" I asked.

"Bad night. Mom had one of her spells and kept me awake. Then I got the call about this break-in." He waved his arm.

"Sorry about that," Nina said.

"You shouldn't be. It's my job." He heaved his shoulders. "Any ideas?"

"Nope. How about you, Winston? Any enemies chasing you down I should know about?" Nina winked.

"Ha. I was about to ask you the same thing. Seriously, this doesn't make any sense." I glanced around. Not a single item was in its proper place. There was more stuff on the floor than on the shelves. "I don't suppose you got a chance to see if anything is missing?"

"I searched some but came up with zilch. I guess, after we're finished, maybe we'll know if the lowlife took anything." Nina raked fingers through her orange and gray curls.

"Okay, I'll start the paperwork, and if you'll come down to the station this afternoon, I'll have you sign the report and give you a copy. Sound good?" Quint tapped his pen on the notebook then slipped both in his pocket.

"Sure thing." Nina turned her head side to side. "I'll need a break sometime. This will take a while."

As Quint passed through the doorway, a line of people filed into the building. I grinned. "Or maybe it won't. Looks like we have some help."

Nina turned. "Well, I'll be. Sierra Pines is full of surprises."

Gladys, Ollie, Minnie, and Meeka gathered around us. They carried mops, buckets, and cleaning spray.

"Tell us where to start and we'll get this job done in a jiffy," Gladys said.

"Lenny and Lucinda from the beauty parlor will be here to help, too. They had to close up their shops first," Meeka added.

"This is . . . you guys are amazing. Thank you." I wrapped my arms around Gladys first then gave each of the others a hug.

NINA CLAPPED HER HANDS. "Okay, cleaning crew. Let's get to work."

We finished cleaning up the mess by early afternoon. I hurried home to take a quick shower to rejuvenate and get ready for round two. I tried to avoid all bad thoughts by keeping busy. It was an uphill climb. Sharp images of Thaddeus lying dead in Julia's bed haunted me, even though I hadn't seen the body, thank goodness. Quint gave us word this morning that the investigation team was through with Julia's room, but I struggled with the thought of going inside. I wasn't ready, and I figured neither was Gladys.

The murder and everything else that happened in the past week gave me a headache and fried more brain cells than I could afford to lose. I had to speak with the Bellwethers about what I'd overheard but couldn't decide where to start or how to help. They said the tiniest gesture was appreciated. This was tiny. I offered to clean the guestrooms. At least Gladys and Ollie could get the rest they needed.

"You'll find cleaning supplies stored in the hall closet, next to my bedroom." Gladys squeezed my arm. "You're a dear. I feel guilty letting you take over my duties. Although, I do need time alone to think this through. It's been such a trying spell since your aunt passed."

"Are you kidding? The way you persuaded all those people to help clean the production building was a blessing. We'd still be at it, if not for you."

She shrugged. "In Sierra Pines, folks help each other. I'm sorry you couldn't figure out who'd do such a horrible thing. Makes me wonder."

"Wonder about what?" I shifted weight from one foot to the other.

"Oh, how everything that's happened this past week all seems connected to Julia." Gladys nodded.

I tensed. "How so?" If she planned to bring up her suspicions of Julia's death, I wouldn't know how to respond.

"Well, let's see." She tapped her lip. "First, Julia dies. Then Thaddeus is murdered. He was Julia's friend and it happened in Julia's B&B, not to mention, right in her bed. And last night, someone broke into the production building where Julia worked. You see? Julia figures into every incident." She wagged her finger. "Don't even try to dispute the point."

My mouth flapped. No, I wouldn't try. I couldn't because I thought of nothing to say. I was flabbergasted by her clever insight.

"Thank you, again, dear." Gladys clasped my hand. "And for offering to make dinner. This free time will give me a chance to better prepare this evening's game. Maybe instead of trivia we could act out scenes from movies for everyone to guess. What do you think?" She disappeared into the library before I had a chance to respond.

I stood only for a few seconds, sorting out what she'd said about Julia and the connections. "Why didn't I think of that idea? You're off your game, Ali Winston." I shook my head then jogged up the stairs to the attic and down the hall, anxious to get started. I had plenty of time to finish all the bedrooms before preparing dinner. If there was a chance I decided to stay, I might as well experience the most of what it would be like to run a B&B.

The closet, stocked with sundry items from top shelf to bottom, was neat and organized. I grabbed bottles of cleaning spray and polish from the middle and towels, brushes, and gloves from the top. My arms were overloaded and piled high. I nestled the stack of supplies under my chin and stepped away, rigid as stone to keep from losing my cargo, but a slippery bottle of glass cleaner popped out and everything tumbled to the floor.

"Just great." I knelt on all fours to gather the items when I spotted a small plastic basket tucked underneath the shelves. It was the perfect size in which to carry everything, with two smaller sections for brushes and gloves. I glowered at the cleaning caddy. "Well, give myself the prize for dummy of the hour."

I slid the caddy out of the closet and loaded my cleaning arsenal. Taking inventory, I blinked then counted again. "Now, where did that can of polish go?" I lowered my head to the floor and peered into the closet. The polish had rolled to rest near the back wall. I reached underneath with one hand and swiped back and forth, my fingers splayed, until I touched something flat, smooth, and rather small. I grasped ahold of the object and slid it toward me and then straightened to stare. Not only smooth and flat but made of clear glass, with gold lettered etching. I took slow, even breaths. Aunt Julia's award plaque. A film of dust covered the surface and blurred the notation. With my fingers, I took a hurried swipe to clean it.

"Ouch." I muttered a couple of choice words and sucked on one finger. The bitter, salty, iron taste of blood filled my mouth. I bent closer to examine the plaque and its jagged edge. A narrow groove formed a cracked line with the jagged corner stained in blood. My blood. I cursed. Had it been cracked before? I couldn't remember. Gladys had mentioned a tiny scratch, but this was much more than a scratch. I absently tapped the side. The plaque sat on the nightstand in Julia's room up until . . . when? Gladys remarked she couldn't find it. No doubt she'd been slightly distracted by a dead body in Julia's bed. I stared at the bloody stain. Maybe the plaque had been there that evening, but why was it in the hall closet now?

Illogical reasoning or not, I wanted to wipe the glass clean, as if the bloody mark desecrated Julia's memory. I grabbed a towel from the caddy and brought the plaque closer. Bunching the towel in one hand I paused. Wet and bright red layered like fresh paint over top of a darker red stain, the texture of it cracked and flaky. I had the urge to touch it, but the idea stalled in my brain and suddenly shot forward as if new thoughts picked up the slack. In a matter of seconds, maybe to a count of ten, the situation became clear. I carefully wrapped the plaque in the towel and shoved it underneath all my supplies in the caddy.

I stood and carried my cargo down to the second floor and straight to Ralph's room. *Clean. Keep busy. Give yourself time to think.* The tiny directives steadied me. "Oh, Gladys and Ollie, what have you done?" I whispered under my breath and kept walking. The muck just got deeper.

I cleaned the rooms within an hour before hurrying to my own. I shoved Julia's plaque into a plastic zipper bag and searched my bedroom corner to corner until settling on a spot. No place was safe enough, but I had to choose. Kneeling down, I slid the bag underneath the bed.

Thoughts passed through my brain faster than I could keep up. Anyone could've hidden it in the hall closet. Anyone besides Gladys or Ollie. That meant Ralph, Dean, Brooke, or Marianne. Or someone from outside the B&B. Obviously, the killer, whoever he or she was, used the plaque as a weapon and hid it in the closet. What other explanation could there be? I shivered. Thaddeus had been murdered with Julia's plaque.

"Gladys being the killer makes no sense. Why would she send me to the closet for supplies if she'd hidden the plaque there?" I reasoned aloud as I took my second shower of the day. "No sane, intelligent person would do that." I raised my brow and shook my head. Maybe sane was the wrong word choice. "Okay, no intelligent person would."

I brushed the tangles out of my hair and pulled it back in a ponytail. I stared at my reflection in the mirror. Dark circles under the eyes, deeper creases in my forehead from worrying, and a sallow complexion hardly conveyed confidence. Mentioning how-to-commit-murder schemes from movies weren't helping the situation. *Thanks a lot, Dean.* And what about Ollie? What if he killed Thaddeus, and Gladys was totally unaware? She'd sent me straight to the evidence that would convict her brother. I popped two chewable pain reliever tablets in my mouth.

"No. Not possible. There isn't anything one of them says or does without the other knowing. If Ollie killed Thaddeus, Gladys would know." I pulled on my sweater and pants and slipped into loafers. I'd have to give Quint the plaque. My conscience wouldn't let me rest otherwise. In the meantime, I prayed for a miracle. The Bellwethers could certainly use one.

I shooed Gladys and Ollie out of the kitchen so they could get ready for this evening while I finished cleaning up the dinner dishes. Snacks for game night were mostly prepared. I slid a tray of jalapeno poppers in the oven then gave Florence a call to talk about SPACA. "Hi, Florence. I've given it some thought, and I think there are a couple ways to turn this ordeal around."

"Well, anything you suggest is worth hearing."

"Great." I sat on a stool next to the breakfast bar and reeled off what I had in mind. "The acting classes for students would be fantastic PR."

"Oh, I love the idea, but who'll teach them? We can't allow the Bellwethers to handle it. At least not for now."

I stabbed a chip into guacamole. My happy mood was losing ground. "The sheriff hasn't arrested either one of them." Though, that could easily change, and soon. My shoulders slumped.

"I'm only trying to douse the flames. People get out of control over things like this."

My jaw paused mid-chew. "Oh? You have a lot of experience with things like this?"

"It's called common sense, Ali. Common sense applied to human nature. It'll take time."

"Yeah, common sense. I should've thought of that." I rolled my eyes. "Now, what about the yearly event? You like the idea of charitable donations in place of keeping all the funds you raise for the SPACA coffers?"

"Absolutely. Your ideas are wonderful, and don't you worry about the Bellwethers. I have a feeling Sebastian will offer to teach the acting classes."

"Oh? Why's that?" I pulled a serving platter from the cupboard and arranged fresh vegies around a bowl of dill dip.

She snorted. "He loves the attention, and any angle that gets free publicity for his ski resort is a win."

"Okay. I guess it's settled."

Footsteps grew near.

I shot a glance over my shoulder and spotted Ralph. "I have to go, Florence. Call me if you need my help."

"You've done quite a lot already by thinking of these ideas. I don't know how you manage. Especially with murder happening right under your roof. Not exactly the way to start running your B&B, is it?"

"It's not my B&B. I haven't made a decision one way or the other. Goodbye, Florence." I disconnected and laid the phone on the counter. "Hi, Ralph. I hope you didn't fill up too much on your dinner. We've got plenty of snack foods for this evening, and Gladys has prepared a fun game of movie trivia." I smiled.

Ralph rubbed his ample stomach. "I'm sorry to say dinner was light on the food and heavy on business talk." He reached across the counter. "So, call me famished. These chips and guacamole look delicious."

"Take them." I slid the bowl and the guacamole dip his way. "I've had plenty."

"So, what's your take on the argument between Lenny Taylor and Sebastian Tubble yesterday?" Ralph arched his brow and swirled a chip around to gather a generous portion of guacamole.

"They certainly weren't enjoying the conversation, were they?" I nodded.

"No, and I think I know why."

"Hmm? How's that?"

"I overheard Lenny talking to the owner of Annie's Florist the other day when I went shopping." Ralph moaned. "This dip should be in stores and restaurants. I have to pry the recipe out of Gladys. She's refused me so far, but I'll wear her down. You help me, and we'll package it and make a fortune. What do you say?" He wiggled his brows.

I snickered and twisted my fingers as if to lock my lips. "You don't know Gladys Bellwether very well, then."

"You just wait. Folks who've gotten to know me think I'm a real charmer. Now, about Taylor. I heard him say that Sebastian—these are his words, not mine—Sebastian is a scheming, no good liar."

"Huh. That's quite a strong accusation. Are you sure?"

"I am. I was standing not more than six feet away when he said it."

I wiped the counter to clear the crumbs. Taylor's claim we overheard yesterday had been just as damaging. *I don't do business with people like you. She warned me, and I should've listened.* Who warned Taylor? And why was Sebastian such a scheming liar?

The timer on the stove dinged and I jumped. "Poppers are ready!" I scooted off the stool and grabbed potholders to remove the pan. I placed it on the trivet. "Would you call everyone down while I carry everything into the parlor?"

"Be glad to." His chest expanded as he sniffed. "The poppers smell scrumptious."

"Oh, and Ralph? Don't say anything about Mr. Taylor's accusation to Gladys and Ollie. All right? I don't want to upset them with anymore unpleasant news."

"Of course. I understand. It's a real shame. Murder in this cozy place doesn't quite fit, does it? Be right back." He jogged down the hall.

I waited while he climbed the stairs and then opened my phone to make the dreaded call. "Sheriff Sterling, please."

"I'm sorry. He's out of the office. May I take a message?"

"Yes, tell him Ali Winston called."

"Ali Winston? Julia Winston's niece? What a coincidence. The sheriff is on his way to your place. He should be there any minute."

"Okay, thanks." A trace of worry slid through me. Quint was expecting a quiet evening of movie trivia. Instead, what he'd get was Julia's cracked and bloodied award plaque. In his past two visits, Quint had been the one to deliver bad news. Now it was my turn. Lucky me.

I placed the poppers back in the oven and set the control to warm. Seconds afterward, the doorbell rang. My breath caught. I took hurried, anxious steps to the front door. "Good evening. You're right on time." I leaned one arm against the doorframe as if the fixture was my life support.

"Evening, Ali." He tipped his hat then stepped inside, brushing my shoulder as he passed by me.

"All ready for a fun night of movie trivia?" I pushed fake enthusiasm to the forefront.

"Not exactly." He removed his hat. "I need to speak with Gladys and Ollie. It's urgent."

I hitched my breath. This wasn't the face of a man looking forward to yummy snacks and a relaxing night of fun. "Oh. Ah . . . what? I mean, is everything okay?"

Quint straightened. All six feet of him towered over me. "I wish I could say yes. Are the Bellwethers around?"

"Um, they're upstairs getting ready. It's been a rough day."

"Anything I should know about?" He crossed his arms.

"No, it's more of a . . ." I paused. Now would seem the time to talk about the plaque. I shuddered. The cracked, blood-stained plaque. "Quint, there's something, that is, I stumbled on something." My throat tightened.

"Ali?" His head tilted sideways.

The thump of multiple footsteps resounded as guests and the Bellwethers descended the stairs.

I stepped to the side and motioned with my arm. "You should go ahead."

He stared at me for an instant before turning. "Good evening, everyone. I know I was invited to your game night, but something's come up." Fingers curled the brim of his hat. "Maybe we could sit in the parlor?"

Gladys leaned toward Ollie, cupped one hand around her mouth and whispered. Ollie nodded and patted her shoulder. I lingered in the hall, waiting for them to follow Quint and the others into the parlor. Everyone escaped to their own spaces as if cocooned in safe zones. I sat next to Gladys and snuggled close.

Quint rested his hands on his legs. Fingers tapped thighs as he studied Gladys. "We've checked Beale's phone, and even though the text you claimed he sent to you is on it, there's something else we found. Voice mails that raise questions." He nodded at Ollie. "From you sent to Beale. I have to say, you used some pretty strong words."

Ollie slouched. His head hung loose as if disjointed. When Gladys squeezed his arm to catch his attention, he raised his eyes.

"I forgot all about that. It was nothing more than an angry spout. Me fuming over how he treated our Julia."

"How do you think he treated Julia?" Quint spoke softly.

"He confused her with all his ideas, making her dream about Hollywood. It made no sense. She was happy in Sierra Pines. I'm telling you, he changed her." Ollie rubbed his face with both hands. "He wanted to take her away from us. I couldn't let him do that. I was only trying to protect her."

Quint cleared his throat. "So, you left the first message warning Thaddeus to stay away from Julia or else. What did you mean by or else, Ollie?"

Ollie shrugged. "It meant nothing. I only wanted to make him listen. I swear, I never planned to do anything more. I wouldn't hurt him."

Quint reached inside his shirt pocket for a notepad and flipped the pages. "You left a second message sent the evening before the murder." Quint took a deep breath then read aloud. "You said, 'I know what you did, Beale. Consider this a warning. You're going to pay.' Does that sound familiar, Ollie?"

Silence thickened and spread its heavy layer over the room. No one spoke. I clutched my stomach as a wave of queasiness took hold. No more speculating on which side Ollie had taken. Support and loyalty just took a disturbing path.

Ollie closed his eyes. "It's like Gladys told you. Julia suspected something was wrong. She confronted Thaddeus, and he murdered her for it. I'm not that brave to do such a thing like killing someone. I didn't like seeing my sister suffer. It made me angry enough to send that message. Nothing more than a warning to scare him off."

Gladys hitched her breath. Letting go, she spoke in a raspy tone. "My brother is telling you the truth. I know him. He's gentle and kind and caring. He cares for me, just as he cared for Julia. That's what friends do." She squeezed Ollie's arm. "But he's not a killer. Nor am I. So, Sheriff Sterling, take your accusations elsewhere."

Quint moved his pen across the notepad and remained silent. Everyone else found something to focus their attention on, anything other than on the Bellwethers.

"People do say things they don't mean. I'll give you that." He tapped his pen, then his attention shifted in my direction. "You had something to tell me, Ali?"

My pulse quickened. What horrible timing. I could lie, but what good would it do? Hiding the plaque, that damning plaque, wasn't going to help matters. I dared a glimpse of Gladys, with her face drawn into worry lines. I prayed she had the strength to handle what I was about to do. "Maybe we could talk alone?"

His head tilted. "Why not here?"

"It's rather delicate." I tried once more.

"Ali, maybe we should all hear what you have to say?" Gladys nodded. "No matter what it is."

It was as if she knew I had bad news to share. But she couldn't know exactly, right?

I cleared my throat. "Well, I . . . Quint, I have something you need to see. Just give me a minute." I ignored his puzzled frown and ran upstairs to my room. Planting my hands and feet on the floor, I lowered my chest to peer under the bed. My arm swept in a wide arc until I touched the plastic bag. With a tight grip, I pulled it toward me.

Clutching the bag to my chest, I hurried down the stairs. "Sorry, Gladys." My lips quivered. "I hope you can forgive me."

When I entered the parlor, everyone was sitting exactly where I'd left them, except for Quint. He stood in the far corner, facing the window, but turned when Gladys exclaimed, "Is that Julia's award plaque? I've been searching for it everywhere."

I ignored her comment. I had to and instead kept my attention on Quint as I stepped across the room. The plaque weighed heavily in my hand. "You'll need this for your investigation." My mind and body resisted, but I raised my arm and handed him the plaque.

His brow creased. "Where did you find this?" Carefully, he took it from me and studied the contents.

I fixed my gaze on Quint's hands. Any distraction, any disturbance, and I would lose control. "On the floor of the attic hall closet, tucked near the back." My words came out in raspy, fractured threads. "I was getting supplies to clean the rooms when I dropped the polish, and it rolled underneath the bottom shelf. I bent down, and there it was . . . the plaque, I mean." My heartbeat raced faster and pounded against my chest as I caught the confused look on Gladys's face.

Quint nodded and studied the plaque. His eyes soon narrowed, and, with one finger, he poked at the bag. "Is this . . . ?" He shot a glance at me for a split second then shifted his gaze to the Bellwethers. "I'll need to send this to the lab." He kept the comment vague with no mention of the blood stain. "Gladys and Ollie, do you have any explanation as to how Julia's plaque ended up in the hall closet?"

Gladys shook her head with a determined amount of force. "I don't. I looked for it that evening when, you know, and I couldn't find it. Really, I have no idea how Julia's plaque ended up in the closet."

Her head wagged side to side as if to deny or erase the suspicion that spread and lingered on everyone's lips. Suspicion was left unstated but clearly evident on their faces. I couldn't blame Gladys, but a heavy, sinking feeling weighted my insides.

"Ollie?" Quint studied his face.

"Not a clue," Ollie said.

"You know, it's possible someone hid the plaque in the hall closet to make Gladys or Ollie look guilty of the crime." My words trickled out, shaky and weak.

Quint thumbed his ear. "You mean someone as in the killer? How would this person know you'd find it, or anyone else would find it, for that matter? It could've stayed hidden for months and not discovered until after the case was closed."

Doubt shadowed Quint's face, and I countered with a defiant stare.

"How is Gladys placing it in the closet and intentionally leading me straight to it any more believable? Especially when she knows I'd never compromise my character by hiding evidence." I searched his face, trying to read his thoughts.

"Unless Ollie did the dirty deed and Gladys doesn't know about it." Dean whistled with a head shake.

I wanted to slap the know-it-all expression off his face. "Those two never do anything without consulting or confiding in one another. If he'd done the dirty deed, as you put it, Gladys would know and try her darnedest to hide the fact. Not lead me to the evidence."

Dean reared back as if my words had teeth.

Quint shifted his gaze from me to Dean. "Let's be civil about this. All right?"

His sharp tone softened when he spoke to the Bellwethers. "I'm sorry, but I'll have to take you into custody. This plaque, Ollie's threatening voice mails . . ." Quint raked fingers through his hair. His face muscles grew rigid with concern. "And the hole you both dug in the backyard, along with the dirt found on Beale's body? You must know how it looks."

Gladys gripped Ollie's arm. Her face was ashen, and her chest heaved and fell in rapid succession. Ollie closed his hand over hers, but nothing in his expression hinted at a reaction. It was more like self-controlled stoicism.

I turned away. "Sheriff, can't it wait until tomorrow morning? They're not going anywhere. You know that." I held his gaze, but tentacles of fear wrapped around me and squeezed when I pictured Gladys and Ollie behind bars.

"That's fine. Besides, it's late, and this way Ollie and Gladys will get a better night's sleep in their own beds." He strained to smile.

"Would you like to stay, Sheriff? After all, you were invited to game night, and we have plenty of snacks." Gladys's voice shook, but she kept a smile in place.

Tears moistened my eyes. This woman could never commit murder. Nor Ollie. They were too decent.

"Sorry. Thank you, ma'am. I'll take a rain check, if that's okay. I have to get this information back to the station." He turned to me and attempted a smile with a slight upturn of his lips. "Plenty going on in Sierra Pines, these days." He stepped toward the foyer. "Try and get some rest, Gladys and Ollie. One of my deputies will stop by in the morning."

"Let me walk you to the door." I hurried to keep pace with him. We reached the hallway when I added, "Is this really necessary? Taking them into custody when you can't positively tie them to the evidence yet?"

"With everything we've found, how can I avoid it? This is my job."

"What about Gladys's theory? Doesn't it make you wonder? I mean, first Julia dies, and then a couple days later, Thaddeus is murdered. Pretty big coincidence, if you ask me." This desperate situation called for my desperate, though rather implausible, measures.

"Coincidences happen all the time. I have nothing to connect the two. No credible evidence at all." He rubbed his jaw. "Look, Ali, I didn't want to say this in front of the Bellwethers, but there's angry talk in town. People want someone to blame. They're demanding answers. Unfortunately, rumors are flying, and all of them are aimed at the Bellwethers. I don't know who started them, and it worries me."

"But . . ." First Florence and now Quint. How did I argue with their reasoning?

He held up a finger to stop me. "However, I'm trying to keep the situation from spiraling out of control. Taking the Bellwethers into custody might be the safest way to go about it." He reached out to take my hand, but I pulled away.

"I guess you know what's best, Sheriff. At least I hope you do." I pointed at him. "Let me warn you, though. If anything happens to them while they're in your care . . ."

"Like what? It's not as if a lynch mob will stampede in and break down the jailhouse door." He rubbed the back of his neck. "Please, Ali. Trust me. Just this once, will you trust me?"

I hugged my chest to quell the shaking. "I don't really have a choice, do I?" Before he could answer, I opened the door and motioned him outside. "Have a pleasant evening, Sheriff." I pivoted on my heel and marched away, leaving him to close the door.

I clenched my lower jaw to keep from trembling, and instead, let anger take over the worry that built inside me. With my hands balled into fists, I marched to the kitchen. Whoever tainted Julia's B&B with bloody murder wouldn't get away with it. I planned to find answers and quick. Quicker than Sheriff Quint Sterling might. I had a team to assist and an agenda to follow. As long as the answers led us away from the Bellwethers. I grabbed potholders off the counter and pulled the pan of appetizers from the oven. "Not caving. Not wavering. Not doubting. Only positive action, Alexis Winston. You've got this."

Armed with a cheerleader's smile and bowls of snacks scrumptious enough to uplift the downer mood we'd been put into, I marched into the parlor where the guests sat staring at the floor while Gladys and Ollie put on a brave front with smiles on their faces.

"Who's ready for fresh guacamole dip and jalapeno poppers?" I quipped.

"I'd like to make a suggestion." Gladys dabbed her mouth with a napkin. Her hand shook as she rested it next to her plate. Despite the depressing mood brought on by Quint's news, everyone gobbled up the appetizers.

"Sure, Gladys. What do you have in mind?" My voice lifted.

The sadness in Gladys's face stopped me from crumbling into a sniveling mess because that would hardly help or save anyone.

"I think we all agree the time and mood for game night has passed. However, to help raise our spirits, I suggest we watch a Cary Grant movie, one of Julia's favorites. It seems we owe her that much after all that's happened." Her voice quivered. "I was thinking *Notorious* would be fitting."

We all followed her lead, moving out of the parlor and across the hall to the library. Ollie and Ralph trailed behind as they carried the bowls of chips and dip.

"It's the film she won an award for and . . ." Gladys's voice hitched. "Those were her last days with Cary. Ollie, would you?" She motioned toward the cabinet filled with DVDs as we reached the library doorway.

"Sorry, everybody, but I don't have time to spare. I have to finish my article. Deadlines can't be broken. Enjoy the movie." Marianne hurried up the stairs.

Gladys dimmed the lights and then took the seat closest to the television. Her expression and words lighted with excitement.

"You can't imagine those days. Hitchcock at his prime and the three of us right there to experience and enjoy every second of it. I told you, didn't I? Julia kept a journal, notes on every gala, every movie, every award show, and all the trimmings of Hollywood society. She planned to turn the journal into her memoir one day and have it published." Gladys nodded.

I tilted my head. "Huh. I remember you mentioned her journal the other day. Sounds wonderful, Gladys." Behind me, a phone buzzed. I turned to look over my shoulder.

"Oh boy. I wish I could stay." Brooke waved her phone. "But the great and powerful Thomas O'Neil wants to shorten the scenes we filmed today." Brooke shoulder-shrugged, and then sprinted to the front door.

"Guess that leaves us." My expression pleaded with Dean and Ralph.

"Maybe I'll stick around for a while. There's nothing else going on." Dean plopped on the sofa. He grabbed a movie magazine from the end table next to him and flipped through the pages.

I regarded Ralph with wary eyes. "If you bail, I'll understand." I kept my voice to a whisper, hoping Gladys didn't overhear.

"Nonsense. I love the classic movies. Especially a Hitchcock production." Ralph patted the empty seat next to him. "Sit. Enjoy."

I twisted my mouth into a grin. "Thank you. I believe I will." By now, the introductory credits filled the screen. Gladys and Ollie sat cozily together. The tops of their heads nearly touched as they whispered and nodded, most likely to reminisce. I envied them and their lifelong relationship. I didn't have siblings. Not even close cousins or friends from childhood with whom I could share memories. What the Bellwethers possessed was quite special. I prayed nothing would ruin it.

# CHAPTER EIGHT

I PEEKED OUT OF MY BEDROOM. Streaks of morning sunlight played across the hallway floor and reached the far end, where Ollie stood in Gladys's doorway. He chattered incessantly, and the volume crescendoed every so many words. Loud enough to penetrate through the walls of my room, but that wasn't what wakened me. Visions of murder and jail and snippets of movie dialogue did. Those images stirred and frightened me. I couldn't sleep. The *Notorious* cast members, Cary Grant, Ingrid Bergman, and Claude Rains had stepped inside my head with dramatic overture.

The moose clock cuckooed seven times. I yawned, and, with a final glance at Ollie, who continued his conversation with Gladys, I stepped back into my room. I planned to spend time with Gladys and Ollie this morning before the deputy showed up. Nina would forgive me for being late to work. After yesterday and all the crew pitching in to clean up, she'd be in a great mood today. Just in case, I left a quick voicemail to let her know I was running late.

If I hurried, there'd be time for a tête-à-tête, plus one with the Bellwethers, before Quint's deputy came to haul them away to jail. I cringed at the thought. This was becoming a living nightmare. I pictured Sierra Pines B&B turned into the Norman Bates Motel. I reached down for the pants and shirt I'd worn yesterday, piled and tangled together in a bunch. With a firm snap, I shook them out in an attempt to erase the wrinkled look. Quickly dressing, I slipped on my flats and rushed out of the room. No sign of Ollie or Gladys or the chirp of noisy conversation. At once, I skipped down the stairs to look in the kitchen. Gladys carried her plate and Ollie's to the table. Steam trailed from the stack of pancakes as she poured maple syrup on top. She'd set a plate loaded with crispy bacon in the center. My stomach growled.

The usual warming trays filled with breakfast goodies were on the counter, waiting for guests to devour them. My heart sank. Despite their date with a jail cell this morning, Gladys had taken the time to fix a grand meal with all sorts of dishes for our guests. Of course, I had offered to take over the task, but Gladys had dismissed the suggestion and said cooking kept her mind off her problems.

"Hey, you two. Why are you up so early?" I grabbed a mug and poured freshly made brew and then filled my plate with a heaping stack of cakes before joining them at the table.

"I could ask you the same." Gladys grinned. "Didn't you wear those clothes yesterday?"

It was comforting to find her spirits cheerful. "Funny you. I turned in late last night, and yes, these are yesterday's duds. I hurried down here because I wanted to have a talk with you while there's time and we're alone. Is that okay?" I pulled out a chair and sat next to Ollie. I gave his hand a gentle squeeze.

"Of course. We'd love that." Ollie winked. "Pleasant conversation with our special girl before we get thrown in the pokey."

"Oh, stop it, Ollie. This isn't a time to joke." Gladys cast him a stern look for a second. She scooted her chair closer to the table and shifted her attention to me. "Now, what would you like to talk about?"

"Hmm, okay. Maybe you could describe those last few days before Aunt Julia passed. The comings and goings of you all, guests included? Perhaps there's a clue we've overlooked." I took a deep breath and leaned back.

"You mean someone Julia might have spoken with or a place she might have gone which would lead us to her killer? What an excellent idea." Gladys's face brightened. "Let me think." Her finger tapped her lower lip.

"Well, not exactly." I cleared my throat. "Look. Under the circumstances, and considering how Thaddeus died, maybe you should rethink your theory." I hoped they got the message. After all, Quint hadn't discovered any reason to investigate Gladys's claim. He made it perfectly clear last night.

"Ah, I see. You still believe Julia died of natural causes." Gladys nodded then sipped her coffee.

"It seems like an obvious conclusion." I munched on a piece of bacon.

"But you can understand my sister has a point. Even murderers are sometimes murdered. I call it karma or justice for the dead."

I opened my mouth but at once clamped it shut. *Talk about a motive for murder.*

He smacked the table and laughed. "Well, I'll be. That didn't sound too incriminating, did it?"

"It certainly did." Gladys waved her fork at him. "I do think Alexis is onto something, though. We should consider whoever killed poor Thaddeus Beale also killed our dear Julia."

I blinked. No, that wasn't what I meant. Did she even hear what I'd said? "Gladys." I cut my losses and gave up the argument for the time being. "Why don't you start by telling me about Julia's last days? Especially her time with Thaddeus. Maybe she shared a secret with you? Anything you feel is worth repeating." I was overwhelmed and unsure what I expected to gain from this. Desperation had hijacked my rational self.

Gladys shook her head. "Julia would never tell us anything you'd call secrets she might have shared with Thaddeus or anyone else. She only mentioned how he tried to convince her to return to Hollywood with him."

"Pompous, arrogant fool." Ollie grumbled and wagged his head as he sliced through the tall stack of cakes.

"Now, now. Show some respect for the dead." Gladys patted his hand then moved on. "However, we couldn't help but overhear some of their conversations when Thaddeus visited the B&B."

Ollie screwed up his face. "Always boasting. The braggart never stopped."

"Oliver John Bellwether, enough." Gladys's eyes flashed with impatience before she turned to me and smiled sweetly. "I've told you. Thaddeus charmed her with his stories about Hollywood and how wonderful it would be for Julia to join him there. But we heard no secrets. Nothing worth mentioning."

I bit down on my lip. "What was her schedule like? Maybe she mentioned visiting someplace unusual. Someplace where she normally never went?" I forked the last piece of hotcake and chewed.

"She spent most of her time here at the B&B." Ollie poured creamer into his coffee.

"She attended to SPACA duties, too. Oh, and her time on the movie set, of course. Nothing more to her days, or at least none we know of." Gladys twisted her napkin. "Oh dear. We aren't helping much, are we?"

I squeezed her hand. "It's fine. You're doing great. Now, was there anyone you can think of who caused Julia a problem? Someone who had a grudge against her?" I recalled Nina's comment. Julia claimed not everyone in Sierra Pines was trustworthy or kind. "Maybe someone on the movie set?" Thomas O'Neil and his abrasive personality, for one. Could he and Julia have argued or maybe had a falling out?

Gladys tapped her lip and hummed for a second. "No one comes to mind. I mean, I can't imagine a single person who'd carry a grudge. Julia was kind to everyone."

"Of course, we never visited the set," Ollie added.

"Anyone else in town you can think of who raises a question?" I dropped my shoulders, losing hope.

"Well, Julia did have a difference of opinion when it came to SPACA," Gladys said.

"Oh?"

"She insisted on her ideas of how the alliance should be run." Ollie nodded.

"The money raised from events should benefit the community first and the SPACA coffers second. It's what she always said," Gladys added.

"Who did she argue with about this?" I guessed the answer but needed reassurance.

"Florence and Sebastian." They chimed in at once.

"Did the arguments ever get heated? I mean, out of control?"

"Oh, no. Never. SPACA matters are always settled in a civil manner." Gladys gathered my plate, along with hers and Ollie's, then stepped away from the table.

"We vote on them. It's the democratic way." Ollie dabbed his lips with a napkin.

"Okay. If you think of anything else, you need to tell Sheriff Sterling. Any piece of information, no matter how small, could be useful." I struggled to keep my mood calm and cheerful, but when the doorbell rang, I flinched.

"There's our ride to the big house." Ollie guffawed as he made the announcement.

"Hush, Ollie." Gladys reached out to hug me. "I'm sure we'll be home soon."

"I count on it. With everyone working together, I bet we'll have this case figured out before dinner." I squeezed both hers and Ollie's hands.

I walked them to the front door and waved as Gladys slid into the passenger seat of the cruiser, next to the deputy, while Ollie, who exclaimed what a thrill it'd be to ride to the station like a true criminal, quickly slipped into the back. Gladys was right. This wasn't the time to joke, but levity was a way for Ollie to cope. He had to be frightened for the both of them. Humor could hide a lot of emotions, including fear.

Once the guests were finished with their breakfast, I reminded Ralph and Dean about our plan. "Since the Bellwethers aren't free to help, we'll need to adjust our assignments. I'll be at the movie set today to work on props with Nina. I might as well take over questioning folks there, if you two wouldn't mind talking with the business owners and shoppers? With any luck, you'll find one who saw the Bellwethers that evening." I dug inside my shirt pocket. "Here's a photo Gladys gave me, in case you run across people who don't know them. Any questions?"

Dean's bottom lip stuck out. "I was hoping to visit the set today. The director mentioned a role in his next film. He thinks I'd be a perfect fit."

"Well, there's no reason you can't wait and talk to him later, after you and Ralph finish questioning people, is there?" A ripple of irritation filled my voice.

His spoiled, immature attitude tapped my patience.

"Sure. I guess." He shrugged but the pout remained.

"I'm out of here. Call me if you come up with anything." I passed Brooke and Marianne on the way. My lips curved into a stiff smile as I waved goodbye. I didn't want to hear any more excuses. Help or don't help. I couldn't care less about excuses.

I sent off another quick text to Nina, saying I'd be at work by eight-thirty. Stepping outside, I hugged my jacket closer to my chest. The temps had dipped below freezing last night, but clear skies and sunshine would warm the ground and plant life by lunchtime. The hint of winter would be forgotten.

I grew anxious with every second. My longing to free Ollie and Gladys from behind bars, even though I agreed with Quint it was the safest place for them at present, burned a hole inside me. I needed to squash those inklings of doubt about their innocence and not forget a killer was on the loose. A killer who might decide to strike again, if anyone got in his or her way. I shuddered. *Anyone.*

I revved up the engine and let the car idle for a few minutes. A perusal of my phone showed no calls or messages from Mom or Dad. I frowned. More than two days without contact was unusual, but not a cause for alarm. My family dynamic played like a true paradox. I wanted independence, but then I didn't. I needed advice, but then I refused to take it. My emotional actions and reactions yo-yoed constantly.

I tapped the screen, hesitated, and then tossed the phone on the seat. "I can handle this. Parental guidance not required." I shifted into gear and motored down Englewood toward Main Street. Trapped inside my car, and with all this stillness around me, I couldn't escape thoughts about murder, about the Bellwethers, about Julia's will, and the list went on, replaying and spinning like a hamster wheel in my head.

Of course, one of those thoughts pushing that hamster wheel was Quint Sterling. I couldn't handle him on top of all the other things going on in my life. Still, whether I liked it or not, avoiding him was impossible. We were in the same town. He investigated a murder which unfortunately occurred in Julia's B&B, *my* B&B at the moment. I wasn't leaving Sierra Pines anytime soon. For one thing, I hadn't decided what to do about my inheritance. Secondly, Julia would want me to stay and support the Bellwethers. Yes, running into each other was a given.

"Which isn't really all that bad, right? He drives me crazy, a little. We argue sometimes. Who doesn't?" I drummed my fingers on the steering wheel.

I turned at the next light and parked in front of Meeka's shop. "Does it matter? I might be leaving eventually. Who cares if he's nice and caring and funny and . . . who cares? I don't want that kind of a relationship with him. Relationships are complicated and sticky. I didn't come to Sierra Pines for complicated. I came to relax, even though murder had to throw all things out of kilter." With an angry swipe, I brushed an unruly curl from my face and tipped my chin a couple inches higher. "Not a problem."

I swung open the door, grabbed my bag, and shed all thoughts about Quint. If I allowed myself an hour or so to snoop around the lot and talk with a few of the workers, I'd get to the production building by half past eight.

I stepped up to the sidewalk and faced the display window of Meeka's shop. I hadn't bought my souvenirs yet but planned to after work today. I stood in one spot and mused over a glass vase resting on a china plate.

Next to it sat a doll with rosy cheeks, dark hair, and dressed in nineteenth century garb. Two more great ideas. It would be hard to choose. I tapped my chin with one finger and contemplated.

Within seconds, the stampede of footsteps caught my attention. In the window, the reflected profile of a young boy running in my direction blurred past. I gasped and clutched my bag close to my chest. This big city girl had a skeptic's attitude about would-be criminals and the impulse to protect anything personal or valuable from being snatched away. I was wrong, in this case. He brushed my shoulder, but without mishap, and kept running. I teetered side to side, barely keeping my balance.

"Are you all right?"

"Oh!" I wobbled and twirled around to face Quint Sterling. "Hi there. How are you?" My words released in breathless wisps. So much for avoiding all things Quint Sterling.

His wry laugh came with a shake of the head. "I'm great, but it seems you're not."

I snorted and lifted my arm in a careless wave. "That? Nah. Happens all the time in New York."

"Kids running into you?" A smirk teased the corners of his lips.

"Sort of. People bumping, walking, or running into each other. It's a crowded place, you know." I shrugged.

"Well, I'm glad you got out of there unharmed." He waited, and when I didn't respond, he added, "You have a good day." Tipping his hat, he turned to leave.

"Wait. How are Ollie and Gladys adjusting?" It had been little more than an hour since the cruiser drove away, but my concern for them didn't measure time.

"Ollie and Gladys are fine. Everyone at the station treats them like royalty. Especially Minnie. She generously volunteered to fill in for Margie, who called in ill."

I rolled my eyes. "Oh, boy. I bet Ollie loves that idea."

Quint laughed. "She dotes on him. That's true enough. I think Gladys is jealous of all the attention he gets. Don't worry, Ali. We'll take good care of them. I called in my deputies to do double duty, so the Bellwethers will have twenty-four-hour protection. Besides, it's the safest place to be. Judge Wilkes in Placerville will see them in court this afternoon to set bail." His brow wrinkled.

"Which you'll argue against?"

"I'll state my case. Not that it matters. I can't keep a close eye on them if they're back on the outside."

I skirted around his comment and returned to Judge Wilkes. "The judge has a soft heart where the Bellwethers are concerned. Did you know he tried dating Aunt Julia a few years ago?"

"From stories the judge shared with me, it sounds like he must've given it his best shot."

"Gladys playing matchmaker is never a wise idea. Julia wanted nothing to do with romance." I glanced at my watch. "I should go."

"Absolutely. I'll be in touch." He pushed back his hat to scratch the top of his head. "About what happens with Judge Wilkes, I mean."

"Ah, right. Until later." I finger-waved and pivoted on one heel before he caught me flushed with heat, and then I hurried down the sidewalk. "See? Who cares? Yeah, Ali Winston, let's go with that." Keeping my mission in mind, I marched onto the movie set, stormed past the SPACA trailer, then pulled to a stop. After retracing my steps a few yards, I ended up back at the trailer. I drew in air to steady my pulse. With one fist raised, I rapped on the door. "Florence? Are you in there?"

Dean and Florence had a secret. After witnessing Dean sneaking out of O'Neil's trailer, leaving Florence a sobbing mess, I was sure of it, and I intended to find out what that secret was. The label nosy body came to mind again. No one liked a nosy body, but sometimes it was how people discovered evidence. Or maybe not. I shrugged. I'd never know unless I tried. *Rap, rap, rap.* "Florence, if you're inside, please open the door. We need to talk." Besides, the opposite of nosy body was a concerned friend. I could be that person.

The door hinge creaked with a long-winded moan. Florence peeked through a six-inch gap. "What do *you* want?" She sniffed and dabbed at her eyes with a hanky.

My face creased into serious concern. "Florence, you've been crying. Again."

"Genius observation, Miss Winston," she snapped. The door opened wider. "Since you're insistent on snooping into my business, come inside. No point letting the whole world eavesdrop."

I nodded and squeezed by her to enter the trailer. Wrappers from fast-food burgers and fries lay on the counter, while a bag of chips sat open on the table.

Florence dug into the bag and pulled out a handful of chips. She crammed most of them into her mouth and chewed. "No good son of a gun. How could my genes and blood run through his veins?" Words tumbled out in a garlicky scent.

I deciphered the chewy-chip verbiage in silence. It didn't help. Her words left much unsaid. "Whose veins are we talking about?"

"Oh, forget it. You wouldn't understand." She swiped the tabletop with her arm. A bag of chip confetti showered the floor. "Your life is perfect, isn't it? Oh, sure, you lost your aunt, but she was ninety-something. She lived a full life, and her reputation was exemplary, even if she sometimes put on airs, like she was better than the rest of us. Besides that, you have perfect parents. People who'd do anything to help you." She threw up her arms. "Who cares about me? My life is crap."

Like a ping pong ball bouncing from word to word and thought to thought, I attempted to follow her comments. When her voice trailed off and the rampage dwindled to silence, I dove in. "Florence, nobody's life is perfect, but I'd like to help you because, well, you seem to need it. Why don't you tell me what's happened?"

Florence waved her hanky. "Sit. It's a long story. You see, Dean is a distant relative. My poor cousin, second or third, I can't remember which, is an imbecile who married some trollop with air for brains. She ran off and left him to raise Dean. You can see how that turned out."

Her hands rolled the hanky until it looked like a pretzel twist.

"Wow. I didn't see that one coming." I leaned back and stared at the ceiling while I processed.

"Now he's threatened to spread horrible rumors about our family, including me, if I don't give him fifty thousand dollars." She whimpered and pressed a hand to her lips. "I don't have fifty thousand dollars. What am I supposed to do?"

Her pitch elevated and reached notes I don't think my ears ever experienced.

"Well, what does it matter? It's all on your cousin. None of it's your fault." I bit my cheek. "It's not . . . right?"

Her chest heaved. "Of course it's not, but that isn't the point. People believe what they hear. This will destroy me."

She stood and paced the twenty-foot length of the trailer, back and forth, marking her path. My gaze followed.

After several laps, I extended one hand and snapped my fingers. "Stop. Please. Sit."

She did without question.

"I can't give you money. I'm broke as a homeless person. However, maybe there's another way to stop him."

Florence dried her eyes. "I'm listening."

"How much do you know about the reason Dean left Hollywood?"

"Why, it's because he's broke and came here to blackmail me. That's obvious."

I grinned. "Let me tell you the other half of the story." I filled her in on the tabloid-worthy incident involving Dean and the critic.

She snorted. "What a surprise. You say his agent sent him here until the soap opera execs calm down and the public forgets it ever happened? I doubt it. Probably another one of his lies, but if it's true, that might be the leverage I need to shut his trap and send him packing."

The old Florence had returned, bold and sassy.

"Never know." I stood and turned to the door. "I think my work is done here. Good luck, and let me know how it goes."

Florence shook her head. "I'd rather forget the sordid incident, if it's all the same to you."

"Got it." Before I took another step, the door swung open. I hopped backward, avoiding a forehead collision with a mass of metal. "Whoa." I was face to face with Dean. Seeing him contorted with anger and hands balled into fists sent a shiver of fear down my back. I squeezed my eyes shut and braced for a knockout punch in a repeat performance of the Hollywood critic fiasco.

When nothing happened, I pried open my eyes, one nanometer at a time. Dean smiled, though his lips were stretched thin over a mouthful of gritted teeth. He wasn't happy, but then again, neither was I.

"Hey, Dean. Aren't you and Ralph supposed to be questioning business owners on Main Street?"

He was either snooping on me or Florence. The little creep.

"I, uh, I need to speak with Florence about an urgent business matter." Dean skirted around me.

Florence gestured to me with an almost imperceptible shake of her head, which I figured meant not to comment. I had to trust she could handle him.

"I guess I'll be going then. Call if you need me, Florence. I'll be on the set for a few hours." I glared at Dean. "*Very* close by."

My feet landed on the ground, and I flew past the row of trailers to reach the crew and cast. Cameras rolled to film a love scene. Soft music filtered through the air while the costars played kissy face. I smacked my cheek as a fly landed, and a crew member turned to me with a finger over his lips. I shrugged my apology.

Waiting for the scene to finish, I mentally recapped what had transpired in the past twenty minutes. Unfortunately, I'd missed my opportunity to question Florence on her thoughts about the murder case. Instead, I left the SPACA trailer with a headache as I imagined all sorts of dirty secrets hidden in her family closet. Added to that were my worries of how big of a real threat Dean was to her. With any luck, I'd turn this sleuthing business around and scrape together a clue or two by talking with O'Neil or one of the crew members. After all, according to the Bellwethers and Nina, Julia had spent a lot of time on the set.

The buzz of conversation nearby roused me from my meandering thoughts. I examined the area and paused when I found my target plus one. Thomas O'Neil's chin jutted out as he stared at Sebastian Tubble with a wrinkled brow. The two men appeared to be in a heated discussion. Suddenly, Sebastian waved his arms wildly until one of his fingers stabbed at the director. I skirted around cameras and crew to get closer and listen.

"I thought we had a deal. You agreed shooting this scene in the evening would paint a different mood. Much more romantic. You can't possibly change your mind. Using the lodge benefits us both." Sebastian rocked back on his heels.

"As long as I pay you for the privilege, you mean." Thomas leered. "I read your contract, and yes, I've changed my mind. You're a shrewd negotiator, Tubble, but a lousy businessman. It's ridiculous to pay that much to film for—what? One hour? And that's only from the outside of the lodge."

Sebastian's chest puffed out. "My lodge is one of the best in the world. It's been featured in *Ski Resort Getaways* and television's top-rated *Travel by Snow,* carried by over one hundred channels, both nationally and overseas. I don't need the publicity, but you obviously do. I'd be doing you a favor." His rant spouted with increasing volume.

I shrank behind someone wielding a camera. "Is he always like that?" I whispered.

"O'Neil?" The linebacker-sized camera man shrugged.

"No, I mean the other man. Sebastian Tubble." It was more of a rhetorical question, when I thought about it. I'd witnessed several Tubble moments and none of them were much different than this. "Sorry, I was thinking out loud. Enjoy filming." I wrapped up my apology with a good-bye and tiptoed around him.

"I don't need your lodge for my movie. In fact, I don't need anything from you. So, please get off my set. I've got work to do." O'Neil's arms flailed.

"Maybe this isn't the right time to talk." I reversed my direction and headed toward the trailers once more. My mood deflated, and my confidence in getting any useful information to help the Bellwethers collapsed along with it.

"Well, good morning, Ali. What a pleasant surprise." Sebastian stepped into my path.

"Holy . . ." Hand to throat, I power-stepped in reverse to avoid a collision. "Sebastian Tubble. You're here."

His laughter bellowed. "As you can see with your own eyes."

My fingers curled to grasp my purse strap. Of all the places he could've chosen to walk? "So, what brings you to the movie set? Plan on making a comeback?"

Confused and surprised, he widened his eyes and remained speechless.

"Oh. Didn't Florence mentioned my suggestion to have SPACA offer acting classes to kids? Since she remarked how you might want to teach them, I assumed you had some acting experience."

"Eh, well." His gaze flickered for an instant while he adjusted his collar. "Call me a fascinated spectator of the arts, which is one of the reasons I joined the alliance. Acting classes, heh? It sounds like a wonderful idea. Excellent PR for our organization." He cleared his throat and tipped his chin higher. "I love working with young people. We have a special kindred spirit. Must be my superb enthusiasm and ways of communicating that inspire them."

"Oh, certainly. Enthusiasm and persuasive communication. Those are winning qualities." A tiny twinge of sarcasm peppered my voice.

He brushed the lapel of his jacket with one hand. "I do try."

"I'm sure you do." Who was he kidding? "Ah, look at the time, would you? Nina's expecting me."

Sebastian moved once more to block my path. "I heard about the Bellwethers' predicament. How are they taking it?"

"As you'd expect. I'm sure they'll be released soon. Not much to keep them behind bars as far as evidence goes." I moved to the far edge of the path.

"Oh? That is good news. You've spoken with Sheriff Sterling? He has leads, I take it. Did he share any with you?"

I chewed on the tip of my finger as his face muscles tightened like stretched rubber bands ready to snap.

He quickly added, "I'm only thinking of the poor Bellwethers. Hopefully, any discovery will clear their names."

"We're all hoping for some kind of breakthrough, but I can't tell you anything. Sheriff Sterling won't share information about an ongoing investigation. Not even with me. Now, if you'll excuse me, I really need to go." I hurdled around him, clearing the distance between us within seconds, as I sprinted down the path. "What a nosy body. He and Florence sure make a pair."

"I'd love to hear more of your ideas for SPACA," he called out. "Why don't you drop by my trailer after work? I'll be there until dark."

"We'll see." I threw the comment over my shoulder. "If I have time." The notion of being a one-woman audience for the overbearing Sebastian and his stories curdled my insides and left me nauseous. On the other hand, if I wanted to learn more about the man and his secrets, his invitation provided an opportunity. What perplexed me was his reaction when I suggested he'd been an actor. He seemed embarrassed and uncomfortable. What could he be hiding? One thing for sure, I needed to learned as much as possible about everyone who'd been in contact with Julia, as well as with Thaddeus, and that included Sebastian. As they said, knowledge was power, and in this case, it could help solve a murder.

I'd come within ten yards of the production building when I spotted Nina with her bag slung over one shoulder as she powerwalked toward the parking lot.

"Hey, Nina. Wait up." I jogged toward her.

"Sorry, kiddo. I made a doctor's appointment for this morning. Do me a favor, though. Would you work on the statue of John Sutter? It needs to be done by this evening."

I tensed. "Is everything okay?" Up close, she looked pale. Dark, puffy shadows underlined her eyes.

"You mean on top of the break-in? Just one of my sinus infections has got me down. Unlucky me since we've tons of projects to finish. Anyway, the doctor was able to squeeze me into his schedule, so I'm off to get some miracle drug that, with any luck, will clear this congestion." Her laugh morphed into a cough. She pounded her chest until it stopped. "I'll be back tomorrow."

"Speaking of the break-in, have you heard any more?"

Nina shrugged. "The sheriff told me one man in our crew saw someone sneaking around the building that evening. Meantime, everyone on set is being questioned. Who knows if it will lead to anything?"

"Yeah, who knows." I recalled Gladys's comment about what these events had in common.

"Okay, I'm off. Hey, if O'Neil shows up, keep him away from our work. Can't let him muck it up. He's like a disaster zone when he gets his hands on a prop and tries to add his ideas. Acting and directing are the only skills he's good at." She coughed some more. "Well, maybe not the only things." She winked an eye then turned and stepped toward her car.

My face grew hot. This wasn't the visual I wanted to have so early in the day. I glanced toward the production building. Working alone wasn't as fun. I shivered as the cool autumn breeze gusted. With chin down, my fingers curled around the collar of my jacket, and I pressed it closer to cut off the wind. Something white fluttered across my feet. I bent down to retrieve a piece of paper and closed my hand to crumble it when a word scribbled across the top stopped me. Curious, I smoothed the wrinkled paper and read aloud. "Keep searching for answers and don't let anyone stop you." I gasped. "What in the world?"

My gaze darted back and forth, from the parking lot to the production building. No one. Not even a passerby to validate my gripping paranoia. I shoved the message in my pocket and marched with long strides to the comforting shelter of the production building. Or at least I hoped it proved comforting. Had the note fallen from my pocket? But who would have placed it there and when? Even more importantly, was it meant for me?

Once inside, I slid the wide door closed and sat at Julia's workstation. More like hunkered down, as if this were a duck-and-cover drill during an air raid. I licked the sweat beaded on my upper lip and drew in several deep breaths. Flexing my hand until it was steady enough, I fished the message out of my pocket and took another peek. *Keep searching for answers.* But how did someone slip me the note? And who? "This is downright creepy." I tapped the paper while visions of murder scenes flashed in my head.

Taking a mental walk, I sorted through my morning and each step from the moment I awoke and took my journey from the B&B to the movie set. Nothing unusual happened. Just a normal, boring day. Other than the Dean and Florence fiasco, with disturbing skeletons in family closets. Oh, and my encounter with Sebastian. Could one of them have found the opportunity to slip this into my pocket? If so, the act was weird and rather unlikely. What else? I folded and unfolded the edges of the paper, prodding my brain for answers.

"The incident in front of Meeka's shop?" I paced the floor, forgetting for the moment about lurkers or killers. Some kid who ran down the sidewalk and collided with me because I was in his path? Not weird. Not unusual. Just random. I was clueless and no closer to a plausible answer.

I reached for the half-finished statue and grabbed a sander. Keeping busy with work was a better use of my time. More constructive, anyway. I pulled on safety glasses and powered up the tool, determined to polish the statue until it shined. Captain John Sutter, the owner of Sutter's Mill where gold was discovered, was a California native who fit into O'Neil's movie perfectly.

The hum and whir of the machine calmed and distracted me from my endless ramble of worries. However, the message and its urgent warning stuck in my head. *That* I couldn't dismiss.

# CHAPTER NINE

THE SANDER WHIRRED THEN SPUTTERED INTO silence. I toggled the on/off switch, which did nothing. I touched the casing, but the surface was barely warm. "Huh." I pushed the safety glasses to the top of my head and leaned in to take a closer look.

"You won't find anything wrong with it."

I gasped and twisted around. Quint grinned at me as his hand dangled the electric cord. "Sorry. I couldn't think of any other way to interrupt and let you know I was here. Any safe way, I mean. I'm sure you value all of your fingers."

"Guess you're right, but you haven't interrupted." I patted the statue. "I've polished and smoothed John Sutter enough. Any more and he'd be shedding pounds." I chuckled.

"Captain Sutter." Quint tapped his lip while studying the statue. "A fair likeness, I guess."

I straightened in my seat. "Fair? You guess? I'll have you know; the Captain and I have become quite close the past few days. I memorized every wrinkle and every inch of his jaw and cheek bones." I wrapped an arm around my work of art and pulled it closer. "In fact, there are things I know about him that no one else does or ever will."

"Oh? Like what?" A smile teased the corners of his mouth.

"I repeat, no one ever will. Emphasis on the ever will part." I gave John a peck on the cheek then set him on his feet. "His secrets are safe with me."

"I'm sure he appreciates it." Quint erupted with pleasant laughter.

I brushed dust off my jeans and stood. "So, what brings you to my little hideaway?" My voice might have sounded light and playful, but it only disguised my worry. I prayed this wasn't a visit to deliver more bad news.

His hand rubbed the back of his neck. "I need to have a word about the murder case."

"Oh?" Starting with "I need to have a word about the murder case" wasn't a good sign. "New developments?"

"More like no developments. Not since the last time we spoke."

"Then, what is it?"

"I've heard rumors." He shuffled his feet. "You formed a team to investigate the murder? Ali, please don't. I'm asking you to please stay clear of my investigation. I don't want anyone else getting hurt. Especially . . . what I mean is your interference muddies the waters."

My brows inched up. "What waters?" I puzzled over who must've snitched. Obviously, none of my volunteer sleuthing team, which left every other person in Sierra Pines.

"It's an expression." His words grew edgy to match his stern face. "You interfering or anyone else interfering doesn't help me. I can't have everybody in town doing their own thing. Too many hands in the pot tampers with a job that authorities should be doing. Is that clear?"

"Muddy waters and hands in the pot are a no-no. Got it." I rolled my tongue as the cheeky tone in me rose to the occasion. "Or how about this. You could say thank you. Yeah. Words like 'thank you, Ali, for doing some of the footwork so my deputies and I are free to handle the heavy lifting and solve the case' would be nice."

He pulled his hat off and slapped it against one thigh. Mussed hair stood out in an array of spikey tufts. "Now, there's no need to be indignant."

Plaster dust stirred as I pulled the apron over my head. I breathed in the powdery taste and gagged and then pursed my lips as I glared at Quint. "I'm not indignant. I'm being reasonable while you're being whatever that is." I waved my arm at him then grabbed a towel and spit into it.

He rubbed his face. "Why don't we start over again? As the sheriff of Placerville, I'd like you to—"

"Oh, for Pete's sake, stop. I heard you." I plopped back into my seat. "Tell me, Sheriff, what have *you* found to help close this case?"

"Until the coroner releases his report—"

"Oh, so you have nothing?"

"I didn't say that, exactly."

"So, you do have something?" I grinned.

He wagged his finger. "You're mocking me."

"Maybe a little." I brought my hands together, palms facing in, and then stretched them farther apart. "Or I guess it's a lot."

"You're one challenging lady." A gleam brightened his eyes.

"Thank you. Seriously, can we forget this argument ever happened?"

"As long as you stop interfering." He walked toward me and slid a chair sideways to sit close. "You've got to understand I can't be keeping an eye on you twenty-four seven."

"I'm not asking you to."

He rubbed the back of his neck. "If you refuse to listen and get into trouble, I won't be there to help." The voice softened, but his face muscles tightened. "This is murder we're talking about."

"I know."

We were inches apart, closer than comfortable for me to relax. Sheriff and concerned citizen. That was the relationship we had.

My voice lowered to match his. "Gladys and Ollie could never commit murder. You do realize this, don't you?"

"I do. Like I said, jail's the safest place for them right now. The townsfolk are still fired up."

I glanced at my lap. "I feel badly for them. This is too much to deal with, especially at their age." I tilted my chin upward to take a peek at his face. "Have you considered the real killer wants to frame the Bellwethers? And has had many opportunities to do so, planting evidence and . . ." I jerked at the warmth of his hand on my arm. "Oh! I . . ." In one swift move, I jumped out of my seat. "You know, I'm late for an appointment. I have to go. Sorry."

Quint grinned. "You do that quite often."

"Do what?" I scrambled to shove brushes and sandpaper into the supply box.

"Hurry off someplace. You said it this morning. Remember? In front of Meeka's shop."

"Oh, that. I—Say, did you recognize the kid who blew past me?" I quieted my voice, hoping I didn't sound too anxious.

"Not really. He whizzed by like Taz the cartoon devil. Too fast for me to note any details. Other than his clothes. He looked fly. Isn't that the word kids use nowadays?"

I snorted and laughed at the same time. "Ah, no. Looking fly is nineties slang. You're showing your age. The current phrase would be to say he looks sick."

"Sick?" Quint shook his head. "Good thing I don't have kids. I'd never understand them."

I patted his arm. "It's okay. They don't understand grownups either." I hesitated, waiting for him to carry on the conversation.

Instead, a goofy grin spread across his face.

"What?"

"Nothing." He shrugged. "I like your humor, Ali Winston."

"Okay, well, I'm leaving, so . . ." I waved to motion him toward the door.

"You're kicking me out. That's nice. Well, you have a wonderful meeting, if there really is a meeting."

My brows shot up.

"Not that you need an excuse to get away, mind you." He winked.

"Right. Same to you, Sheriff Sterling. You enjoy investigating all on your own. Without any help from me." I muttered under my breath as he wheeled around the corner. "Stubborn, independent male ego. He wouldn't take a helping hand if he was hanging from a cliff and ready to fall."

"What was that?"

I squealed and clutched my throat as Quint peeked around the edge of the doorway. "Gotcha." He clucked his tongue and winked again before disappearing.

"Moron," I shouted, but with a smile on my face.

After closing up the building, I made my way toward the movie lot. The early evening sunlight had turned hazy with a soft covering of clouds, but at least the wind had calmed. I steered a path along the row of trailers on the opposite side of the lot, stopping at each to search for something to identify Sebastian's. Ollie informed me how Sebastian complained the SPACA trailer wasn't up to his standards and that the commute between his ski lodge and movie set was too inconvenient. He needed private space and comfortable lodgings to spend the night on occasion. Seemed fitting. His had to be the most ostentatious of them all, even more than O'Neil's.

The time inched past six. He might've left for the day, but it was worth a shot to stop by for a chat. I had an itch to explore the inside of his trailer. All sorts of goodies could tell me more about him because I suspected he kept a closetful of secrets about his past. Maybe even shady ones. A man as conceited as Sebastian would never willingly confess his weaknesses or flaws.

I stopped at the last trailer and gawked at a Rockwood Signature, probably the latest model camper, complete with fireplace and patio. My face brightened with a smug grin. "That's *sooo* perfect."

I rested my head against the structure to listen for any movement. I shrugged then knocked on the trailer door. Footsteps shuffled and the door swung open. Sebastian greeted me with a beaming smile.

"Hope I'm not too late."

"Not at all. I'm having a nightcap while settling in for the evening." He straightened his shoulders and tilted his chin. "I've been spending several nights on set since O'Neil asks for my expertise quite often. Anyway, would you care to join me for a drink?" He waved me inside.

"Ah, no thanks. I'm good." I skirted around him while I digested and catalogued every detail of the expansive room. Not many personal items, which was disappointing. I raised my brows as I studied the closet door.

"I have a confession."

My breath hitched. "Oh?" I pried my attention away from the room décor to face him.

"I wasn't quite honest with you. In truth, I have done a bit of acting, but that was years and years ago. Theater mostly." He sipped at his nightcap. Setting the tumbler on the counter, he added, "Tell me more about your ideas to save our precious alliance."

I laughed. "I wouldn't say it needs saving. This is more of an image makeover. Offering acting classes at the youth center is one suggestion."

"What else?"

"What if SPACA donated money earned from events to the town's nonprofit organizations, like the theater guild and the children's museum? You know, instead of filling SPACA's bank account, which I suspect is not hurting for money." I flavored my tone with a hint of slick sarcasm and turned to glance from one end of the trailer to the other. "Nice Rockwell."

Sebastian stroked his chin and remained silent, which made me even more suspicious about his handling of SPACA funds. In all fairness, he might earn plenty from the ski resort to easily afford a fancy trailer, but I recalled the Bellwethers' story. Julia disagreed with Florence and Sebastian on how to spend the funds. Had she suspected or found something?

He picked up his tumbler and took another sip. "Your suggestion deserves some thought, but I'll have to crunch the numbers."

"That's only one of my ideas. I'll think of more." I moved around the room to avoid his glance. "When I first spoke to Florence about the acting classes, I suggested the Bellwethers would be a fit choice to teach them, but she believes the further SPACA distances itself from Gladys and Ollie, the better." When I finished speaking, I turned to gauge his reaction. I needed to know where he stood.

He tapped the counter. "She's right. This situation needs to be resolved. Murder is messy and ugly and not the sort of thing we deal with. If, that is, when the Bellwethers are cleared of all charges, we'll welcome them back. After all, SPACA's reputation and that of Sierra Pines remain my first concern. I'll teach the classes. At least to get them started."

His authoritative manner was smug and annoying. There'd be no point in arguing, though his comments reeked of fake overtones. The ski resort and the money it brought in were his true concern, I'd bet. I backstepped toward the door, disappointed my sleuthing earned me no clues about Thaddeus's murder.

"Guess that's all for now. If you have any questions, call me." My rear end bumped into something other than the door. I winced at the rattle and clink of objects colliding and falling. I closed my eyes for an instant until silence resumed. "Oh, I'm so sorry. How klutzy can I be?"

I scrambled to pick up a picture frame that had landed on the floor. "I hope it's not broken."

"It's fine. I can take it from here." Sebastian drew closer, his hand extended.

"I'll pay for any damaged items, of course." I examined the glass and relaxed. No cracks or chips, but something caught my eye. The photo behind the glass. A group of people stood in front of a building. The word Starlight was scrawled above the doorway in huge letters.

"I'll take that." Sebastian snatched the photo from my hand, which left me curious as well as disappointed I hadn't had a chance to examine it further.

I wished him a good evening and jogged down the path to the parking lot, relieved to be alone. That photo. At the very least, it meant something to Sebastian. Why else would he grab it from me so quickly? This man acted more and more mysterious every time I encountered him, and it bugged me enough to find out why.

I pulled the convertible into the drive and entered the house with somewhat deflated enthusiasm and energy. I'd spent the day polishing a sculpture of Captain Sutter, finding the note with its portentous message, being lectured by Quint to leave his murder case alone, and having a mostly unproductive visit with Sebastian. Nothing to help lead me to Beale's murderer. I shuddered. That note. Somebody was watching me. Guess who'd be looking over her shoulder twenty-four seven?

"Hello, dear. I'm glad you're home."

I came to an abrupt stop in the foyer and widened my eyes to saucer-sized orbs. "You're here."

Gladys grinned at me while Ollie stood behind her with a plate as he shoveled pie into his mouth. He nodded a garbled hello.

Gladys hugged me. "Yes, we are and so lucky to have such loyal friends."

"Friends are wonderful." I agreed, though confused.

Ollie laid the fork on his empty plate. "Judge Wilkes is a real pip."

"Ollie, I don't think Alexis understands pip. No one uses that word nowadays. Besides, I'd never compliment a man with pip." Gladys admonished with a headshake.

"Age of equality. Woman, man, old, new, what difference does it make?" He shrugged his shoulders then looked at me. "I'm saying he's a good soul who helps his friends when they're in a pinch."

"Pinch meaning . . ."

"She knows what in a pinch means, Gladys. Stop spouting off like Webster's dictionary." Ollie rolled his eyes.

I pressed my lips together to stifle a laugh and waited while they sorted out their opinions and settled the argument.

"Ollie, why don't you take your dirty dish to the kitchen?" Gladys smiled sweetly.

"Don't mind if I do. Women and their prattle, not the least bit interesting to me." Ollie stomped off down the hall in his uneven gait.

I scoffed. "He's more into female prattle than he'll admit."

"Or realizes. We'll leave that discussion for another day."

"Now, tell me the story. How did you get released so quickly?" Obviously, our sleuthing team couldn't take credit. We'd found nothing to support the Bellwethers' case.

"The judge took pity on us. You've heard your aunt speak of him. We've been close friends with Judge Wilkes since Julia, Ollie, and I arrived in Sierra Pines."

"He set bail in the amount of one dollar. How's that for drama in the courtroom?" Ollie returned from the kitchen.

"Women's prattle not interesting, hmm?" Gladys tossed him a wry smile.

"I can tell the story better than you. Has nothing to do with prattling." He shifted his gaze to me. "The judge stated the charges were out of line."

"What he said was the town's tax dollars shouldn't be used to place two kind and elderly model citizens behind bars," Gladys corrected.

I grew tired from volleying my attention back and forth between them. "That's good to hear. I suppose Sheriff Sterling wasn't too happy with the judge's decision."

"He didn't say much of anything, in court or on the drive back to the B&B, which seemed odd to me," Gladys said.

"Oh?"

"Yes. He seemed in a hurry to leave. Even passed on my offer of apple pie and coffee. He warned us to be careful, though." Gladys nodded.

"Quint is anxious to get out there, find the killer, and put the case to bed." Ollie sat on the foyer bench and rubbed his bum leg.

"I don't think people use the phrase put the case to bed, Ollie."

"What does it matter?" Ollie's voice rose.

My cheeks puffed as I sucked in air. "Please." Both of them turned and stared blankly at me. "Sorry. It's been a tiring day, and I'm grimy with plaster dust covering me top to toe. I think I'll just . . ." I pointed toward the stairs.

"Yes, certainly. We can chat later." Gladys patted my sleeve. Dust particles scattered and she waved an arm in front of her face.

"Sorry." As I jogged up the stairs, the doorbell rang. Pivoting on one heel, I paused. If it was Quint, I'd express my gratitude for him taking care of the Bellwethers.

"I have a delivery for Julia Winston." A male voice outside the door spoke.

"Oh, oh my. Would you look at that, Ollie? It's a rosy teacup dogwood." Gladys clasped her hands together.

My breath caught hearing Julia's name. I descended the stairs and into the foyer. "Who's it from?" I stared at the tree with its roots covered in burlap that now rested against the doorjamb.

"Would you like me to take it around back, ma'am?" The deliveryman held out a clipboard and receipt for Gladys to sign.

"No, it won't be necessary. I can't imagine who would do this, can you?" Gladys asked.

"Not a clue." Ollie bent over, examining the tree top to bottom. "Not even a card to explain."

We all turned to the deliveryman. He shrugged. "I just deliver the merchandise."

"Can you at least tell us when the tree was ordered?"

"Nope. No date on this receipt. I suppose you could ask someone at the delivery service office. I'm sorry." He tucked the clipboard under his arm, grabbed the dolly cart, and powerwalked down the drive.

Had Julia ordered the tree? If so, what were we to think? The idea of it gave me goose bumps, considering the Bellwethers' plan for a memorial. No, it had to be someone else. Someone Julia knew.

My mind shuffled through names—people with a kind and generous heart, those who loved Julia and would possibly buy the dogwood tree the Bellwethers had been hoping to plant. Plenty of folks in Sierra Pines were kind and generous, plenty who knew Julia Winston and the Bellwethers, but how many of them were aware a rosy teacup dogwood was Julia's favorite? Only a few people had been in the house the day Gladys divulged that particular detail. Even more curious, the sender must have known the Bellwethers' plan to plant a tree in the backyard.

"Did you talk to Mr. Digmoore about a tree?" I asked Gladys.

"No dear. I haven't called him or anyone. Much too busy with, well, you know how it's been."

I studied the tree and how Gladys gleamed with pleasure. Did it matter who? Maybe not. Maybe I was paranoid. Afterall, a tree was innocent enough. Plenty of gifts were given anonymously, weren't they? A prickly sensation shivered its way through me. I rubbed my goose-pimply arms. Quint had better work overtime to get answers, and, despite his objections, he could use our help. The more the better. He was right to worry about the Bellwethers and their safety, but his concern fell short. All of us had to worry because none of us were safe as long as the killer was out there.

# CHAPTER TEN

I SPLASHED COLD WATER ON MY FACE to stir me awake. Sleep, at least peaceful sleep, hadn't been on the agenda because I couldn't erase from my mind what happened to Julia or Thaddeus. I certainly couldn't stop a killer from planting misleading evidence or perhaps planning yet another murder. On top of that, I worried about the B&B. I was clueless how to keep it and run it.

Hand to throat, I gasped as my phone rang and vibrated on the sink counter. An involuntary hiccup came out of me as I stared at the familiar face on the screen. I tossed the towel clenched in my hand to the side. With only a moment's hesitation, I pressed the answer button. "Hi, Mom."

"Sweetie! I thought for sure you'd send me to voicemail."

The reproachful comment colored with her cheerful tone triggered a warning. "Good morning, Mom. If you called to talk about me coming home, don't bother. I haven't made up my mind." I pressed the speaker button and set down the phone then yanked a brush threw my hair.

"Of course you haven't." She sighed. "Your Dad contacted the appraiser he knows. Also, the owner of the remodeling and construction company. Both are located close enough to Sierra Pines. One in Placerville and the other in Folsom. I'll text you the names and numbers."

"Mom." I dragged out the syllable in my own reproachful tone.

"This way you're covered whether you decide to sell or you stay and make improvements."

I winced. Her cheery tone had taken on a sharper edge. "Tell Dad I said thanks, but really, I can handle this."

"We'd fly out to help you, but this play we are in won't close until next month."

I gritted my teeth. Was she even listening? "Gotta go, Mom. I have lots to do. Thanks for calling, and give Dad my love. Bye." I jabbed the end call button. I was free for another month. However, after the play finished, they'd take the first flight out of La Guardia to get here, whether I protested or not. "Parents. Got to love them, no matter how smothering they get."

The phone dinged with a text message. I clicked to open. The screen displayed the information she promised to send. I shrugged and entered both names in my contacts. Why not? No point in being a stubborn fool. Besides, my parents weren't the only relationship problem bothering me.

I studied myself in the mirror. Bright red cheeks contrasted with dark spots under my eyes, and my chest heaved at the thought of Quint Sterling. I pictured his face and my insides fluttered. "Oh for—stop it. You're tired and emotional, and it's messing with the part of you that doesn't need attention right now. So, stop." I jabbed a finger at my mirrored reflection.

To avoid the image, I turned my head, chin to shoulder, then marched into the bedroom. "It's not like he's into me." I pulled my hair into a ponytail. "Good lord. What am I saying?" I tugged my legs into a clean pair of jeans and pulled a shirt over my head. "I don't want him into me. I'm selling the B&B as soon as this horrible nightmare of a murder case is solved, and the Bellwethers can go back to normal lives. After that, I'll be on the next flight to New York, but not because Willa and Robert say so." I shoved both feet into my sneakers. "No more Quint Sterling. No more problem."

Hitting the bottom stair, I skidded to a stop. Rubber soles gripped the hardwood floor. I teetered forward and barely grabbed the railing to steady myself. My breath held for the count of ten while I stared past the parlor doorway. Quint sat on the sofa, conversing with Dean and Ralph. Talk about horrible timing. I fanned my cheeks then moved across the hall.

"Good morning." My gaze settled on Quint. "How nice of you to drop by."

"Ralph was telling me the Bellwethers received a surprise delivery yesterday," he said.

"Yes, the dogwood tree." I sat in a chair across from Ralph, who seemed preoccupied as he leafed through a book. "Strange how no card came with it, though."

Quint shrugged. "Possibly nothing strange about it."

"Possibly." I nibbled on my bottom lip. "Still, after two people died under this very roof and one of them murdered?" I shivered. "Maybe I'm overreaching, but an anonymous delivery seems hokey to me."

"Hokey?" A smirk teased Quint's lip.

I puffed out my cheeks. "It's one of Julia's expressions. Hokey means fake or suspicious."

"Does anyone even use hokey nowadays?" His smirk grew into a mile-wide grin.

I volleyed with a stony stare. "Can we move on? What I'm saying is how many could've known Julia loved rosy teacup dogwoods?"

"More than you'd imagine." Quint dropped the smile and relaxed in his chair.

"Oh?" I leaned forward, curious.

"She talked about her garden to anyone who'd listen, including me. Her favorite flowers, her favorite tree, and what vegetables grew best in this climate."

I mulled over that piece of information and recalled similar conversations with her. "Yeah, but how many others knew the Bellwethers intended to plant one in the backyard as a memorial? Hmm?"

"True. Even more curious, why keep any of this a secret?"

"Exactly. It's like the person wants to sound mysterious," I said.

Dean moved from his place by the window to sit next to Quint. "Maybe the person was a creepy admirer or stalker who had feelings for Julia but kept it a secret because, well, he's a creep. Get it? That reminds of me of an episode in *The Young and Beautiful*. I'd come out of a coma and . . ."

"Maybe it's nothing." Quint leaned back.

"Or it's the sender's way to distract us from the murder case." I scratched underneath my chin.

Quint shook his head. "You're reaching. This has nothing to do with the murder."

"As I was saying, this is like that episode in my soap. After I came out of the coma, the killer—" Dean raised his voice.

"This isn't a soap opera, Mr. Thornton. I'm conducting a murder investigation. With a real killer, not some make-believe nonsense." Quint's tone was tinged with annoyance.

"I know that. I'm not stupid." Dean stood.

I blinked, not sure what was happening.

Quint ignored Dean and turned to me. "Ali, the reason I stopped by was to ask you about something. Can I speak to you outside?" He glanced at Dean for a second. "Alone?"

"Um . . ." I gazed at each of them and neither one seemed happy to be in the room. Especially together. On the other hand, Ralph had his head buried in a book. Literally. His chest moved in a steady rise and fall as the slight hum of snoring quivered from his lips.

"Sure. Let me grab my sweater off the coat rack." I narrowed my eyes at Dean as I stepped cautiously around him. If looks were weapons, his would've sliced, diced, and skewered Quint, and I had no clue why.

We reached the front porch. I was relieved to escape the tension building between the two of them. "That was awkward and strange."

Quint leaned against the wood post. "Not so strange. I think Dean is jealous."

"Jealous? J-j-jealous of what?" I sputtered and blinked. No way would I leap into that frying pan of personal embarrassment. Not after what I'd dreamed last night.

"Of you and me." His voice softened to a smooth, velvety tone, almost seductive, if not for the vulnerable, childlike expression he wore.

I fussed with my sweater, struggling to fit buttons into holes as my hands trembled. After a few seconds of silence, I looked up. "You wanted to ask me something?"

"Ah, sure." He shoved both hands into his pockets and straightened, no longer leaning against the post. "First, I want to apologize for yesterday. I was rude. I should've never said what I did. Not in that way."

"No, you shouldn't have. It was also condescending and chauvinistic." I forced my lips to hold a straight line. "You should be ashamed."

His jaw tensed. "Hey, if we're to be honest, you took a turn lashing back at me. I don't . . ." He smiled and tilted his head to one side before he settled against the post once more and crossed one leg over the other. "Ah, I see what you did there. Got me good. Props to you."

"Props to me, huh? Nice expression. You'll be communicating with the younger crowd before you know it." I winked. "If there's nothing else on your mind, I should go." When I reached for the door handle, I caught sight of Dean.

His face scrunched and eyes glared as he peered out of the parlor window. Maybe Quint was right.

"Wait."

I turned when Quint's hand rested gently over mine. At least I didn't flinch or pull away this time.

"I'd like to take you to dinner Monday evening. That is, as a gesture to make up for my rude, condescending, and chauvinistic behavior." The words tumbled out and, afterward, he whistled. "Whew. That wasn't so hard."

"Dinner?" I clenched the door handle with a white-knuckled fist. Not a big deal. Two friends sharing a meal hardly raised concern. As if that argument had a chance to work, I repeated the thought a couple times until my breathing evened. "Sure, though you've got nothing to apologize for." I pointed at the door. "Okay, I've got to, ah, it's getting late and I'm . . . I should go."

"Because you're in a hurry and have someplace to be?" His eyes sparkled and the dimples in his cheeks deepened when he smiled.

"Hah. Yeah. Touché." I pointed a trigger finger and grinned. "See you later, Sheriff." I lingered on the doorstep as Quint jogged to his cruiser and drove away.

One dinner wouldn't hurt. I had no intention of changing my mind. I had to be practical. Running a B&B wasn't in my skill bank. Not to mention, if I was leaving Sierra Pines soon, starting a relationship made no sense either. "There you go again. Assuming. He's only being courteous because he's a friend. He's not interested in you any other way. And who cares, right?"

Stepping inside the house, I collided with Dean and yipped. "Good grief." My breath hitched at the sight of him.

A twitch had formed in the corner of his eye. "Did he say anything about me?" He delivered his words in an edgy, staccato-like clip.

I tilted my head to one side. "Pardon?"

"Did your conversation have anything to do with me? Why else would you go outside where I couldn't hear?"

"Yeah, ah, no mention of you. Nada. Zilch. So, you can chillax, Hollywood. Now, if you'll excuse me." I tried skirting around him, but he sidestepped in front of me.

"You're sure? You'd tell me if he happened to say something, right?"

"I told you. He said nothing." I peeled off my sweater and turned to hang it on the rack. I chewed on my bottom lip as the thought came to me. On impulse, I spun around. "He did make one tiny remark, though."

"He did?" Dean straightened and every muscle tensed.

"Yeah, let me think. I want to get this right." I tapped one finger against my cheek while Florence's confession played like a video recording in my head. I pictured the fear on her face as she spoke. "You know, it's really nothing." I shrugged.

"You sure?" His shoulders relaxed while a nervous laugh spluttered from his lips.

"Yeah, but I should tell you this much." I leaned close enough to gag on the musky odor of his pricey cologne mixed with breath minty freshness. "It would be a shame if the press got word you were hiding right here in Sierra Pines. I'm sure they'd love to write your story. Threatening old ladies with blackmail? Not exactly a fan pleaser."

Witnessing the speechless look on his face was satisfying in so many ways. Petty, maybe, but I couldn't stop defending the people I cared about when they needed it. People like Florence.

A stiff smile stretched across my face as I patted Dean's chest. "Now, why don't you go look for someone else to pester? I've got more important things to do with my day than to spend it consoling you." I nudged him sideways and traveled toward the kitchen. Suddenly, I craved one of Gladys's tomato and cheese omelets.

I lifted my nose and sniffed. The faint odor of bacon wafted throughout the kitchen. A plate filled with a thick omelet and two biscuits rested on the counter. A sticky note with my name was attached to it.

"Gladys, you're the best." I poured a glass of OJ and grabbed my plate.

Setting at the table, I gobbled my egg omelet and a buttered biscuit as I wondered where Gladys and Ollie could be. They usually hung around the kitchen while Ollie finished his second breakfast serving and Gladys planned meal choices for the next morning. I cut a few apple slices. With those in one hand and a mug of coffee in the other, I made my way out to the atrium.

I set down my mug, pulled off the black cover and opened the cage door. "Hey, pretty boy. How you doing?" I held Blackbeard's beak while I scratched behind his ear. "Would you like an apple treat? Hmm?" I placed the apple slices in his tray and filled the other with water. Glancing to the side, I caught sight of some movement in the yard.

"So, that's where you two are." I closed the cage, grabbed my coffee, and made my way toward the rear exit of the screened porch. I stopped at the screen door and took in the backyard scene. Gladys and Ollie knelt next to the rosy teacup, gently patting the soil around it.

My heartbeat hiccupped. Gladys stood and joined hands with Ollie. They bowed heads as they spoke.

"Julia, I hope this tree gives you peace and a bit of happiness. We miss you and will never forget your kindness." Gladys's voice quivered.

"Meet you on the other side someday soon, dear friend." Ollie's chest heaved.

I swiped my eyes with the back of one hand. Once they'd picked up their tools and turned to face my direction, I opened the screen door and stepped into the yard to meet them halfway. "Good morning. The tree looks beautiful."

"Just you wait. The dark pink blooms in the spring are a glorious spectacle." Gladys sniffled and brushed away tears, leaving a smudge of black on her cheek.

I felt my heart break just a little. She'd have to send me pictures when the time came because I would be in New York by then, resuming my life, hopefully with a new job, and not sponging off my parents. "I can imagine. Let me carry that for you." I reached for the shovel in Ollie's hand.

He pulled his arm out of reach. "Nonsense. Wouldn't be the gentlemanly thing to do. Besides, you're carrying hot coffee. What if it spilled? We don't want to spoil the morning by having to run you to the emergency room for third degree burns."

"Now who's the fussy one?" A wry grin widened Gladys's face.

"I'm only watching out for Julia's niece. It's what she'd want us to do."

"How about we go inside and have coffee together?" I twisted the kitchen door handle.

"Excellent idea." Both chimed in at once.

I led the way and held the door open while they passed inside.

"There you are," Ralph exclaimed. "Ali, your phone has been ringing for the past several minutes. Whoever's calling must have something urgent to say."

I winced. Right now, I craved some pleasant downtime with Gladys and Ollie and maybe a second cup of coffee. "Thanks, Ralph." I grabbed the phone off the kitchen counter and shoved it into my back pocket.

One of Ralph's bushy eyebrows traveled skyward. "You're not going to check?"

"Not yet. I want a moment of nothing but friends and pleasant conversation."

"Couldn't agree more." Ollie held out one hand. "Let me pour you another cup. Cream and one teaspoon of sugar, right?"

I grinned and nodded. "Like I said, Ralph, friends and pleasant conversation. It's therapy."

He shrugged. "Not about to argue. In fact, if it's not an interruption, I'll join you."

"Of course you'll join us. This is a B&B and you're a guest." Gladys handed Ralph a mug.

As we sat at the table and discussed the Halloween festivities happening soon, the buzzing vibration from my back pocket tickled my rear. I clenched my jaw. Best made plans or intentions never worked when some persistent person was determined to mess with you.

I stood with phone in hand and stared at the screen. Florence. How about that? Not a surprise. I smiled at my breakfast table companions. "If you'll excuse me for a minute, or maybe two? Don't go away, though. Please."

I hurried out into the hall and pushed the button to answer. "Good morning, Florence. How can I help you?"

"You can throw that despicable, conniving Dean Thornton out of the B&B. That's what you can do."

Her voice was screechy, and I shoved a finger in my ear to stop the ringing. "Why? Has he threatened you again?"

"What do you think? That I act this hysterical all the time?"

I eyeballed the phone screen. "I can't kick him out, Florence. Maybe if you gave me more information about the blackmail. Somehow, I get the idea you haven't told me everything." If she was going to involve me, I deserved answers.

"I think I've told you plenty." Her voice lowered. "Do you know how difficult it was to divulge such a shameful family secret to you? Please, Ali. He could destroy me, if this gets out to the community. I need . . . I *want* him gone, far away from Sierra Pines."

"It could backfire. He doesn't seem the type who walks away from a threat or, in this case, after being kicked out of the B&B." Suddenly exhausted, I plopped down on the hall bench seat. Exhausted from dealing with out-of-control, needy people like Florence and Dean. Exhausted from worrying over this thing between Quint and me. Yeah, I was exhausted and out of patience. "Let's change the subject. I spoke with Sebastian and shared your suggestion. He's offered to teach the acting classes. He claims his acting experience in the theater would be helpful. That and how well he gets along with young people."

"Acting experience? Huh. I never knew."

"Oh? That's weird. Why would he keep it a secret from you?"

"I'm sure I don't have a clue since every time he opens his mouth, it's all boastful blathering spewing out. And as far as getting along with young people? Total hogwash. He despises children and has no patience for them." She paused a short beat then snapped, "Are you going to boot Dean out of the B&B, or not?"

"I'm not forcing Dean to leave the B&B."

"Fine. Thank you so very much for your kind and generous help."

The phone clicked, ending the call, before I could question why she suggested Sebastian was qualified to teach the classes in the first place. I shook my head. Maybe now wasn't the time to ask. Florence's present state of mind was filled with worrying about Dean.

I stood, ready to head back to the kitchen. The photo on the wall directly across from me was a candid shot of Cary Grant and Joan Fontaine in a scene from the movie *Suspicion*. I recalled the scene clearly. Cary and Joan were in the car, driving on a twisted stretch of road, high on a steep cliff with the ocean hundreds of feet below. Joan believed Cary planned to murder her for her money. Ironically, she had it all wrong but never confronted Cary, only suspected his intentions.

Florence suspected Dean would reveal her secret. Did he speak to anyone else about it? Or if he talked to Florence while visiting the movie set, someone might have overheard their conversation and later confronted Dean, maybe threatened blackmail. The question was, who. Possibly someone on set. The crew. The actors. Any one of them. Even Thaddeus. He'd been on the movie set every day. He enjoyed taking walks and getting to know the crew and cast. *I learn all sorts of things that way.* His words. And the trailer he shared with Jax was only steps from SPACA's. I shuddered. He had numerous opportunities to see and hear any confrontation between the sparring cousins. If Florence knew he listened and she went totally bananas—her go-to reaction to most every situation—she could have panicked and murdered Thaddeus to keep him quiet. Permanently. Sure, my theory was a bit melodramatic, but, after all, it involved Florence.

I shuffled through events from our evening at the theater, trying to recall Florence's whereabouts throughout the play. Had she left at any time? I couldn't say with any certainty. I rubbed my temples. All this speculating gave me a headache. What if she talked someone into committing the heinous crime for her? In my opinion, murder wasn't her style. "Get a grip, Ali. Your imagination is way out in left field." In any case, it couldn't be easy to keep secrets in a small town like Sierra Pines.

Once more, the movie played in my head. Fear in Joan Fontaine came to a startling climax when the car swerved and her door flew open. She believed Cary would push her out of the vehicle, but he didn't. He pulled her to safety. Imagining the worst was what people did when they were afraid. Florence was afraid of anyone discovering her secret. Especially anyone close to her. Try living with that.

I lifted slowly from the bench and walked down the hall. "Okay, this is ridiculous." I was desperate to find a scapegoat, anyone to blame and take the focus off of the Bellwethers.

I returned to the kitchen and forced a smile. Gladys and Ollie were alone at the table.

"That was Florence. She was having one of her moments and needed to vent, I guess."

I peered out at the porch. Ralph sat in a sunny spot with his newspaper and coffee.

"Isn't that every day?" Ollie asked.

"Shush, Ollie. You're unkind. What did she want to vent about, Alexis?" Gladys sipped her coffee.

I debated on how much to tell them. Less was better. "Oh, her usual complaints about life not going the way she'd like. Nothing too important. I did find one of her comments strange, though." I tapped the handle of my mug. "When I told her how Sebastian mentioned he'd done some theater acting years ago, Florence was surprised. She'd never heard that about him. Did you know?"

Both Gladys and Ollie shook their heads.

"Then again, if he was in stage theater, we didn't travel in that circle," Gladys explained.

"And it would've been after our time there. What is he? Around sixty-something?" Ollie added.

"Oh, that's an excellent point. We left Hollywood in forty-eight, you see. Sebastian wouldn't have been born yet, or no more than a toddler. Did he say when he was in the theater?" Gladys asked.

"No. Only that it was years ago. It doesn't matter." I shrugged. "I was only curious." I dismissed the topic from our conversation, but one detail stuck in my head. Why hide his theater background from everyone but me?

"Maybe we should have a party to celebrate the tree planting. What do you think? I could bake Julia's favorite cookies and use her recipe for hot apple cranberry cider." Gladys beamed.

"Sounds like a great idea." I patted her hand. "I do have one more question. Does a business with the name Starlight mean anything to either of you?"

Gladys raised her eyebrows. "Starlight? No. Do you recall anything, Ollie?"

"Doesn't sound familiar. Why? Is it important?" Ollie rested both hands on the table and laced his fingers together.

"I'm not sure. I found a photo in Sebastian's trailer that made me curious." I stood. "I should be going. I promised Nina I'd stop by this morning to help with a new project. It's Sunday, but I guess in Nina's mind, every day is a work day. You need anything from town? I could pick it up on my way home."

"No, dear. We plan to go out this evening, stop at the diner for a meal, and then do a bit of shopping," Gladys said. "We certainly need some pleasant distraction, don't we?"

"You certainly do."

"So do you. I hear the guests are traveling north to a winery this afternoon. You should go along," Gladys said.

"Can't. I promised Nina I'd stay until the project is finished, which will most likely mean until evening since it's huge."

"You're dedicated, just like Julia." Gladys smiled. "Have a good day."

I bid them goodbye and grabbed my sweater off the hook before heading outside. With any luck, it would be a good day, an uneventful one. Funny how boring could be a welcomed relief.

I TOSSED MY BAG ON THE BENCH SEAT and shrugged off my sweater. The clock chimed nine times. I could barely hold my head up, and my body ached. The project Nina and I worked on had fallen apart. On the third attempt, we succeeded. By then, it was after eight. I helped clean up the disastrous mess we'd made then dragged myself to my car and drove half-asleep to the B&B, fortunately without crashing. So much for uneventful.

"Hello? Anyone here?" I remained in the foyer. My body protested the slightest movement, every aching inch of every muscle. My voice echoed into silence. I shuffled up the stairs and dragged myself to bed. I stripped off my dusty shirt and pants and dropped them to the floor. A shower would have to wait until morning. Sleep pulled me under, and the last thought running through my head was how big and lonely the B&B felt when nobody else was here.

I awakened in a groggy stupor as silence in the house broke with a resounding bang. My breath hitched in a sharp, painful gasp. Hand to chest, I willed my heartbeat to steady its uneven pace. "Is that you Gladys? Ollie?" I called out, but it came in a raspy whisper that most likely no one could hear.

Within minutes, I slid out of bed and into my robe before tiptoeing across the bedroom floor. Curiosity trumped fear at this point. Most likely one of the guests or the Bellwethers caused the raucous sound. Maybe. However, tired or not, I'd never fall back asleep without checking. Besides, the noise was loud, too loud to ignore.

Peering out of my doorway, I shifted my head to glance from one end of the hall to the other, which was pointless since darkness made it impossible to see six inches in front of me. I raised my voice. "Gladys? Is that you? Anybody here?"

Growing fully awake with my faculties sharp and alert, the faint sounds of paper shuffling and drawers sliding open caught my ear. I tiptoed into the hall and listened. The sounds came from my left and in the direction of Julia's room. I picked up the front of my robe to keep from tripping and stepped quietly to her door. At the bottom, a faint crack of light shimmered out into the hallway. I hesitated. Perhaps Gladys was inside, stealing a moment to mourn. She'd said how being in Julia's room made her feel closer to her. Since Quint had removed the crime scene tape and given the all-clear sign to enter, Gladys might have been anxious to take a look.

I knocked softly. "Gladys? Are you in there? I don't want to bother you, but I heard noises and figured I should check." I inched forward until my lips brushed the door. "I'll go away if you want me to, but say something so I know it's you in there." My breath quickened as silence met my ears.

I turned the knob, both relieved and frightened to find the door unlocked. I braced my shoulders then inched the door open and stepped inside. Papers had been scattered across the floor and drawers turned upside down on the bed. I gaped at the disarray. “What in the—” My voice broke, the words abruptly cut off, as a sensation of falling overcame me and everything turned to black.

# CHAPTER ELEVEN

I PRIED OPEN MY EYES. A huge, blurry image hovered over me. I blinked and my vision cleared somewhat, enough to recognize the shiny badge on his chest and the wave of jet-black hair. "Hey, Sheriff." I slurred my words as if in a drunken stupor. I attempted a smile, but stretching my face hurt. "Ouch." I reached up, but Quint pulled my hand away and rested it on the bed.

"Not to touch. Doctor's orders."

"What doctor?" I wanted to shake my head and clear my brain, but something warned me that would hurt, too.

"You've got a lump the size of Pluto on the back of your noggin, compliments of whoever ransacked your aunt's room." He tensed and his eyes darkened.

"Oh—Oh wow." I dropped my jaw, at once remembering what transpired before my blackout. "Did you catch him? Or her? I couldn't see, but there were noises and such a mess in the room." I squeezed my eyes shut. Julia's room.

"No. By the time the Bellwethers returned home and found you on Julia's bedroom floor, the trespasser was nowhere around." Quint tucked my arm underneath the covers. "Have to keep you from getting a chill. Doctor's orders."

"The doctor sure has plenty of orders. Seriously, I'm fine. Other than the Pluto-sized lump on my head." I winced.

"All the same. You're to stay in bed to rest, at least through tomorrow morning."

I thrust out my lower lip. "But I have work to do. The Bellwethers need me. I can't stay in bed doing nothing."

His smile grew into an ear-to-ear grin.

"What are you smiling about?"

"You whine like a baby. Anyway, you're not leaving this room until the doctor gives his okay." He pointed at me.

I crossed my arms tightly over my chest. "I'm not a baby. I'm quite capable of making my own decisions. Now, if you don't mind, I'd like you to get out so I can dress."

Quint shook his head. "Nope. Not going to happen. Besides, as sheriff, I have to ask you some questions." He removed the notepad and pen from his pocket.

"Questions? Someone broke into the B&B, wrecked Julia's room—obviously looking for something—and then knocked me over the head because I interrupted. There's nothing more I can add." I threw off the covers, which he immediately replaced. "Oh for . . ."

"Question. How do you know someone broke in? I have to consider all possibilities. One of the guests or the Bellwethers could've rummaged through Julia's room. I've asked, and, as expected, all of them deny having been here when you were attacked. So, why do you think it was an intruder?"

"I . . . well, because I called out and no one answered."

"Hmm." He tapped the notepad with his pen. "If you were an intruder, especially a B&B guest or employee, and went through someone's belongings when you had no right to, would you answer to let anyone know?"

My mouth flapped like a fish, but no words came out. I failed to think of one reasonable argument.

"Exactly. So, we can't rule out anyone staying here. Meantime, we're dusting for prints. Who knows? Maybe we'll get lucky with the results. Now, what time did you arrive home?" He waited with pen tip to paper.

I grew more anxious with each question. "Around nine." I paused then pointed my finger. "You know, the timing of this strikes me as suspicious."

"How so?"

"Thaddeus was murdered only days ago. This place has never been broken into before. Why now?"

"And robbed." Quint nodded.

"Robbed?"

"Yes. Gladys checked the other rooms and found a few items from Julia's collection missing."

"Oh, no. That's . . . those can't be replaced." Julia kept all her collection pieces on display in a separate room that adjoined her bedroom so she could visit and reminisce in private. Thankfully, she wasn't alive to witness the theft. She'd be heartbroken.

"Still, I'd say it's a stretch of logic if you're suggesting a connection between the murder and the robbery."

"And Julia's death. Mustn't forget that." I bit down on my lip. Why did I go there? I was trying to put that theory to bed.

Creases deepened his brow. "Julia's death isn't a mystery. She died of natural causes."

"As far as you know." I shivered, bordering on fear and suspicion. I had become Joan Fontaine. Could Gladys be onto something with her theory that all these disturbing incidents connected to Julia? Thaddeus, his death, the break-ins at the production studio and in Julia's room, and the stolen items from her collection. How much weirder could it get? Whatever the explanation, we all needed to keep a watchful eye until Thaddeus's murder was solved. "Forget it. To tell you the truth, I'm convinced Julia died of old age. Mostly convinced, anyway. Call this my reaction to a horribly unpleasant experience. Did the doctor leave any meds? I need sleep."

"No meds because you might have a concussion. He says you should be wakened every couple of hours until tomorrow morning. Gladys and Ollie volunteered to carry out his instructions. So, no tranquilizers for you."

"Yes, mother." An impish grin curled my lips.

He laughed. "Honestly, I'm counting on you to get better. We have a dinner date, which I'll have to postpone if you don't recuperate soon. And I'm not a patient man." His eyes smoldered, deepening in color.

"Is that all? You're worried about a dinner date?" I teased.

"That, and I'd miss all your insults and arguments. I'm just getting used to having you around, Miss Winston." He smiled while his voice shifted into a smooth and sultry timbre.

I shivered, despite the layering of bedcovers. "I don't know if you have much time, Sheriff. After all, I'll be leaving soon. I have a life and family in New York waiting for me."

The smile wavered. Slowly, he stood. "That's a shame, but let's make the best of it while you're still here. Dinner tomorrow evening at six? I'll pick you up. Got to ride in style."

"Wait. You mean the cruiser? My coupe might be a better choice."

"I didn't say cruiser. Let's make it a surprise, shall we?" The smile returned.

"Sheriff Sterling, I think you should let Alexis get some rest. Don't worry. We'll take good care of her." Gladys stood in the doorway with hands on hips and a stern expression pasted on her face.

"Yes, ma'am. I'm leaving right this minute." He tipped a hand as he stepped toward the doorway. Turning to me, he winked. "Tomorrow. Dinner. Get better or else." With that, he disappeared into the hall.

"Now, you rest while I fix you a cup of tea. Got to keep you awake." Gladys rearranged my covers. "I'm so sorry, dear. If we'd been home . . ." She sank onto the edge of the bed.

"Don't apologize. What if the intruder had come on another night and attacked you instead?" I shuddered, imagining how that scenario could have turned tragic. "It's a shame about the collection. Are the stolen items valuable?"

She shrugged. "Moneywise? Not terribly much, but every item in that room is cherished and irreplaceable. I'm so glad Julia isn't here to see it." Tears welled in her eyes.

I handed her a tissue. "I thought the same thing."

"It's odd, though. You'd think a burglar would take the pricier collectibles. Why, the papers Sal gave us that day in his office were laying on the center table, in plain sight. Anyone could read how much each item is worth. Very strange."

"Yeah, it is, isn't it?" I digested her comments. My head pounded from more than the bump. Each day delivered a downpour of puzzling details to solve. It was like treading water with the shore nowhere in sight. "Gladys, do you think you could bring me that tea? Maybe it will help this headache."

"Oh, of course. How rude of me to sit here babbling. I'll be back in a jiffy." She hurried out of the room, leaving me to mull over her words.

"Why take something of no value? Unless it means more in an altogether different way." I ran my fingers across the edge of the bed quilt. What if the burglar wasn't some random stranger? And like I suggested to Quint, what if this person had a connection to Julia, the B&B, and the murder? Scarier yet, this person could be someone we all knew.

To sleep like the dead, like a rock, or like a log wasn't the way to describe my night. As promised, Gladys and Ollie, and even Ralph took turns waking me every two hours, asking me questions like what was my mother's name and did I know who starred in the 1960 movie *Psycho*, not the horrible remake. Two guesses as to who asked that one.

At nine a.m., I woke from a groggy two-hour stretch of mostly fitful slumber. My head still throbbed, but at least I could see straight. No more blurry images or doubles of anything. My legs wobbled, but I managed to stand and walk to the bathroom. However, one glance in the mirror and I grimaced. "This won't do." After taking a quick shower and dressing in clean clothes, I scribbled a quick note for Gladys. I left it on the dresser then tiptoed downstairs and out the door.

Determined as ever, I planned to go forward with my agenda. If I passed out at any time, plenty of people on the movie set were close by and would send for help. On the way there, I'd stop at a few stores, talk to proprietors, and ask about the Bellwethers' rendezvous at Bagels and Buns the night Thaddeus was murdered. When Ralph came to wake me during the night, I'd asked him how his mission had gone. Unfortunately, Dean ditched him, which I'd suspected would happen, and, with most of the stores closed, the task went uncompleted. Now it became *my* mission.

"Good morning." I smiled and greeted the owner of the Taffy House.

Julia had been one of her favorite customers. Taffy candy in numerous tasty flavors filled the B&B's snack bowl every day.

"Why, if it isn't Julia Winston's niece." Margie erupted into a belly laugh. Her round face and ample chins jiggled.

As if an afterthought caught up to her, she quickly sobered. "You poor dear. How are you doing? Everyone in Sierra Pines cherished your aunt. She'll be sorely missed."

She didn't comment about Thaddeus's murder, though I knew she was aware. Small towns equaled plenty of gossip. Maybe their type of etiquette required the affected party to mention it first. I wasn't sure since this was my first murder experience.

"Thank you. I'm fine. It's been a rough week, though. We're all adjusting, including the Bellwethers. Losing someone you've been friends with for so many years makes it hard to cope." I shifted my weight from one foot to the other. "Speaking of the Bellwethers, I don't suppose you can recall seeing them outside Bagels and Buns the night of the play preview at the Sierra Pines Theater?"

"Hmm, let me think." Margie scrunched her forehead as she stared beyond me. Seconds passed. Suddenly, she gasped. "Yes. I do believe . . .

wait. No, that was another day." Her head wagged back and forth. "Sorry. I closed early the evening of the premier. It was on a Wednesday, right? Yep. Early closing on Wednesdays. My daughter has ballet practice, and little Henry goes to kickboxing class. I'm Super Mom." She chuckled.

"That's too bad. I mean, bad as in you didn't see the Bellwethers. Not the super mom part. Go super moms." I punched my fist skyward with cheerleader enthusiasm.

Margie frowned.

At once, I dropped my hand to scratch behind one ear. "Um, thanks, Margie. Guess I should go. I have a few other shops to visit. You have a great day." I waved and, after a few deep breaths to clear my head, moved slowly down the sidewalk.

The next three owners were of no help. One had closed early for a family emergency. The other two had been slammed with customers and had nary a second to be gawking out the window. Their words, not mine.

I had time for one more stop. Schumacher's Hardware. Mr. Schumacher had to be near Minnie Short's age, which would make him close to ancient. He'd been sweet on Julia for decades. During a visit one autumn about five years ago, I was sure there'd be wedding bells. Julia talked about feeling lonely and regretting she'd never seriously looked for a companion after her heartbreak over losing Cary.

During that time, Clive Schumacher came by the B&B once or twice a week. He brought Julia flowers and other gifts. In the end, she'd said no to his marriage proposal. Clive never came around the B&B to visit after that, according to Gladys. She'd claimed it was for the best. Clive wasn't good enough for Julia. In Gladys's mind, few men would be good enough.

The tiny gold bell attached to the door jingled as I entered. "Good morning, Mr. Schumacher."

Clive glanced up from the cash register, an antique Royal, which he claimed traveled by covered wagon to Sierra Pines with his great-grandfather who opened the hardware store back in 1845 before the town was established. He never tired of telling customers that story and ones about the famous California gold rush. I braced myself to hear them again.

Clive squinted. "Ali Winston, is that you? As I live and breathe, when did you get to town?" He slammed the register drawer shut and it dinged.

"A few days ago." I walked up to the counter.

"I bet your aunt is sure glad to see you. She talks of nothing else when you come to visit. Beams and smiles, she does. Enough to light up the whole town." He tittered.

Confusion left me without words. A long awkward silence followed.

After a moment, Clive blinked and then reached up to adjust his glasses. "That is, she would've been glad. Sorry I missed the funeral. I hear the pastor gave a fine eulogy."

My chest eased as I let go of my breath. "It was. Thank you. Mr. Schumacher, I need to ask you an important question." I scanned the store and found no sign of customers. "Do you have time?"

Clive straightened authoritatively, despite his frail and elderly build. "I need to stock shelves, but I guess it can wait."

I set the scene for him, the evening of the play premier when the Bellwethers waited in front of Bagels and Buns. "I realize it's been almost a week, but do you recall seeing them standing outside the shop that night?"

"Oh, I can say exactly that. It was well past sunset, but the full moon brightened the evening and those lights in the trees help. Yes indeedy, Gladys and Ollie were out there, standing in front of Taylor's store." He nodded.

My breath hitched, anxious for some good news. "You're sure? I mean, this is really, really important, Mr. Schumacher."

He pulled back his shoulders and lifted his chin. "Sure, I'm sure. I've got my head on straight. They were outside, standing right there." He pointed across the street.

"For how long, would you say?"

"Oh, maybe twenty minutes or so. I was washing my display window at the time. It gets pretty grimy after a couple of weeks. And there's a tiny crack at the top where water gets inside. Meaning to have it fixed, but I—"

"Yes, Mr. Schumacher. Did you happen to notice if anyone joined them while they were waiting?"

"Let me think." He gave his head a slow shake. "No, no one joined them. I'm sure of that, too."

He narrowed his eyes as if challenging me to disagree.

"Thank you. You've been very helpful. I'm sure Sheriff Sterling will stop by to ask you about this. I hope you don't mind."

"Why should I mind?" A single brow arched as he cocked his head. "I'll be here if he does. I'm here every day."

"Thank you, again." I stepped toward the door. "You have a great day."

"I always do." He called out as I landed on the sidewalk.

What a lucky break. Excited to share the news, I pulled out my phone and called Quint. Instead of praise, an explosion of laughter met my ear. I glared at the screen. "Why exactly is this news funny?"

"Funny doesn't begin to explain it. Clive Schumacher can't see ten feet in front of him, even with his glasses, which most times he refuses to wear. That's what Emma Schmidt claims."

"Who's Emma Schmidt?" This wasn't good news. It was horrible news. It was the return-to-square-one-and-start-over kind of news.

"She's Clive's widowed sister who moved to town this past spring. She's been living at his place, and Clive hired her to work in the shop so she could earn her keep," Quint said.

All the elation from moments ago drained out of me and landed in a puddle at my feet. "Well, this is disappointing. I hoped we had an eyewitness."

"Even if we did, such news wouldn't completely put the Bellwethers in the clear."

"It would help. Even a tiny bit of proof would help," I argued without my usual thunder.

"Wait a minute. When did you have time to speak with Clive? Where are you, Ali?" The voice on the other end of my phone grew sharp.

"Oops. Gotta go. I'm late to, ah, I'm so late." My words stumbled over each other, rushing to get out before I stabbed the end call button. "That was too close." I raised my chin and focused on the traffic light, willing it to turn green.

When the phone rang, my face tightened, and I scolded myself for not turning the darn thing off. I'd bet a nickel Quint wanted an encore performance to scold me for not following doctor's orders. My finger hovered, then I clicked the button because he'd just keep calling. "I don't want to argue with you."

"I don't want to argue with you, either."

After a quick glance left to right, I spotted my opportunity. I darted out into the road. Halfway across, I jumped at the squeal of tires and the blast of a car horn as a sports van careened around the corner. I winced then waved before hurrying to the other side. "Sorry," I shouted.

"Sorry for what?"

"No, not you. Never mind. You were saying?"

"I wanted to confirm our date this evening since obviously you're feeling better."

I scoffed and rolled my eyes. "Do I detect a hint of sarcasm?"

"Only making an observation. Is six still a good time?"

"Sure thing. Looking forward to it, Sheriff." I slowed my pace as I neared my destination. I had one more stop before heading to the movie set.

"So am I, Miss Winston. Oh, and bring a heavy jacket along. The weather will be chilly this evening."

The receiver clicked before I could ask why a heavy jacket was necessary for a dinner date. I rushed inside Sierra Pines Office Supply and up to the counter. "Hi. Do you have a copy machine I can use?"

The clerk, a boy who couldn't be more than sixteen, kept his head down while pushing buttons on a game device. It zapped and dinged with uninterrupted frenzy. With a slight head tilt, he motioned to the left. "Clear to the back."

"Okay. Thanks so much." I directed my path down the closest aisle. After laying the sheet of paper with my agenda for SPACA on the glass surface, I stuffed quarters into a machine that had to be older than me, but it worked. Within a few minutes, I had the copies I needed to give to Sebastian and Florence.

Streaming past the counter, I hollered goodbye and received a grunt for a response, followed by a couple of dings and zaps. The thought didn't come to me, until I reached the intersection, that Sierra Pines Office Supply was only one door away from Bagels and Buns. Not a direct view from the front window, but if someone were standing near it or maybe just outside the door, he or she could have seen something.

I retraced my steps and studied the image of Game Boy through the window for a moment. Chances were he never paid attention to the comings and goings of customers in the store, let alone someone outside the store. And none of that mattered if he didn't work Wednesday evening. Still, asking him was worth a shot. I ran back inside.

"Excuse me. Again. I have another question." I waited and mustered as much patience as my damaged head could take while he punched buttons. The throbbing pain returned, but the bump on my head wasn't the issue. I released a long-winded groan and snatched the device out of his hand.

His head snapped up and a scowl wrinkled his face. "Hey! You can't do that."

"And you can't seem to do your job. You work here, right? Or do you only occupy this space to play your stupid game?" I huffed and glared back at him. Mine was much more effective.

"Yeah, I work here. What can I do for you, ma'am?"

I proceeded to tell him about the Bellwethers meeting with Thaddeus. "Did you happen to see them or hear anything?"

"Yeah, sure. They're cool. Old man Bellwether gives me a nice tip every time I deliver to the B&B." He nodded.

"Wait. You mean you saw something that evening? You saw the Bellwethers?" The throbbing in my head tunneled down to my chest as my heart quickened.

He stared at the ceiling, and his brow scrunched in deep lines. "I'd say near closing time, between seven thirty and eight. I always close the window shade. Mr. Hummel is picky that way. He wants the display light in the window dimmed and the window shades closed. Anyway, when I walked to the door, I noticed the Bellwethers standing outside the bakery."

My tongue traced along my upper lip. "Were they alone?"

"When I looked, yeah. It's like they were waiting for someone."

"What makes you think that?"

"Well, they just stood there, didn't talk or anything, and kept staring at the bakery. Oh, and Mr. Bellwether looked at his wrist several times, like he was checking something. Probably his watch. He wears a really nice watch. I've seen it. Anyway, that seemed to me like they were waiting."

I smiled. "That's really helpful . . . ah, what is your name?"

"Jason."

"Thank you, Jason. I'm really sorry for snapping at you earlier. Would you be willing to tell your story to Sheriff Sterling if he came by?"

"Sure." He straightened and grinned. "Is this like important evidence in a case or something? Would I get to testify in court? That'd be so cool."

I smiled. "Let's not get ahead of ourselves. Okay? I'll let the sheriff know, and I'm sure he'll be in touch. You have a good day, Jason."

"You, too, ma'am. And I'm sorry for being such a tool."

"We all get like that sometimes." I waved goodbye and headed for my car.

As soon as I parked in the movie set lot, I called Quint.

"Backing out on our date so soon? I should've known. You actor types are a fickle bunch."

I snorted. "Such a biased opinion. Remind me to set you straight about us actor types someday. No, I'm calling about business."

"What kind of business?"

"The kind where I find a credible witness, one with perfect eyesight, who saw the Bellwethers waiting in front of the bagel shop the night of the play. That kind." A low, drawn-out whistle sounded in my ear.

"Do tell."

I filled in the details about Jason who worked at Sierra Pines Office Supply and his story. "So, you'll follow up on it, right?"

"I will, but like I said . . ."

"I know, this doesn't prove they're innocent of murdering Thaddeus. But Jason's story backs up their alibi for that evening, and the phone evidence confirms Thaddeus wanted to meet with them, right? Don't you see? If Thaddeus didn't show, he must've been sidetracked by someone else who led him to the B&B, and then murdered by that someone. Not the Bellwethers." I fell quiet, waiting for his response.

"All of that's plausible."

"You're not convinced." I sighed. "Fine, I'm hanging up, now. My job is waiting. I'll see you this evening." I ended the call before he could comment further. Even if he didn't agree, I was convinced the Bellwethers had nothing to do with Thaddeus's murder. When the coroner came back with a conclusive time of death, it would prove they couldn't have killed him. I didn't need Jason's testimony or a coroner's lab results to tell me the outcome.

In the meantime, a killer was on the loose. A deathly chill shivered through me. Skirting around several cars, I made my way to the production building. I'd keep myself busy and not dwell on worries about the other evidence threatening to put a noose around the Bellwethers' necks. My only hope was to steer the case in another direction. In other words, I'd find new evidence to clear them.

"Hey, good looking. What brings you here?"

I gasped and pulled to an abrupt stop.

Dean beamed with a smile stretching ear to ear. Quite the opposite effect from the last time we were together.

"I'm doing what I do every time I come here. Work."

"Me, too."

"Say what?"

"Work. I snagged a role in this movie. How about that? Awesome, right?" His shoulders jiggled. "I'm totally psyched."

"A role in the movie?" My skeptical eye emerged.

"Yep. Aren't you going to wish me luck?" A smirk rearranged his smile.

I patted his arm. "I'm sure you'll do fine without it."

"Say, listen. I know somebody who sure could use some luck." Dean leaned back on his heels with arms crossed.

I rolled my eyes. "I suppose you want me to ask who. Okay, who?"

"Brooke, our B&B-slash-camera lady, who's been busted for criminal trespassing."

I tilted my head. "What are you talking about?"

"Unreal, right? I heard one of the crew reported seeing her outside the production building." He snapped his fingers and pointed at me. "Say, isn't that where you work? You and the orange-haired chick?"

I blinked. "Nina. Her name is Nina. So, what you're telling me is Brooke Seale broke into the production building?

Dean shook his head. "No. What I said was somebody on set saw her near the production building the other night."

"Okay. Was she arrested?" I scrambled to think what this could mean. Brooke disappeared the night Thaddeus was murdered. Of course, she claimed she was with O'Neil, and Quint was able to get him to confirm her alibi. This news that she could be the one who trashed the production building put doubts about her in my mind all over again.

He shrugged. "Don't know. Don't care. Well, gotta practice my line. See you later." He yelled over his shoulder as he jogged across the lot.

"Line? As in one?" I threw out the retort but got only a wave in return. "Figures."

Nina was at her station when I entered. "How's it going, boss?"

"Oh, up and down and around." She laughed. "Almost done with the waterfall. Would you rummage in that supply box of Julia's? I'm pretty sure she took my tube of aqua blue and forgot to return it. Either that, or our intruder has a thing for aqua and stole the paint."

"Speaking of our criminal-at-large, I hear a witness ID'd one of the camera crew. Brooke Seale?" I stepped over to my work area.

"Oh yeah. Almost forgot. Sterling called me and said he's bringing her in for questioning."

"Huh. Interesting." Interesting, as in Quint never mentioned Brooke when we spoke less than fifteen minutes ago. I pulled out the box, buried underneath bags filled with dozens of diagrams for prop projects. The other day, I'd combed through a few. Most were sketched on thin tracing paper, rough sketches without attention to details or precise dimensions. I remembered following Julia's initial efforts, her fragments of ideas which came at a frenzied pace. She'd sketch them on paper straight from her imagination. The final diagrams would come later, placed on graph paper, except for complex or difficult props. Those required a 3D miniature model.

I wiped off the dusty cover of Julia's treasured supply box. Opening it, I carefully removed each item until I uncovered the paint tube Nina wanted. "Found it." As I sifted through what remained in the box, my hand touched a gummy surface. Definitely odd, and it didn't take more than a second or two for me to grab hold and pull it out of the drawer. I stared at a sticky note, partly covered by a glob of paint.

"Ali Winston, do I have to come over and get it? My hands are kind of busy."

"Sorry." I laid the note on my worktable and hurried across the room to hand the tube to her. "You want me to start on the next project or help you paint?"

She waved me away. "Next one. The supplies are on the top shelf behind your desk." Her head remained bent while her brush moved with broad strokes across the foam structure.

*Now, what could this be about?* I tapped my foot as I sat down at my station. Carefully, I picked the paint blob off the note without tearing or destroying the words. Some were already watered down to nothing, but I recognized Julia's familiar handwriting. The message read like a reminder of sorts, and I skimmed through it twice in an attempt to make sense of the sparse content.

*Tell Thaddeus about my new discovery this evening. Research: forgotten movie companies, scandals. Source verified. Definitely about . . .* I frowned. About what? I held the note up to the light. Whatever else she had written had been destroyed by that glob of paint. Deep in thought, I stroked the edges of the note. "Well, what do I make of this?" I muttered under my breath. I glanced at Nina, who continued working, seemingly oblivious to everything around her. I stuffed the note inside my bag. Forgotten movie companies and scandals. Could this be related to the message Gladys found in Julia's pocket? A thought hit me. What if Julia only meant to share the information with Thaddeus, but not necessarily accuse him of it? Gladys had been so intent on her theory; she was blinded to any other explanation.

I pieced a plausible scenario together. Julia and Thaddeus had Hollywood in common. Maybe this had been merely an innocent topic to discuss over dinner. Like Quint suggested, it could've been part of the research for her memoir. I sucked air through my teeth. But what if she'd stumbled across something dangerous?

I gathered supplies and studied the prop diagram while mulling over the note. Did Julia have a chance to share her discovery with Thaddeus before she died? And if she did, was he murdered because of her news? Too bad these were questions neither of them could answer.

One thing was for sure, I refused to mention anything about the murder or Julia's notes or Brooke Seale being guilty of B&E this evening because I had a date.

# CHAPTER TWELVE

I PRIMPED AND PAMPERED MYSELF FOR AN HOUR before my date. I was embarrassed to admit how long it had been since my last one. Dating and romantic evenings seldom filled my calendar these days. My breakup with boyfriend number three this past spring continued to sour my attitude, and I'd built a wall of defense. Wes Carson had been smooth as well as handsome. His Oscar-worthy lines kept me in denial, and no matter what friends and family said, this dopey, dreamy-eyed girl ignored all their warnings for months. That was, until the last time Wes and I spoke. The meeting hadn't been pretty, but I won the battle and walked away with dignity. As of now, we could actually have a civil conversation. We'd both moved on, or at least, he had. I was still working in that direction. It was weird how relationships went. Both platonic and romantic.

At least after a glass or two of wine and my walk down memory-dating lane, I managed to push thoughts about Julia's note out of my head. Besides, her words really didn't give me much to think about or analyze. Later this evening, I planned to share my discovery with Gladys and suggest both notes implied nothing more than one friend sharing a story with another, certainly nothing to do with murder. I gripped the gold heart necklace hanging from my neck. In truth, I was pretty sure I needed convincing more than Gladys.

The doorbell rang and I hurried down the hall. "I'll get it." Clip-clopping on heels, I descended the stairs, grabbed my coat and bag off the rack, and threw open the door. A frown furrowed my brow. No one stood on the other side.

"Seriously. Who rings the doorbell and runs away?" I glanced at my watch. It was five after six. I leaned forward, glanced left and right, and then straightened to peer out at the street. The curved outlines of a horse and carriage formed pale silhouettes against the darkened background of twilight while the lean form of a man stepped onto the pavement and strolled up the drive. I smiled as he reached the porch. "I would've never taken you for such a romantic."

"Oh, I'm full of surprises."

"Yeah?"

"Absolutely. Stick around and I'll show you."

My smile wavered. "Nice ride. Are you going to tell me where this carriage is taking us?" I took his hand as he led me off the porch. The horse pawed the ground and snorted as we approached.

"You'll see." He helped me into my seat.

"More surprises." Warmth spread through me, despite what I was thinking. This could lead nowhere. This was temporary.

"It will be worth the wait. I promise." He snapped the reigns and clucked his tongue.

We made a U-turn and headed toward town. The soft, rhythmic clip-clop of hooves lulled and soothed me. The cooler air of evening carried on the breeze. I draped my coat over my shoulders and leaned closer to Quint. "This is nice."

"I'm glad you think so." He pulled the reigns to lead the horse left at the next turn. In the distance, a redwood sign formed an archway, supported by two iron posts. The words "Sierra Pines Park" scrawled in white across the board welcomed its visitors.

We passed underneath and I squeezed his arm. "I know. We're having a picnic, right?"

"You spoiled the surprise." He covered his frown with a laugh. "But that's only part of it." He parked the carriage close to the gazebo, also carved from redwood, and then hopped down. "Now, I want you to stay put and cover your eyes."

"I already know it's a picnic."

"Please?"

"Fine." I cupped both palms over my face to block the view and squirmed in my seat, ticking off the seconds.

"Okay. Open."

My hands dropped and I gasped. Light strands penciled an outline on the curves of the gazebo. The soft glow of white and gold reflected on every square inch of the floor. My heartbeat quickened at the sight of a white tablecloth and wicker basket placed in the middle of the table with a bottle of wine and two goblets next to it. I gestured with a thumbs-up. "Not bad, Sheriff Sterling. Not bad at all."

He bowed. "I aim to please." He clasped my hand in his and we walked across the lawn.

I settled on the bench across from him while he poured wine. "Is this where you bring all your dates?"

He paused for an instant before handing me a goblet. "I'm not into redundancy."

"Hmm? How's that?" I tasted the wine and moaned over the California Chardonnay.

"I never use the same idea twice."

"Oh, I see. So, there have been lots of dates?"

"No, not lots."

"Only a few, huh? Is there something wrong with you?" I hid a smile behind my glass.

"Heck no there isn't." Deep creases furrowed his brow as he shook a finger at me. "You're toying with me again. And you're pretty good at it."

"I am, aren't I?"

"What about you?"

I ticked off all my fingers, but then held up two.

"I don't believe you."

"You absolutely shouldn't." I tipped my head. "Tell me about yourself. Other than your lack of dates."

"Funny lady. Why don't you start? Tell me one thing about you."

"Did I mention how much I hate acting? Me being one, that is." I leaned both elbows on the table and cradled my chin in upturned palms. "It took a daring move to convince my parents the stage wasn't for me."

We sat through servings of fried chicken, potato salad, and pie, while chatting about favorite movies, books, and music and our childhoods.

I pushed away my empty plate. "Thank you. This was so nice. Did you cook or is this takeout?"

He covered his chest with one hand. "You can't know how much that hurts."

"Ah, okay. I'm right, aren't I?"

"Maybe a little. I put together the checkered napkins and matching plates. Does that count for something?"

I rolled my eyes and hid a smile. "Guess it'll have to do." The napkin sailed across the table and soft-landed on my face. I tossed it into the basket. "Childish."

Quint stood and came around to my side of the table. He took my hands in his and pulled me up. "I don't think this would be childish."

He leaned in until his lips brushed mine. I breathed in the musky scent of cologne. Maybe this was moving too fast. However, at this moment, I didn't care.

"Ali. Sheriff Sterling. Help me!" A voice wailed and the pounding of footsteps thundered across the gravel parking lot.

I gasped and pushed away from Quint. Florence stopped in front of me with both hands locked on her knees as she bent to catch her breath.

When Florence lifted her head, I reared back and clutched my throat. "Oh my." Her hair swirled and spiked in total disarray. A smudge of lipstick covered one cheek while lines of mascara blackened her eyes. She'd delivered Halloween a week early.

Holding up one arm, she took a final gasp of air. "I need you to hurry to my trailer." The words rushed from her mouth before she gasped for more air.

"Why don't you tell me what's happened?" Quint spoke calmly.

To keep busy, I gathered up the contents of our picnic and placed them in the basket. Once finished, I glanced at the parking lot and raised my eyebrows. Except for our carriage, it was totally empty. "Florence, how did you get here?"

"I took an Uber." She waved her arm. "What does that matter? Dean. He's . . ." She shot me a worried glance. "He attacked me for no good reason."

"Florence." I narrowed my eyes. My tone condescended to warn her I wouldn't go along with covering up the truth. I knew too much already.

"Oh, very well." She huffed. "He's been threatening me with blackmail, and then this evening, he demanded his money. When I told him I didn't have it, he threw this." She pulled a glass paperweight out of her pocket. "See? I have the evidence."

"Blackmail?" Quint's eyes narrowed. "For what?"

I rolled my eyes. "For goodness sake, Florence. Tell Quint the whole story."

"What does it matter why? He tried to kill me with this. You need to arrest him. If you need more reasons, I have plenty." She glared at Quint.

"Now, you say this happened at your trailer, you mean the SPACA trailer parked on the movie lot?" Quint helped me with my coat and then cradled the basket on one arm.

"Well, of course it's on the movie lot. Where else would it be?" She waved an arm, impatience written on her face. "Now hurry. Before he gets away."

A thought came to me. Dean had a quick and fiery temper. He was also stronger and years younger than Florence. "Speaking of getting away, how did you manage?"

Florence swiped wild tufts of hair from her face. "I ducked when he threw the paperweight. Then I grabbed the Persian rug with my hands and pulled it out from under his feet. I didn't wait to see if he was okay, and I really don't care." She shook the paperweight at us. "He tried to *kill* me."

"Huh, you're full of surprises, aren't you?" At this point, I didn't know who to feel sorrier for, but clearly Dean should be behind bars. His reckless behavior could only lead to a bad ending.

We walked to the carriage, and Quint held out one hand to Florence.

"You've got to be kidding. Where is your squad car? This won't do at all." Florence lifted her chin. "By the time we get to the movie lot, he'll be halfway to Canada." Her voice screeched.

"This is all we have, Miss Greeley. Now, you can either come with us or walk. Up to you." Quint's voice remained calm.

"Walk? Probably make it there quicker if I did." She threw a steely-eyed glare at Quint but took a seat in the carriage. "Can you at least put out one of those BOLO calls? Maybe your deputy, who I pray has transportation that runs on gas and not horses, can catch that despicable man."

"Already done." Quint clenched his jaw, but his temper appeared to be in check.

I wished I could say the same for mine. "Now, look here, Florence . . ." I pressed my lips together and clenched my side of the carriage. I turned to Quint. "Maybe you can drop us off at my place? I think Florence needs a time out."

Quint smiled. "Two minds thinking alike." He steered the horse toward the B&B.

Whether subdued or satisfied, Florence fell into silence on our ride home. I did the same while going over her story. My suspicions grew. She was hiding a few important details and maybe lying about Dean and his blackmail. She wouldn't want her reputation tarnished. The family secret must be scandalous, but what was it?

I turned to look over my shoulder. "Florence, you mentioned there were other reasons to arrest Dean. Like what?"

Florence chewed on her fingernail while staring out at the road.

"Florence?"

She leveled her eyes at me. "Don't you find it suspicious Dean was the only one at your B&B the night Thaddeus was murdered? Hmm?"

"Florence, I don't know if—"

"Dean has a plane ticket to L.A. dated the day after the murder." The words tumbled out in a rush. She slapped a hand to her mouth.

The carriage pulled to a halt in front of the B&B. Quint calmly laid the reigns in his lap. "How do you know this? . . . Florence?"

"I searched through his pockets." Her voice shook.

"When?" Quint stepped down from the carriage and came around to my side.

"Oh, dear. I've said too much. Maybe we could wait until after you arrest him."

"Florence, when?" His words tensed.

Her chin jutted out. "You keep asking questions that don't matter. The ticket is incriminating. Why leave Sierra Pines without a word to anyone? I'll tell you why. When you commit a murder, you don't stick around to get caught." She crossed her arms over an ample chest and snapped orders in Florence Greeley fashion. "Ali, I need a hot bath, with oils or salts, if you keep any, and brandy to help me relax." With that, she scooted to the other side, jumped out, and marched toward the front porch.

I managed a smile. My arms wrapped around Quint's shoulders as he lifted me from the carriage. "That was certainly interesting."

"It was." His jaw exercised side to side as he stared beyond me.

"You think she's on to something?"

"Maybe. Who knows?" He shrugged. "It's worth a follow up."

"Well, if you find him, let me know his answer." I recalled Dean's flippant behavior. Not much to joke about in this situation. "Speaking of follow ups, I heard you brought Brooke Seale in for questioning about the B&E."

He ran a hand along his chin. "Yeah, I did."

"And?"

"I'm not ruling her out as a suspect. Her story was rather, what's that word you used? Hokey?" He grinned.

I scrunched my nose. "Okay, wise guy. How was her story hokey?"

"She claims she was looking for Nina, but it was late at night, after everyone had gone home. So . . ." He shrugged.

"Does Nina know about this?"

"She does. I called her before I came over to your place. Funny, she didn't sound surprised or curious. Women. Your behavior is impossible to read sometimes."

"Oh, yeah?" I winked. "It's called mystery. A necessity in all relationships."

He stroked my cheek. "Relationships, huh?"

I blinked and my mouth went dry. "Yes, well, I should get going. Thank you for this evening, even if we didn't get to finish."

He leaned down to plant a kiss on my cheek. "Maybe we can continue where we left off, after Florence so rudely and hysterically interrupted?"

"I'd like that." I skipped up the sidewalk. "Good luck in catching your man, Sheriff."

"Don't need luck. I have skills." He pitched his words and waved before snapping the reigns. The horse whinnied as it trotted down Englewood.

"Now to deal with Florence." I lifted my chin and entered the house. The hum of conversation trailed from the parlor. Essence of pumpkin spice candles teased me with memories of past visits, like Julia and me sitting by the fire, sharing laughs and family stories. My heart ached for those.

I walked into the parlor. Florence snoozed in the oversized wing chair with a crocheted blanket covering her.

Gladys smiled at me. "The poor dear went out like a light. What did you do to her?"

"Me? Did you talk to her? She has a pretty wild story to tell about Dean."

Gladys giggled. "I'm only kidding. I know the story. Florence stopped here before she left to search for you, screaming how Dean wanted to kill her. Then again, this is Florence. I didn't take much stock in what she had to say."

"*You* told her where we were?" I puckered my brows.

"Ruined your date, did we? I'm sorry for that, but we couldn't take much more from her." Ollie slapped his knee. "The woman's off her rocker."

Gladys wrinkled her nose. "Now, Ollie. Play nice."

I gave Florence's shoulder a gentle nudge.

"Oh, please let her sleep. She's pleasant this way." Gladys pouted.

"Can't. She needs to explain some things." I stabbed harder with my finger and she stirred awake.

"Dean, I won't give you a penny. You're rotten, just like my sister." A pinched expression tightened her mouth as she tossed her head side to side.

Ollie whistled. "Now, we're getting somewhere."

Florence clutched her throat and cowered in the chair. "What did I say? I don't remember. Oh, goodness." She bolted out of the seat. "I have to go."

I grabbed hold of one arm. "No. I think you should stay. You're in no condition to be roaming the streets. Why don't you sit down and tell us about Dean?" I guessed the scandalous family secret involved someone closer than a distant cousin. No wonder she carried on so.

Florence threw back her shoulders. "I need my bath, first."

"No way. I want you to tell us about Dean. This time, don't leave anything out because my patience is spent." I led her back to the wing chair and gently pushed her to sit. "Now, spill."

A sigh trembled from her mouth as she nestled into the corner of one wing. "Dean is my sister's son." She sobbed and flipped her arm. "I had no idea Doris even had a son. When our parents had had enough of her wild behavior, they kicked her out of the house. She left and never came back. Not even . . ." Her voice broke off.

"Not even what, Florence?" I coaxed.

"Our father died when I was only eighteen. Then our mother grew ill." Florence glared while she clenched her fists. "I had to take care of her all by myself, for so many years, until she died. I gave up on the idea of marriage. What was the point? No man would want a wife with a sick mother. At least that's what I thought.

"Anyway, I tracked down Doris's number and last-known address and tried contacting her several times. I snail-mailed and left voice messages begging her to come home to help. Do you think she bothered to answer? Even one little letter or phone call?" She smacked her hands on the chair arms. "No, sir. Not one word."

My voice softened. "I'm so sorry, Florence. It must've been really hard for you."

"Darn straight it was hard." Her shoulders quaked. "Maybe not as hard as Doris's life. Dean told me she had him when she was sixteen. Pregnant and penniless with a newborn. His dad, a hippy rock star with an eye for excitement, never planned to stick around. Sure, Doris found jobs, but none that paid much. Dean swears he doesn't remember seeing any letters from me, but he figures Doris would've hid them or thrown them out. He claims she was ashamed of her life, but why should I believe him? Why believe anything that blackmailing loser has to say?"

Gladys patted her shoulder. "There, there. It's not your fault."

Florence straightened and lifted her chin. "I know I was bitter and resentful. Maybe I should've tried harder to find her, but none of it gives Dean the right to blackmail me. Or make me feel like a horrible sister." She stared at Gladys. "He didn't even know about me until a few weeks ago. How's that for sisterly love?"

"Sometimes it hurts to face the past," Gladys said.

Florence laughed. "I doubt this had anything to do with facing the past. Doris never was a fan of sappy sentiment. You know what I think? She sent Dean here to blackmail me. She figures I owe her."

"Did he tell you that?" I asked.

"Not in so many words." Florence wagged her finger. "But I know my sister. She always put herself first. I'd bet every last dime in my pocket she sent him."

"Still, you're only guessing." I considered the alternatives. He could've found out about Florence by accident. Maybe come across one of her letters.

"It doesn't matter, does it? Blackmail is dirty business. Not to mention illegal," Florence said.

"Dean has a lot of explaining to do when Quint finds him." I couldn't wait to hear Dean's story.

"Whatever excuses he makes, I don't care. He needs to be in jail and stay there for good." She stood once again and paced the parlor floor.

"Florence, don't you think you're being a bit too dramatic?" Gladys said.

"If you'd gone through what I have, you'd be just as dramatic and hysterical as me." Florence puffed out her chest.

"Humph. I doubt it." Ollie moved to stand by Gladys.

Florence ignored the jab and went on. "He's been harassing me since the day he arrived in Sierra Pines. Two weeks of not knowing when he'd turn up at the trailer. It's a miracle I've kept my cool this long. He deserved more than a tumble to the floor." She shuddered. "If this gets out, what will it do to my image, I ask you?"

"Not much worse than it already is." Ollie scrunched his forehead.

"Ollie, stop." Gladys pinched his arm.

"Ouch. No need for that." Ollie stepped several feet away from her.

"Anyone on set might have overheard you two talking." I voiced my opinion aloud.

Florence grew quiet for a moment. "I imagine so."

"Seems to me if the situation is such an embarrassment, you'd keep your mouth shut." Ollie zippered his lips with a finger and thumb.

"Maybe we should table the conversation for now," I said. "Florence, I'm going upstairs to draw you a bath. You've had enough action for one day. Gladys, why don't you pour her a glass of something strong?"

Ollie's expression softened. "You're right. I'm sorry, Florence. Quite a day you've had."

Gladys nodded while Ollie moved to the far side of the room and stood in the corner. He stared out the window. "I think I'll go for a walk and get some fresh air."

"Wear a coat. It's chilly this evening." Gladys called over her shoulder as she moved toward the kitchen.

"I'll let you know when your bath is ready," I said to Florence then climbed the stairs. I puzzled over Ollie's behavior. He shifted and bounced from one emotion to another, agitation to concern and back again. Odd, to say the least.

I found a box of bath salts tucked away in the hall closet. Glancing at the bottom shelf, I flashed on the image of Julia's cracked and blood-stained award plaque. It stirred the dregs of my fear and worry until they emerged to the surface. I drew the bath and sprinkled a generous amount of salts in the water.

I sat on the edge of the tub. What if Thaddeus had overheard them arguing and decided to do his own bit of blackmailing? He worked on set and had plenty of opportunity to pass by the SPACA trailer. He'd told me as much. Besides Julia, had any of us really known him that well? The Bellwethers certainly had their suspicions about his character. I tried picturing Florence, the plaque clutched in her hand, pounding Thaddeus over the head. I shivered. Or Dean could have found out and become angry that Thaddeus wormed his way into Dean's blackmail scheme. I sprang to my feet and paced back and forth. "Like Florence said, Dean was here at the B&B that evening, giving him a perfect opportunity."

Quint wasn't aware of Dean's blowout with the critic, but maybe he should be.

I pulled out my phone with an unsteady hand. It occurred to me I was desperate and ventured over the line of reason, but part of me argued it could be true. Take Dean and his hot temper, add motive, and you had plausibility. We only needed real proof. A few rings later, an answering click brought me back to the present moment.

"Hello? Ali?"

I opened my mouth to share the Hollywood story about Dean when a deafening boom rumbled throughout the house. "What in the world?" I sprinted across the hall and down the stairs, my hand gripping the phone while Quint hollered my name. I raised the phone to my ear. "I can't talk right now."

"But you called me."

"Yes, I did." I'd landed on the floor. By now, screams and shouts filled the parlor. "Did you find Dean?"

"He wasn't in the trailer. My deputy is covering the south side of town while I search the north. Don't worry. We'll get him."

I stepped into the parlor. My jaw dropped. Not one thing about this scene was normal. "Ah, no need to look any longer. He's here. And . . . well, you should come to the B&B. *Now*." I shoved the phone in my back pocket. "What's going on, here?"

"Seems we've got front row seats to a live shoot-em-up western." Ollie tossed his coat in a chair then rolled back on his heels and grinned.

I drew in a deep breath to calm myself. Dean had surpassed his own level of uncontrolled, crazy rage. "What are you doing with that rifle?"

He didn't answer. No one did at first, but fingers pointed to the wall behind me. I turned to follow their direction. A huge gaping hole blemished the framed painting of Sierra Pines clean through the caption which read, "Welcome to the friendliest town in the west."

# CHAPTER THIRTEEN

I STRUGGLED WITH THE SIGHT OF DEAN, as if I didn't trust what my eyes were telling me. "A rifle. You shot a rifle?" I squeaked out the words.

"That's not just any rifle. It's a prop from the movie *Dodge City*." Gladys's face beamed.

"Nineteen thirty-nine, starring Errol Flynn. Not many folks know he filmed a western. It wasn't a great box office win for him." Ollie wagged his finger. "And that rifle is one of the items missing from Julia's collection room."

Dean shook his head. "I know what you're thinking. I didn't steal it. I found it."

"Is that so?" Ollie scoffed.

Dean clamped his mouth shut.

I raised my hand and lightly touched the sizable gap that scarred Julia's favorite painting, ignoring Ollie's comment about missing collectibles. "What happened? I mean, I see what happened but . . ." I turned to Gladys, avoiding Dean and the crazed look on his face. "What happened? And where's Florence?"

Gladys tipped her chin toward the floor. At once, someone moaned. The sound came from below me, on the other side of the sofa. I peered around it and blinked. "Florence?"

"She's fine. The shot flew clean over her head by at least six inches. Not so handy with firearms, are you, Son?" Ollie took the glass of water he'd been holding and poured the contents directly on Florence, who woke with a loud, choking gasp.

"Good lord." She coughed and cleared her throat. "How did I end up on the floor?" Turning sharply, she caught sight of Dean, who held the rifle at his side. With a whimper, she fainted again.

"Huh. Guess I better fetch more water." Ollie raised the glass and left the room.

I swallowed hard. I was face to face with a crazy man. Dean's wild-eyed stare darted from the floor to me. In an uncomfortable silence, I locked my attention on his trigger finger, until commotion from the foyer interrupted. The front door flew open, crashing against the wall. Footsteps pounded across the hallway.

"Thank goodness." I dropped my shoulders and let out a long breath as Quint entered the room.

Seeing the man in uniform, Dean dropped the rifle and collapsed into the chair. Meanwhile, Ollie returned with the second round to douse Florence. I swear he grinned with pleasure.

Quint pulled up a chair next to Dean. With one foot, he slid the rifle across the floor and out of Dean's reach. "Maybe you'd like to explain what this is all about?"

"I'm not saying anything without a lawyer present, and especially with her in the room." Dean crossed his arms and narrowed his eyes as he glared at his intended victim.

Quint turned to Florence. She'd come to, sputtering between complaints. "How about you? Care to tell me what this is all about?"

"Gladly." She waved an arm at Dean. "He tried to kill me. *Again*. How many times will it take before you arrest him, Sheriff? Or do I need to die first?" Florence pushed Gladys's hand away from her head. "I certainly don't need your help. I can fix my own hair, thank you."

I caught the angry glare flash in Ollie's eyes and hurried to add, "Florence, I think the sheriff could use some clarification on what happened." I nodded at Dean.

"You can bet I have a lot to say." She stood and threw back her shoulders in a defiant posture. "My so-called nephew can't make up his mind if he wants to blackmail me or kill me. Can't have it both ways, you Hollywood has-been."

"You should've tried harder. You should've searched for her. Anything. Instead, you stopped caring. Well, it's too late now. She's dead. Your sister, *my* mother, is dead." Dean swiped away the tears with the back of his hand. "You're a cold and selfish woman." Dean stood and stepped toward the rifle, but Quint caught his arm.

"Not a wise move, my man," Quint said.

Ollie moved in to grab the firearm.

"I didn't know." Florence trembled as she sank onto the sofa. Gladys snuggled next to her and squeezed her shoulder.

Slowly, Dean sat in the chair and dropped his head into upturned palms. "Get her out of here, would you? I can't look at her any longer."

"You don't tell me what to do." Florence hiccupped. "And I did too love her. She was family."

Quint raked fingers through his hair. "How about we all take a breather."

Florence shoved away Gladys's hand and stood. She walked to the far side of the room and sat in a rocker next to the fireplace.

"Gladys and Ollie, why don't we go to the kitchen and get some refreshments? I'm sure everybody could use a drink." I glanced at Quint, who gave his nod of approval. "Great. Refreshments coming up. Oh, and by the way, Quint? You should ask Dean where he happened to find that rifle. It belonged to Julia's collection."

Dean raked fingers through his hair. "I told you. I won't talk until my lawyer is present."

"I guess, in the meantime, you'll be waiting behind bars." Quint's jaw clenched.

"I want my phone call then. I have rights."

"Don't worry. You'll get one. As soon as my deputy arrives and we haul you off to the station."

"I'd like to stay for the rest of the show, if you don't mind," Ollie said.

"I do mind. Kitchen. *Now*." I narrowed my eyes and gave him the don't-argue-with-me stare.

Surprisingly, he followed alongside Gladys, carrying the rifle. With a defiant pose, he lifted his chin and penciled his lips in a tight line. I pulled out my chair and motioned across the table. "Please, sit down."

Gladys widened her eyes. "I thought we were here to pour some refreshments."

"My guess is this was her way to get us alone to talk. Isn't that right, Ali?"

His smile failed to hide the worry in his faded blue eyes. Anyone who didn't know him well might be fooled. I wasn't one of them. Underneath his cajoling, sometimes sarcastic manner, rested a kind and caring soul and a soft heart I couldn't help but love. However, the lengths he'd go to defend what he held dear worried me.

"Sharp deduction, Ollie." I rested my arms on the table. "Here's another one. You were acting strange back there in the parlor, and my gut instinct tells me you're hiding something. Now, what is it?"

Ollie pressed his lips and locked them shut.

My agitation flared while he remained silent. "Ollie, please. I'm trying to piece this puzzle together. Anything you can share might help."

"I doubt anything I say will fix it." His arms crossed tightly over his chest.

I leaned over the table. "Ollie, I overheard you the other night assuring Gladys she didn't need to worry and how Sheriff Sterling would never find the proof he needs to pin the murder on you both. You remember that? It sounded pretty incriminating."

My nerves tensed. I didn't like playing this card, but, fair or not, he pushed me. "If Sterling found out, it would look bad for you."

"Oh, Ollie. Please tell Alexis. It does no good to keep quiet." Gladys squeezed his arm as she pleaded.

Seconds crawled by before Ollie moved to nod.

"Good. Now, my guess is you knew about Florence's secret. How? Did you hear her and Dean arguing?"

"I might have." Ollie raised his chin.

"When?"

"At the SPACA trailer, a couple weeks ago, when Dean first got to Sierra Pines. I stopped by to drop off the flyers for the theater play. You know Florence. When she wants something, it's ASAP and not a minute later."

"You're saying Dean was in the trailer?"

Ollie scratched behind one ear. "Well, I heard shouting. So, I was ready to skedaddle out of there. I can't stand it when that woman gears up into one of her rants. Screeching to the high heavens." He looked at Gladys. "You know what I mean. She frazzles the nerves. I think Julia was the only one who could handle her well. God bless her soul."

"But you stayed and listened to what Florence had to say. Why?"

He shrugged. "I recognized Dean's voice. I didn't know the man well or what he might be capable of. So, when he started threatening Florence, I couldn't leave. Florence might deserve many things but not threats."

"That's when you heard about the blackmail." I nodded.

"I did. He spouted off how she needed to pay up or else, how Florence would lose her precious reputation if the townsfolk found out she'd abandoned her sister. I admit I was feeling sorry for the guy."

"That's why you didn't say anything. You figured Florence deserved his anger and revenge. Wow, Ollie." I shook my head.

Ollie held up one hand. "I'm not finished."

I raised my brows.

"Don't get me wrong. Blackmail isn't right, no matter who's on the receiving end. But I know Florence. She's no pushover. Give her time to handle it, I told myself. So, I left the box of flyers on the doorstep and walked away."

Gladys patted his shoulder. "I know you would've stepped in if Florence needed help."

"I suspected Dean was trouble the minute he threatened blackmail. Always about money. Sad, isn't it? His generation of Hollywood doesn't measure up. Nothing like we were in the old days. Back then, the love for acting was most important," Ollie said.

"We met Doris once." Gladys threw Ollie a furtive glance. "It was awkward. Ollie, Julia, and I were invited to dinner at the Greeley house. This was a few years after we'd moved to Sierra Pines. I remember Florence and Doris were just children."

Ollie rubbed his jaw. "The Greeleys were nice folks, but those daughters argued like alley cats. Their mother ordered them out of the room. Florence went without a word."

"Not Doris, though." Gladys tapped the table with one fingernail. "She had spirit. I'll give her that."

"Doris was only a teenager when her family kicked her to the curb." Ollie shook his head. "I don't understand how you do such a thing."

"Me neither, Ollie. Me neither." Gladys clucked her tongue.

I scratched my forehead. "Family dynamics. They're not easy to figure out sometimes."

The quiet murmur of conversation from down the hall amplified to shouts and screeches, Florence's screeches. I stood and rushed to the parlor. Ollie and Gladys pattered close behind me.

"You're a poor, pathetic excuse for a human being." Florence wielded Gladys's cane above her head.

Quint grabbed it out of Florence's hand.

"That's enough, Florence." I gripped her arm and led her across the room. "What happened?" My hand pressed on Florence's shoulder to keep her seated and away from Dean. He looked battered and beat up enough for one day.

Quint raked fingers through his hair. "It appears Florence has some crazy notion in her head that Dean murdered Thaddeus. Says she has proof."

"What?" I steadied my attention on Florence.

"It's not crazy. When I was on my way to deliver a message to O'Neil, Dean and Thaddeus were arguing on the movie lot, behind the SPACA trailer, loud enough for anyone nearby to hear."

"Did Dean threaten Thaddeus?" Quint asked.

"Well, no. But . . ." Florence threw up her arms. "If he'd stoop to blackmail and try to hurt me, why not murder?"

"Aw, come on. Are you going to believe this? She's bat-crazy. We argued. So what?" Dean spouted.

Florence pushed against my hand to rise.

"Eh, eh. Stay where you are," I warned.

She waved her arm. "You and your hot temper. That's what. Oh, yes. I heard all about your tangle with the critic. Must be a curse to carry around so much anger. Who knows how far you'd go? Maybe take it out on some old man. You coming here to blackmail me was bad enough. Did you ever think what it would do to your Hollywood golden boy image?" Tears welled in Florence's eyes. She swiped them dry with the back of one hand then continued.

"Maybe Thaddeus knew and threatened to tell. Or do you have some other dark secret, something he hung over your head? No matter what it was, you had the perfect opportunity, didn't you? Thaddeus came to the B&B, where no one was at home, but you. Did you arrange the meeting?"

"That's ridiculous. I had no idea he was here." Dean wagged his head. "No idea."

"You told him to meet you at the B&B. What did you argue about? Hmm? Something damaging to your career? After all, you both come from Hollywood. Actors make up a pretty small circle when it comes to gossip. That's it, isn't it? To keep him quiet, you murdered him." Florence turned and stared with glossy eyes at Quint. "It makes perfect sense."

"What we argued about had nothing to do with dark secrets or my reputation. I can tell you that." His attention landed on Quint. "Like I said, bat-crazy. She's the one you should arrest."

Tension in the room pressed down on us like a suffocating layer. I eyed Gladys. She paled to ashen white.

"I think we've heard enough." My words seemed to fall on deaf ears.

Florence pushed. "What about that plane ticket to L.A.?"

Dean blinked. "What do you know about that?"

Florence flapped her mouth as her complexion flushed deep red.

Quint rushed to speak. "My deputy found the ticket in the trailer. You must've dropped it during your altercation with Florence. Care to explain why you were leaving in such a hurry?"

"I'm here, aren't I? Why would I stick around if I'd murdered the guy?" Dean answered through gritted teeth, but his voice remained calm.

Florence stuck out her arm, wagged her finger, and sputtered as she talked. "You stayed because O'Neil dangled the pretty little movie role under your nose and you couldn't resist. With all the evidence against the Bellwethers, you had no reason to hurry out of town, right? But it was you. *You* murdered an innocent man."

"That's insane." Dean's tempered anger had burst.

"How about both of you zip it." Quint's professional demeanor was gone.

"Come on, Florence. Let's get you something to drink." I nudged her arm.

"I have a perfectly good explanation for that ticket. My agent called and said it was time to return to work." Dean rambled on. "After the murder, I couldn't leave because the sheriff claimed we were all suspects. But you're right. I wasn't about to pass up a chance to star in an O'Neil movie."

Florence snorted. "Star. What a crock."

No love lost in this relationship. "Maybe we can pop open the cork on that California rosé I spotted in the wine cellar. What do you say?"

Footsteps trudged across the foyer, and one of Quint's deputies entered the room.

Quint nodded to him then turned. "I'm going to have to take you in, Dean, for unlawful possession of a firearm and discharging it to endanger lives. You understand?" He pulled out a pair of handcuffs.

"Look. I found the gun. I didn't steal it, and I didn't know it was loaded. I swear." With deliberate force, he rubbed his jaw. "I only wanted to scare her."

Florence laughed. "Like he's going to buy that story."

Quint's jaw clenched. His wall of patience had crumbled.

"We'll continue this discussion down at the station. Then I'll check out your story and go from there. Okay?" He cuffed Dean, who grew quiet.

"Florence? I'm heading to the kitchen. You coming?" I motioned with a head jerk to Gladys and Ollie. Gladys took the lead.

"I think I'm having a heart attack." Florence placed two fingers on the side of her neck. "My pulse is racing. Do I look flushed?" She placed her hand on one cheek. "I feel hot. Oh, my. Should we call nine-one-one?"

Gladys touched Florence's face then eyed me with a slight shake of her head.

This was Florence. No other way worked to calm her. "Sure, we'll call for the medics to check you out." I gave her an encouraging smile.

Quint motioned to me as his deputy led Dean toward the front door. While Ollie got on the phone to dial emergency, I followed Quint.

"I'll call you tomorrow." Quint bent down to kiss my cheek.

"Ah, geez. Get a room already." Dean rolled his eyes before the deputy shoved him out the door.

Quint squeezed my hand. "I'll call you and we can talk. Okay?"

I nodded. "Tomorrow." I stood in the doorway as he caught up to his deputy and Dean. The three of them walked toward the cruiser. A cool breeze lifted fallen leaves and stirred them. Their dry and brittle texture crackled as they moved across the yard. I waited until the cruiser drove away, while the faint scream of sirens grew louder and the EMT unit approached.

I stepped back and closed the door as Gladys and Ollie guided Florence out into the foyer.

"Maybe I'm overreacting." Florence sat on the foyer bench.

"Maybe? I'd say it's more like—" Ollie started.

"Ollie, hush. It's always better to be cautious," Gladys said.

"I can take it from here. You two should go on to bed. You look exhausted." I sat next to Florence and patted her hand.

"Thank you, Alexis. Come on, Ollie. We've got a busy day ahead of us tomorrow," Gladys ordered.

"Doing what?" Ollie's shoulders sagged.

"It's near the end of the month, and Halloween will be here soon. We need to clean the house, top to bottom, and put up the decorations, and—"

Ollie held up his arm. "No need to tell me every detail. I'm tired just listening."

I laughed. "Good night, you two."

"Good night, Alexis. Thank you." Gladys smiled.

Within minutes, the paramedics wheeled Florence to the van and drove away. I locked the door and turned off the lights before dragging myself upstairs. Florence's theory had merit, but was it true? I'd had similar ideas. However, mine placed Florence at center stage. She had as much at stake as anyone in her position. With her reputation stacked up against Dean's, I questioned who had more to lose? The answer depended on one person's story. Only he couldn't answer because he was dead.

# CHAPTER FOURTEEN

I STIRRED FROM A DEEP SLEEP WHEN the phone rang. Through squinty eyes I read the unfamiliar number on the screen but answered anyway. "Hello?" My voice croaked.

"O'Neil here. I need you to come to the movie set, ASAP. I can't find Nina anywhere. She hasn't answered my calls, and there's a prop emergency."

I scrunched my nose. People who barked orders annoyed me, especially first thing in the morning. "It's kind of early, and I haven't even showered."

"You can shower later. I'm on a deadline, and it's costing me thousands each day we go over. That break-in already set us back. I swear, when I find her, there'll be hell to pay."

"But . . ." I sat up, fully awake at this point.

"No time to argue, Winston. Get in your vehicle or run if you have to. I need you here, *now*."

The phone line clicked. I stared blurry-eyed at the screen. "What the heck." Nina had to pick this morning to go MIA? Now I had to fix whatever the problem was, ASAP, according to O'Neil. "Seriously?" I slid out of bed and puttered to the bathroom.

"Nobody out of hundreds on his payroll can fix the problem?" I splashed cold water on my face and rubbed it vigorously with a towel.

My tongue ran over a pasty mouth, cheek to cheek. I grabbed my toothbrush and squirted minty fresh gel on top. Nina didn't miss work. She'd bragged as much. Not one day. Other than the trip to the doctor when she'd left early. I tipped my head to one side. Maybe that was it. She was in a fevered stupor and stayed home.

"Why wouldn't she call? That makes no sense." I gargled and spit in the sink. "Maybe she overslept or her phone died."

Shuffling back into the bedroom, I pulled on yesterday's clothes, jeans and a sweater, and ran a brush through my hair. "Nothing more serious than that, right?" I stared in the mirror, forcing my imagination to take a break. No scenarios where Nina got into a car accident or tumbled down a flight of stairs and cracked her head.

I tiptoed across the hall and down to the main floor. It was early, too early to wake up the Bellwethers. Instead, I scribbled a quick note to let them know where I'd be and left it on the kitchen table. I grabbed my jacket and bag and hurried out the front door.

Tiny flakes drifted and coated the ground, melting as they landed. Most of the trees had shed their remaining leaves and stood bare and colorless, like vestiges to remind us it was the end of another season and on to the long months of winter, when they'd hibernate in an eerily peaceful slumber.

I tightened the collar around my neck and shivered. I sprinted down the drive to the car. There'd be no walking to work today, even if I wasn't in a hurry. It was ten past six. Hardly anyone would be on set. Only those actors who belonged in the scene to be filmed, and the crew, and O'Neil. Everyone else arrived at seven or later, which meant the parking lot would be mostly empty.

I grabbed a spot in the front row and sprinted to the production building. I braced myself to face O'Neil and his usual crabby attitude but refused to put up a fight. Just finish the job and leave.

I chewed on my lower lip and studied the unlocked latch. O'Neil had to be inside. Or maybe Nina got the call and arrived here first. I slid the door open. No one was in the building to greet me, but a light glowed near Nina's workstation. I found an eight-foot post leaning against the wall, one from the pergola we'd constructed last week. A splintery crack near the bottom had nearly cut the post clean through. A note was attached. "Fix this and return it to my office at once. T. O." I read it and sniffed. "Crabby *and* impatient."

I pulled out Nina's supply box and immediately spotted tubes of wood glue, putty, and pieces of sandpaper. I worried we'd run out of the matching stain color, and the thought of confronting O'Neil to let him know curdled my stomach. It was too early in the morning for confrontation. After exhausting my search of the box's contents, I turned to the cabinet behind me. Six drawers filled with supplies had to cough up the other items I needed. When I opened the bottom drawer, I grinned. "Thank you, Nina." I picked out the can of matching stain color and a brush.

Cradling the supplies in my arms, I settled in at my station, examined the damage to the post section, and then got to work. This wouldn't take more than twenty or thirty minutes. After dropping off the post, I'd return to the B&B in time for breakfast with the Bellwethers and guests.

I smoothed the rough edges with sandpaper. A splinter jabbed my finger. I winced and pulled out Julia's box to search for a Band-Aid. As soon as I opened it, I groaned. I'd forgotten to show Julia's note to the Bellwethers.

I was nearly finished when the sliding door creaked open. "Nina, it's about time." I didn't look up from the table.

"Sorry to disappoint you. I was passing by and wanted to stop in and say hello."

My head jerked. Sebastian stood in the doorway. His hair was windblown and face ruddy red from the cold.

"Oh. Um. Good morning, Sebastian."

"Mind if I take a seat and warm my hands? It's a bit chilly this morning."

"Sure." I motioned toward an empty chair. "Guess I'm not the only early visitor on set. What brings you out this time of morning?"

"Oh, I stopped by to ask O'Neil some questions about his schedule. Time is moving quickly, and he needs to vacate the park area by early November. We have Christmas decorations to set up and festivities to prepare." He settled into the chair, and, with his hands cupped together, he blew air on them. "More than a bit chilly, isn't it?"

Sawdust flaked and fell at his feet.

My brow creased. I grabbed the tube of glue and squeezed some into the crack. I pressed the sides together then applied some putty to disguise the scar. "What made you think anyone would be in the production building so early?" I raised my head and stared. A disquieting sense seeped inside me. Rational or not, I would never be comfortable around him, especially alone.

He shrugged. "I spotted your car in the parking lot and figured you'd be here."

"So . . . you haven't spoken to O'Neil yet?" I rubbed my finger across the putty until it was smooth and then applied the stain with a couple of quick brush strokes. I fanned the finished product dry, anxious to be done.

"I, no, you're right. I was on my way to visit O'Neil when I decided to pop in here first." His face deepened to an even redder shade.

I didn't contradict him. Something told me to leave it be. "Well, I'm on my way to see him, too." I stood and pointed at the post. "Emergency job. He needs it ASAP, as he put it."

"If you don't mind waiting? I have a matter to discuss." Sebastian stood and shoved both hands into the pockets of his jacket.

"Oh? Sure. I guess a couple minutes won't matter." I detected the quiver in my voice and hoped Sebastian didn't notice. My phone buzzed and I glanced at the text message with Nina's name. I scrolled with my finger.

**Sorry. Be there soon. Went on a wild goose chase to Sacramento. Got a crazy email from the hospital telling me my sister had been admitted to the ER. Turns out she's fine. Go figure.**

I closed the message. Yeah, it was crazy and strange. Who'd make that kind of mistake? I guessed it could happen, though. I looked up at Sebastian. He smiled pleasantly, but it was almost too cheery. The fake kind of cheery accompanied by comments like "Oh, how wonderful to see you" when the person clearly meant it wasn't wonderful.

He pulled his chair closer and sat once again. "You know, it's such a shame. I heard about what went on at the B&B with Florence and Dean. It's fortunate no one was hurt." He shook his head.

I crossed my arms tightly. My voice edged up. "You heard?"

"Yes. It really is tragic. I considered Dean Thornton an upstanding, successful man. Such a shame. These young actors nowadays. Most of them are spoiled and always looking for attention." He clucked his tongue as he rose from his chair once more.

I squirmed. "I believe this was something more personal."

"Oh? And what would that be?" He stepped forward.

"Is that your question? The one you wanted to talk about?" I countered his move with a few steps in reverse. My body grew rigid.

"No. Not really. I only commented because Florence is a friend of mine. You know, in my day, actors kept their self-respect. The media didn't go into a frenzy and spread dirt on their front-page tabloid. The producers and agents made sure to keep bad news quiet. Reputations were at stake. None of this scandalous rubbish."

"I guess times are different." I tapped the brush against my leg.

"You bet they are. When I lived in Hollywood, the industry ran smoothly. People kept a squeaky-clean image, down to the smallest detail. If scandal ever got out, it was bye-bye and good riddance to those involved."

He raised his arms and then let them drop, dangling and limp at his sides.

"Starlight Productions was one of those independent movie companies during the seventies and eighties. One of the best, and it was going places. Greed can ruin a thriving business, you know." He cleared his throat. "I was one of the lucky people. I got out of there before news hit the papers and destroyed Starlight."

My attention sifted through his wordy description to focus on one detail. *Starlight.* My memory leaped to the scene in his trailer and the photo I'd knocked to the floor, the photo of several people posing in front of a building with the name Starlight. Had Sebastian been in that group? If so, it was a younger version of him and not the heavyset, balding man standing in front of me. I swallowed hard. If he was associated with Starlight, what did it mean?

"Oh, I know what you're thinking. Here's an old man, living a quiet, normal life running a ski resort. How is it possible he'd once been part of the glamorous Hollywood scene?" Sebastian chuckled with a nod. "That life was decades ago. I've changed for the better. Don't you think?"

I blinked. Not according to what I'd witnessed. What I saw was a man with an aggressive, possibly volatile behavior, but this wasn't the time to argue. I dropped the brush and wrapped my fingers around the pergola post. "I should get this to O'Neil before he comes looking for me." Maybe he'd get the hint and leave.

"But I haven't asked my question yet." He motioned for me to sit. "I don't suppose you've found anything unusual in your aunt's belongings, have you?"

"Unusual?" Rather than sit, I shuffled my feet back a few more steps until the rough brick surface of the wall stopped me. My heartbeat raced. Something was wrong with this picture. A full-blown headshot of Joan Fontaine floated in front of me, screaming for help.

"Yes, I recall her telling me she kept a journal and did research on the golden years of Hollywood. I'd guess a journal like that would be a real gem and worth lots of money to publishers. Did she say anything to you?" He steadied unblinking eyes on me.

My legs grew rubbery and weak. I leaned against the wall. Julia's journal. Didn't Gladys mention it the other evening? My muddled thinking struggled for clarity. I swallowed to ease the dryness in my throat and tugged at my collar. I worried he'd spot my crumbling composure since I was doing a lousy job of hiding it. "Maybe. I'm not sure."

"Come now. It's not something you'd easily forget. You either know or you're refusing to tell me. Why would you do that, I wonder?" He stepped closer, now within a few feet.

I gripped the post with both hands. As if a post made of compressed wood could stop a big man like Sebastian. If I was lucky, I could land a blow to his face or bust his nose, but that was a longshot since my athletic skills were lame. Desperate times. Desperate measures. This was definitely one of them, and my frazzled nerves never failed to turn me into a chatterbox.

"Well, I'll be sure to look when I get back to the B&B." I glanced at the wall clock. "Wow, I really need to get this prop to O'Neil. He's such an impatient man, right? Didn't you say you're visiting him? Maybe you can deliver this for me. I promised Gladys I'd return to help bake some pies. Pumpkin. Gotta have pumpkin for Thanksgiving, right? Not that it's Thanksgiving yet, but still, a little practice doesn't hurt." A nervous squeak escaped my lips.

By now he'd circled around the worktable. He lifted his hand and pointed. "You're lying. I can sense it." His voice rose. "You know about the journal. You've probably read it and learned all about my past, haven't you?"

"I, I don't know what you're talking about." My voice shook because I did know. Or I guessed. Julia, for whatever reason, must've told Sebastian about what she'd discovered. I widened my eyes and dropped my jaw. "The notes." I struggled with the words as my breath came in weak gulps.

"What notes?" His jaw worked side to side while his hands balled into fists.

Small movie companies. Julia wrote that in both her notes. Gladys assumed the message she'd found in Julia's pocket referred to Thaddeus's background. But what if the information she'd discovered was about Sebastian? I hugged the wall and winced as a sharp object stabbed at me. I brought one hand around my back and touched a switch. I knew what it was for. I'd watched the movie gaff trip that switch to get what he needed for a scene. Lifting my chin, I dared a quick glimpse at the ceiling.

"She threatened to expose me. All her talk about ethics and moral character, as if she was above everyone else." His laugh deepened. "She ranted on how I shouldn't get away with fooling the fine people of Sierra Pines and making myself out to be an ideal citizen, not when I'd stolen money with the president of Starlight." His face reddened as he shook. Both hands clenched at his sides. "If Thaddeus had left matters alone, it wouldn't have gone this way. He blabbed about all the evidence he had to prove what I'd done, which was his first mistake, and he knew it. I spotted the fear in his eyes when I told him I was aware of the journal." Sebastian shrugged. "It's funny what people do when they're afraid, how they flip from one mood to another. The fool laughed at me. Can you believe it? He laughed and rattled on with nonsense that I . . . never mind. It's not important for you to know. What does matter is he's gone and will never talk about this to anyone again."

He nodded and smiled. "My plan couldn't fail. I waited until the timing was perfect. You all attended the play performance. I made sure the director had plenty of tickets to pass around. So, I left Thaddeus a note, explaining how I'd found the journal." He shook his head. "People are so predictable, you know? I hid outside his trailer until he made his move. Then I followed him, straight to the B&B. The pompous idiot underestimated me, and that was his second mistake. He never saw it coming. One blow to the head is all it took."

He pointed at me. "Unfortunately, you all returned sooner than expected. I hid the plaque and planned to retrieve it later. What were the odds you'd find it? I figured that development might work to my advantage, and it did, in a way. One more incriminating piece of evidence to pin on the Bellwethers. Right?"

His eyes glowered and his jaw clenched as he grew nearer.

When he stood within six feet, I gripped the post and wiggled it back and forth in front of him. "Back away, Sebastian. Or I promise you'll regret it."

When he threw back his head and laughed, I winced. So much for bold words and gestures.

"You sure are a sight. Standing there with that pathetic wood post, all full of courage."

I tensed as he took a couple steps away, placing him in the perfect spot.

"Don't you get it? I had no choice. They both threatened to tell the authorities. First, Julia ranted with her holier-than-thou attitude, and then Beale claimed I killed the love of his life. He only needed to prove it." He shrugged. "The irony of that is I did no such thing. Oh, I planned to, but another matter took care of it. Her death wasn't my fault. The both of them forced my hand, like you're forcing mine."

My breath pulsed and pounded. I flipped the switch and, within seconds, the net released the theater curtain. I gasped as it landed on top of Sebastian and dropped him to the floor. A soft moan, muted by the layer of brocade, sounded before he grew silent. The post slipped through my hand and clattered on the floor. The room grew fuzzy. With knees wobbling, I slid down the wall until my rear end landed. I tucked both legs under my chin and forced air through my mouth.

# CHAPTER FIFTEEN

Footsteps pounded across the room and grew louder as they neared. I lifted my head to take a peek. "Oh, thank goodness."

"The Bellwethers told me where I'd find you. Are you okay?" He moved his head from side to side and then back to the rumpled pile on the floor. "What happened?"

"Sebastian." I pointed at the curtain. "He came barging in here, and then he . . ." I choked. Panic rushed back as I replayed the scene. "He told me he killed Thaddeus."

"What?" Quint's head snapped around to face the lumpy form which lay underneath the curtain. His jaw shifted and, in the next second, he walked over to uncover Sebastian, who hadn't moved.

"He admitted it. He admitted how he killed Thaddeus to keep him quiet because he knew about the shady dealings Sebastian had been involved in decades ago. And he said he would've killed Julia, too." I sobbed and hiccupped at once. "The note. Gladys was right to be suspicious."

Quint knelt next to Sebastian and slapped his cheeks.

I drew my knees to my chest and sobbed. "He's alive, isn't he?"

In a moment, Sebastian stirred. He took one hand and rubbed his eyes.

"I think he'll live." Quint's jaw clenched as he helped him to sit.

Spittle covered Sebastian's chin as he ranted and mumbled. With one thrust of his arm, he pointed. "She tried to kill me, and for no good reason."

My breath hitched. "Me?" Adrenaline pushed me to my feet. I stared at Quint. "You aren't buying this, are you?"

Quint helped Sebastian to stand. He didn't answer me.

"Aw, come on. This is insane. He confessed. He told me right to my face how he killed Thaddeus and had intended to kill Julia." I took long strides toward them. "Then you threatened me. Admit it. You schemed to get me here. The text message to Nina. The damaged pergola post. That was all you. Admit it. What was your plan, huh? Kill me too?"

Sebastian cowered against Quint. "You've got a wild imagination, young lady. I found you here by chance and took the opportunity to ask about Julia's journal on Hollywood's golden years. A publisher associate of mine is very interested in buying the rights. Before I knew what was happening, you turned on me. I have no idea why."

"You asked me about her journal and said there was something in it you didn't want to get out." I argued, while my blood pressure spiked. "You stole money from Starlight and escaped before authorities could arrest you. You've been hiding out here ever since. Is Sebastian Tubble even your real name?" I was trying to get around Quint, who blocked my way. "You said Thaddeus threatened to tell, so you killed him."

My bubble of optimism burst. I assumed the case was solved. The killer, who stood right in front of me, would go to jail, and the Bellwethers would have their good name back. That was how this scene should play out, but Quint made no effort to cuff him.

Sebastian smiled and shook his head. "Ali, I didn't kill the poor man. I had a talk with him the evening he was murdered. That's all. I was nowhere near the B&B when it happened." He clucked his tongue. "Your delusions are getting the best of you. I left Hollywood because I was out of a job."

"You . . ." I lunged forward with fists clenched.

Quint caught my arm. "When I stopped by the B&B to find you, the Bellwethers were reading and discussing Julia's journal."

"They found it?" I dropped my arms and stepped back.

"In the library safe. Julia mentioned Starlight movie productions in one entry. Gladys remembered you'd asked about the company, and she found it odd how Julia wrote Sebastian had worked there." He turned to Sebastian. "If you're telling the truth, the story will be easy enough to check out. I'll call the L.A. authorities today."

"Thank goodness." I relaxed.

Quint turned to me. "In the meantime, I can't charge him with anything. It's his word against yours."

I opened my mouth to protest, but Sebastian beat me to it. His expression was smug. "What about the curtain she dropped on me? I believe that's grounds for assault."

"Let's take a breather, folks. I'm not arresting anyone at the moment. Not until I have more information. Okay? Sebastian, I'll check on a few things and call you if I have any questions."

"Fine, but you'll be hearing from my lawyer." He pointed at me.

"Don't push it. No more talk. Just leave." Quint stabbed a finger at Sebastian. "Before I change my mind."

I waited until Sebastian had disappeared outside. I spun on one heel to face Quint. "Are you kidding me? You're going to turn your back and let him walk away? He confessed, Quint. He told me every detail. He killed Thaddeus Beale and maybe Julia."

"I said I'll make some calls. Until I have more evidence, I can't arrest him. As far as testimony goes, the only witnesses who could prove he's lying are dead."

"But . . ."

"No buts. Without credible evidence, I can't make an arrest." He squeezed both my arms. "Ali, I want this case solved as much as you do, but I have to go about this the right way. If I make an arrest on flimsy hearsay—now, don't give me the hurt and offended stare—hearsay is what you've given me, and if I arrested him on that alone, any case against him would get thrown out of court. I need to do this right. Understood?"

I nodded then switched to shaking my head. "What if he tries to run? He did it before, after the Starlight scandal."

"I'll have one of my deputies keep a watch on him until I find out more."

I snapped my fingers. "The journal. If Julia claimed she had a story on Sebastian's criminal past and wanted to tell the authorities, she must have the evidence. It has to be in the journal. When I find—what is it?"

"Gladys showed me the journal entry about Starlight. All it describes is the history of the company, who worked there, and when it shut down. Nothing about a scandal or embezzlement. That's why I need to make some calls."

I chewed on my fingernail and considered other possibilities. "Okay, if it's not in there, information about the scandal and the role Sebastian played must be hidden someplace else. Maybe Julia found the information later and put it where no one but her would find it." My shoulders dropped. If she did, uncovering her hiding place wouldn't be easy.

"If there's more to the story."

"Stop doing that. I know you're the show-me-the-evidence kind of guy, but at least try and take a positive attitude, would you?" I curled my arm around his. "You owe Julia and me that much."

He patted my hand. "Indeed, I do, Miss Winston. Now, let's get out of here."

"Almost forgot." I ran back to my workstation and picked up the pergola post. "I need to take this to O'Neil. By now he must be furious." Mentioning O'Neil reminded me of Nina. "And I should give Nina a call. I can't imagine how angry she is. Work is her life."

Quint blinked. "Angry about what?"

"It's a long story, and right now I have no time to share." We stepped outside the building, and I latched the door.

"If I get moving on inquiries about Starlight and Sebastian right away, maybe I'll have some answers before noon. You'll be okay if I leave you, right?"

I ground my feet to a halt, feeling a bit offended. "Without a doubt I'll be fine. I took care of Sebastian, didn't I?"

Quint grinned. "You certainly did. I'll give you a ring if . . . all right, *when* I've found out something." He jogged backward. "Don't give up on me. I've got this."

"I'm sure you do, but don't trip on the way." With a slight wave, I turned onto the grassy path leading to O'Neil's trailer and picked up speed. There'd still be time for breakfast back at the B&B, as long as I had no more interruptions, scary or otherwise.

THIS MORNING'S INCIDENT CHANGED MATTERS. Even if Quint didn't worry, I did. My gut told me Sebastian's survival instinct kicked into gear the moment Quint said he'd look into his story. Facing charges for his involvement in the Starlight scandal wasn't something he'd risk. As soon as he left the movie lot, he would've gone home and packed his bags. I estimated by this afternoon he'd be halfway to Mexico, leaving authorities twisting in the wind and their chances to arrest him gone. Sebastian loved wealth and power above all other possessions. He probably banked all his money in offshore accounts. Soon, he'd be drinking piña coladas and sitting by the poolside, smug with the satisfaction of his victory. My stomach soured at the thought he'd win.

I fumed and griped on the way home. While dropping off the prop at

O'Neil's trailer, I had bumped into Florence. My quick visit turned into a half hour gabfest, meaning Florence talked and I listened. During that time, Quint called to say Dean's story about the plane ticket checked out. As for the rifle, Dean confessed he'd taken it the day before my head collision with the mysterious intruder. He planned to pawn the item because he was running out of money. I scoffed. The Hollywood star had lost more of his shine. On top of that disappointing news, there had been no word from LAPD about Sebastian. We were batting zero.

Florence, in her usual busybody fashion, put clues together from my end of the phone conversation and bullied me into confessing what happened in the showdown with Sebastian. I gave her the abridged version, minus the juicier bits I suspected she craved. Most likely, as soon as I walked out of O'Neil's trailer, she called to fill Gladys's ear with details of my mishap.

No surprise, by the time I reached my car, a hysterical Gladys was on my line, begging me to come home. It was a proven fact. Tell Florence a story and a nanosecond later the whole town knew it. Life in Sierra Pines had its downside with plenty of gossip and people sticking their noses in where they shouldn't.

I parked at the top of the driveway, closer to the front door. I was anxious to learn more about Julia's journal from Gladys and Ollie, but first I had to calm Gladys and assure her I was fine. Later, I'd sneak in the opportunity to search Julia's room for proof of the scandal and Sebastian's shady past. I was certain she hid it someplace close where she could keep an eye on it. Her bedroom seemed like a perfect spot.

"There you are." Gladys wrapped her arms around me and squeezed as I entered the foyer. "My stars. Thank goodness Sheriff Sterling got to you in time. You're not hurt, are you?" Without waiting for my answer, she took hold of my chin, turned my head side to side, and smiled. "Okay, then. Let's go to the kitchen. I have a fresh pot of coffee made and some chicken croissant sandwiches for an early brunch. Then we can chat." She scuttled down the hall, motioning with her arm for me to follow.

The fragrance of pumpkin spice wafted from burning candles, while the aroma of freshly ground coffee beans awakened my senses. Ollie sat at the table, hovering over his plate stacked with three sandwiches and a mug of coffee alongside. I grinned. At least some things remained constant. No matter how small or unimportant, it was comforting.

I placed a sandwich on my plate while Gladys poured me coffee.

We ate in silence. Sustenance first, then conversation. Besides, I wanted time to gather and choose which details of my morning to share and which to leave out. I'd skip over the frightening moment when Sebastian threatened me and how Quint refused to arrest him because he claimed there wasn't enough evidence. Also, I couldn't forget Dean's alibi, which was solid as a rock, so he'd go free. No point in worrying or depressing them with those details. Knowing wouldn't change anything, but unfortunately, we'd taken several steps back in the case of Thaddeus Beale's murder.

Gladys wiped crumbs off the table then lifted her gaze to me. "I guess I'll start. I'm sure Quint told you about Julia's journal?"

"He did. What I don't understand is why there's nothing in it about the Starlight company scandal when her notes implied as much." I shook my head.

"Notes? There's more than one?" Gladys frowned.

I explained the note I'd found in Julia's desk. "You see? Why else would she mention a Hollywood scandal and fraud? Sebastian told me Julia knew he had stolen money from the Starlight company. That's why she planned to expose him."

"Well, there's something of a surprise." Ollie picked up the conversation.

Gladys clasped her hands. "This must've been what Julia wrote about. There's no other explanation."

"I take it Julia never told you anything about a scandal?" Disappointment hung over me.

Ollie tapped the table with his finger. "Not a peep."

"At least we have the notes," Gladys said.

"Yes, there are the notes." Sebastian wouldn't invent the scandal story. He had nothing to gain and everything to lose by confessing to a crime where there was no proof. Assuming the evidence existed, and Julia or Thaddeus knew, Sebastian would want it kept quiet to avoid any possibility of criminal charges. I figured that was motive enough to kill.

"Now, how about that scuffle with Sebastian?" Ollie's eyes gleamed. "I want every horrid, messy detail. I hope he got what he deserves."

"That's enough, Ollie." Gladys poked his arm.

I laughed. "Nothing horrid or messy about my morning. Exciting and frightening? Yes, maybe. At least Quint will be checking up on Sebastian's record. Tubble's hiding a dark criminal past, and the proof will come out soon enough." I laughed at the disappointment on Ollie's face. "Okay, I'll give you one detail." I shared my victorious moment when Sebastian ended up buried by the theater curtain.

"Well, that's good enough for me." Ollie pivoted in his seat to face Gladys. "Before I forget, speaking of horrid, how about *Night of the Living Dead*? You up for that one on our movie night? It's the Halloween season, remember."

Gladys shuddered. "Absolutely not. I wouldn't mind a ghost story, though. How about *The Haunting*? The original production from nineteen sixty-three, of course."

"Too sweet and no horror, but it's your turn to choose. Besides, it's been a trying day and maybe sweet is what we need. Though, in my opinion, *Rose Red* has more substance."

Gladys scrunched her nose. "That's a TV miniseries, horrid *and* bloody. Now, if you're talking television, I'd say Stephen King's *It* is superior, though we should be discussing movies, shouldn't we?"

I suppressed a laugh. Busy and absorbed in their conversation, the Bellwethers appeared to have forgotten me. I quietly slid the chair away from the table and tiptoed out of the kitchen. I'd seize this opportunity to snoop for Julia's research on the Starlight scandal. The sooner I found the story, the better. Sebastian Tubble should be behind bars.

# CHAPTER SIXTEEN

I PLOPPED DOWN ON MY BED. Two hours had passed. Sweat dribbled from my brow, and, with one hand, I swiped damp strands of hair off my face. Nothing. I'd searched Julia's room and closets and more closets, from the attic to the basement until Gladys demanded to know about my peculiar behavior. I explained my quest.

"It's not like I haven't searched in every corner, except for the occupied guest rooms. I suppose it's possible she tucked the story away in one of those." I was exasperated.

"Not likely. She'd worry one of the guests would discover it and maybe toss it in the trash. Who knows?" Gladys shrugged. She stood near the doorway. "If there are such notes, they would be in her room. I'm almost positive."

"Almost isn't a sure thing, but your suggestion does make the most sense." I wiggled and flexed my shoulders and neck to work out the stiffness.

"Speaking of Julia's room, I won't put off any longer what needs to be done." Gladys's voice was dull and void of her cheery optimism.

I smacked my thighs and bounced off the bed. "I'll help you. We'll get the job finished in a jiff while we chat about happy times." My voice bounced with cheerleader energy. "What do you say? Operation cleanup begins."

Tears filled Gladys's eyes, but a smile tickled her lips. "I'd like that."

She led the way down the hall to Julia's room when my phone rang. I held up a finger and told Gladys I'd be along in a minute. If this was bad news, the poor woman didn't need to hear it. "I didn't expect you to call this soon."

"My contact in LA is mighty efficient and quick," Quint said.

"And?"

"In the late eighties, there was a scandal involving a small movie company named Starlight. The president, Al Reynard, was charged with embezzlement and served a few years in prison. According to the transcript of his interrogation, he claimed someone helped him steal the company funds, a man named Timothy O'Toole. However, his accomplice vanished, and police had no concrete proof Reynard was telling the truth. With no leads, authorities gave up the search after a few months."

"Do you think . . .?" I scratched behind one ear. Gladys came out of the bedroom, a pile of clothes in her arms. She passed by me on her way downstairs.

"Be back in a moment, dear. I want to put these in boxes for the charity drive. I have some stored in the kitchen."

I nodded then waited until she was out of hearing. "Do you think Timothy O'Toole and Sebastian Tubble are the same man?"

"It's likely, but we need evidence to prove it."

"You have to bring him in, Quint. Please tell me that's your plan."

"That's our plan. I'm sending one of my deputies up to the lodge, now."

"I thought your plan was to send someone up there this morning." I clenched my stomach. Images of Mexico, piña coladas, and the smug face of Sebastian sank my hopes.

"Blame it on bad timing. There was a store robbery and then a pileup on the highway."

"We need some good news. Maybe the coroner's report will come today and the evidence will connect Tubble to Beale's murder." My voice trembled. I hated the thought of the Bellwethers spending even one more sleepless night worrying.

"Don't make that leap, not until I get the report."

His words cautioned me.

"I know. I'm playing the role of Gladys's cheerleader right now."

"Come again?"

"Never mind. I have to go. I'm helping Gladys clean out Julia's room. Call me when you learn anything else."

"You do the same. Or call me anyway. It would be nice to hear from a cheerleader instead of getting bad news." He chuckled.

After an exchange of goodbyes, I ended the call. Taking brisk steps, I approached the bedroom when Gladys called out from downstairs.

"Alexis, you should come to the kitchen right now and see this."

I hurried, taking the stairs two at a time, and jogged down the hallway. "What's wrong? Did you find something?" I caught my breath as I reached the kitchen.

Gladys sat with both hands folded in her lap. A camcorder rested on the table, along with an apple-shaped cookie jar, one that looked very familiar.

"Oh my. It's Julia's favorite cookie jar, the one you gave her for Christmas years ago." I traced the side with my fingertips.

"Yes. I was pulling boxes out of the utility closet when the jar toppled from the shelf. I barely caught it. The lid fell off and broke, I'm sorry to say. Then I discovered the camera hidden inside." She shook her head. "Julia told me she'd broken the jar. That's why we bought a new one. But my stars. A camera inside the cookie jar? Why ever would she put a camera in a cookie jar?"

"Even more puzzling, why would she hide the jar in the utility closet and lie to you she broke it?" I picked up the cookie jar.

Gladys turned the jar around. "There's more. Look at the leaf design."

I leaned closer. "What in the world?" A tiny opening marred the tip of one green painted leaf with a perfectly round hole about an inch in diameter.

"This is beyond strange," Gladys said.

I stood facing the closet and shifted my attention from the jar to the shelf and back again. As if it suddenly made sense, I placed the camera back inside the jar and carried both to the closet. "The top shelf?"

"Yes."

"Do you remember when she fibbed about the cookie jar?"

"Hmm, I'd say around two weeks ago."

"Which would mean a few days before she died." I lifted my arms and returned the cookie jar to its hiding place, with the carved-out hole facing our way. I moved backward a few steps to the table then nodded. "The placement is a perfect vantage point to view the kitchen area. The plan was risky, though. She must've counted on no one noticing or shutting the closet door."

"What are you thinking?" Gladys came to stand alongside me, her neck stretched to view the jar on the shelf.

"If Julia wanted to film something—and I have no clue why she'd do it—but if she wanted to, do you see what I mean?" I faced Gladys but extended my arm and pointed at the shelf.

Her jaw dropped and eyes grew round. "Oh, my goodness. It's so clandestine. Like a detective or spy story. You know, in *Rear Window* Jimmy Stewart spied on people with his telescope, and that's when he solved the murder." She nodded solemnly.

I blinked and offered no comment to argue the point. It wasn't the craziest suggestion. Certainly not the worst idea. I stared at the hole in the cookie jar then turned. "Did you check inside the camera for a disc?"

Gladys held up the answer. "I looked first thing. I wonder what's on it."

I wondered, too. Even worse, I worried whether the video contained something unpleasant. In any case, after seeing the carved opening and the camcorder hidden inside the jar, I'd bet a month's supply of Gladys's lemon scones that Julia secretly filmed whatever went on in the kitchen.

I placed a hand on Gladys's arm. "We should watch it. Let's go to the library, okay?"

She handed me the disc, and we crossed the hall to the library entrance at the same time Ollie and Ralph approached from the parlor.

"Starting our movie night, a day early, are we?" Ollie remarked, pointing at the disc in my hand.

"Oh, I love a movie night. What are we watching?" Ralph asked as we entered the library. He quickly pulled a chair close to the fifty-inch flat screen television mounted above the fireplace mantle.

"Home movies, I hope. We shall see." I loaded the disc in the DVD player and grabbed the remote to press play. Nerves sparked like livewire jolting through me. I was too nervous to sit. Instead, I moved to stand behind Gladys and Ollie, who sat front and center.

The first minute or so showed nothing but an empty kitchen, until the squeak of footsteps on tiled floor filled the silence. Gladys grew rigid in her seat as someone entered the picture. Julia walked over to the kitchen counter and turned. "I don't suppose you've come here to apologize or promise to do the right thing."

I gasped when Sebastian stepped into the screen, his back to us. I recognized the tall, hulking form and sparse silver-gray hair without seeing his face.

"Hardly, if that's what you were expecting."

"Then we've nothing to talk about. I told you more than once what I have to do. I warned you," she said.

"Give me the journal, and then I'll leave." Sebastian edged closer.

I squinted at the screen. His right hand slipped into a coat pocket.

Julia raised her arms. "Why would I give up the only leverage I have? So you can . . . what would you do, Sebastian? Hmm?" She turned once again to face the counter and wall. Her head bent to one side. "You're like this clock. Crooked." She reached up to straighten the fixture.

"I'd like to think I'm clever and crafty, a true survivor who wants to win. Julia, it's time you hand over the journal." Impatience clipped his words as one hand moved inside the pocket. The jacket material shifted and rolled.

"It wouldn't matter if I did, though I won't." Julia walked toward Sebastian and stopped within inches. Her chin tilted up to meet his face. "I've made copies."

"I don't believe you." Sebastian glared.

"I did and gave them to trustworthy people. If anything happens to me, they'll take the journal pages to the press. You're done here, either way. Sierra Pines is no longer your hiding place." Julia's face paled. She leaned to one side and gripped the table, and, inch by inch, she lowered herself to sit in a chair.

"You should rest, Julia. You look worn out." Sebastian stepped back and slightly off screen then appeared in front of the sink. Water ran from the tap as he filled a glass.

Julia lay her head on the table, facing toward the camera, and closed her eyes.

The only visible movement I could detect came from the faint rise and fall of her chest.

At once, Sebastian walked into the forefront and stood directly behind her. He pulled a small bottle from his pocket. My stomach lurched and nerves tightened as I grew anxious, too scared to watch more, too scared not to.

"Here. Drink some water. It should help." Sebastian smiled as he held the water in one hand. He tapped the bottle several times and drops fell into the glass. He stirred with his finger then stepped around to face Julia. "Take a few sips. You'll feel better."

Julia didn't answer, and her chest had stilled. I gripped the sofa. Tension wound tighter around my throat with each second and each breath. Julia didn't answer and she wasn't moving. Not her chest, not any part of her.

Sebastian poked at her arm. After a few seconds, he shook both shoulders, but his efforts failed. He picked up her hand and placed two fingers on the inside of her wrist. "Well, well. Isn't that convenient." His lips spread apart as he laughed.

Tears moistened my eyes. I pressed one hand against my lips to silence any sound desperate to escape. Through blurred vision, I followed Sebastian's path to the sink, where he poured out the water, rinsed the glass, and stuffed it into his pocket, along with the tiny bottle of what I could only assume was poison.

None of us said anything as we watched Sebastian disappear from the screen and heard a door slam shut, until only Julia, with her head on the table, resting, silent and still, remained. The DVD played through, leaving only the eerie quiet of the kitchen and still form of Julia for us to see. I stabbed the remote and hit eject, willing the image to vanish from my mind, but I failed.

Ollie braced his shoulders and growled. "I'll kill him myself."

I didn't object, nor did Gladys or Ralph. A second later, though, Ollie crumbled back into his seat and lowered his head into both hands.

Gladys finally spoke. "At least there's one thing. She didn't suffer."

"Wow. That movie must've been a real tear jerker." Dean snickered as he stood in the doorway.

Gladys's jaw tightened. "Mr. Thornton. I hear you'll be leaving soon. Would you mind settling your bill this evening?"

"Sounds good to me. I've had enough of this town. Course, I'll be back soon enough. Can't skip out on my court date, can I?"

The slick, charming smile returned. With that, Dean left us to jog upstairs.

"Yes, well, looks like we have some answers to our mystery, don't we?" Ralph interrupted to steer us back to thoughts about the video.

"You mean how Sebastian tried to poison Julia but she died from, well, perhaps it was a heart attack." Gladys sank into the sofa cushions. "How wrong I've been, Ollie."

"How wrong we both were, you mean." The corners of his eyes crinkled as Ollie smiled. He grasped her hand and squeezed. "She died peacefully, Gladys. We have that much to be thankful for. And I didn't mean what I said. I'll let the sheriff take care of Sebastian. I promise."

I pressed my lips together to stop from commenting. I hoped he meant it.

Ralph moved the conversation along. "That leaves us with Thaddeus's death."

"Whom Sebastian admitted murdering." My voice shook. The video proved he was capable of foul play, but we needed more. Julia must have suspected Sebastian and his criminal past for several days, maybe weeks. At least since she'd found the information on Starlight. What if she noticed the framed photograph in Sebastian's trailer and later came across the same photo in her research? In a newspaper, for instance. Articles often included photos captioned with names, a name like Timothy O'Toole, for instance. I swallowed the lump of fear growing inside.

One thing was for certain. She'd been clever, clever enough to put the clues together and come up with at least one answer—Sebastian Tubble was a thief and a fraud. Unfortunately, I'd bet Julia never suspected how her plan to expose him would end in tragedy, that Sebastian would kill and her good friend would end up dead. Worse now, the murderer was probably on the run. Who knew when and if authorities would catch him?

# CHAPTER SEVENTEEN

A BLUSTERY WIND WHISTLED AND MOANED and rattled the windows as if in a struggle to win the battle by pounding its way inside. I cupped both hands against the glass pane and peered out the front window. Tiny flakes of snow drifted sideways, and only a scattered few stuck to the ground but enough to coat it with a thin layer. Though early, autumn was taking its first bow to winter.

I grew more anxious with each passing minute. Quint would arrive shortly. I'd told him on the phone about the video. He promised to be here as soon as he put out a BOLO on Sebastian. As I feared, the killer was on the loose. According to the lodge manager, he'd packed a bag and said a quick goodbye to his staff.

I took a deep breath as Quint parked his vehicle out front and jogged across the lawn. I threw open the front door. He stepped inside and immediately wrapped his arms around me in a tight embrace.

"Thank goodness." My voice trembled as I mumbled words into his chest, not caring to move. The image of Julia's head resting on the table and Sebastian hovering over her with that cold-hearted stare haunted me.

"Where's the video? I need to see it." Quint hadn't let go of me.

I finally broke the embrace and pulled away. "In the library, but I don't want the Bellwethers to watch. They've had enough shock for one day."

"Wise decision." Quint held my hand as we traveled down the hall. "Where are they now?"

"Resting in their rooms, the last I checked. Although, with Ollie, I think it's more of a time out to cool down." I shook my head. "He's in defensive mode and ready to destroy Sebastian."

"Let's hope we catch Tubble and place him behind bars before Ollie gets to him."

I shivered. "Yeah, let's hope." Once inside the library, I hit the button to play the DVD. I settled next to Quint on the sofa and watched him rather than the screen. His facial expression barely changed, hiding any response to Sebastian's actions as they rolled out in living color and cinematic horror. When the video finished, I hit stop and ejected the disc then handed it to Quint.

He tapped the disc against one palm. "No doubt, it appears he meant to harm her."

"He meant to kill her."

"Without knowing what he put in the water glass, I can't assume that."

I was exasperated. "Oh for . . . you heard him. He said 'well that's convenient.' What else could he mean besides her death solved his intention to kill her? I don't know why you're being so bullheaded."

Quint's jaw tensed. "One step at a time. If Sebastian's DNA matches Tim O'Toole's, I'll have enough to keep him behind bars until LAPD can arrest him to face charges for embezzlement."

"Quint . . ."

He raked his fingers through his hair. "I know all this is frustrating, but I have to go by the letter of the law. The video shows he might have intended to do your aunt harm, even if it wasn't to kill her. At the very least, I can haul him in for questioning about that. As far as the incident in LA? We'll wait and see."

"But what about Thaddeus?" Frustration barreled through me.

"Yes, and Thaddeus. As sure as you are about it, I have to go by the evidence, not my gut. We need solid proof that makes it easy for the prosecution to convict him for the murder."

Proof like Julia's notes on the Starlight scandal I'd failed to find. They had to exist, and I had to find them. I refused to leave the case like this. Sure, plenty of murders went unsolved, but Thaddeus was Julia's friend. If she were alive, she'd stop at nothing to get justice. I planned to do the same.

Quint's phone rang, interrupting further discussion. Whatever words came from the other end of his phone didn't sit well with him. His brow creased with worry and lips tightened into a thin, colorless line.

"I'll be there in five minutes." He finished the conversation and pocketed his phone.

"What happened? Did they catch Sebastian?" I grew tense and worried as Sebastian and officers in a shootout played a scene in my head.

"Deputies from Calaveras county spotted Tubble traveling south in his vehicle. They're giving chase. Don't worry. They'll catch him. He won't get far."

"I'm not worried, but he must be. Worried and desperate." I shivered.

"Look, I have to go. If they catch him, I want to be close by when they bring him in." He leaned closer, and his lips touched mine.

Pulling away, he smiled, a warm and sensual smile. The expression brightened his face and stirred my heart.

"We should talk. Before you decide anything, or make any plans for the future. You okay with that?" He stroked my cheek.

"Sure. We can talk." My voice lifted. For a brief moment, murder wasn't at the forefront of my thoughts. On impulse, I grasped his arm. "Be careful. All right?"

"Always am." He held still, his gaze intent, his chest rising and falling in rapid rhythm. Then he smiled and stepped outside. "Looks like the almanac was right. Winter's come early this year."

Snow covered his hat and coat within an instant as it came down heavier and thicker now. The front lawn had become a blanket of white.

I shivered and quickly shut the door after the cruiser sped away. My heart shouldn't interfere or influence my decisions. That was what my sensible side argued. But who was I kidding? My heart, my feelings, all my emotions pushed to take control. I exhaled and leaned against the door. Enough problems encumbered my life and needed to be resolved first.

I took steps toward the kitchen when Dean tromped down the stairs. A duffle bag hung from his shoulder. He clutched suitcases, one in each hand.

"Dean." I greeted him, but his scowling face came with a warning. I didn't bother with niceties.

"My flight leaves in an hour. I'll send for my other things tomorrow." He reached to open the front door.

"I'm sorry about your mom." The words stumbled out. I felt awkward.

He shrugged. "She was in a lot of pain, but not any longer." His smile quivered. "Besides, I'm used to being on my own."

"You shouldn't blame Florence. Her heart's in the right place, most of the time. Anyway, it looks to me like she's the only family you've got left."

"She posted my bail. Go figure." He wiped one hand across his face. "I need some time. So does she, after the stunt I pulled."

"More than one." I chuckled.

"Yeah. Boy, the gunshot. Not my best performance." He shook his head.

"Did Doris really want you to carry out your revenge?" I had to ask, even if it wasn't my business.

"No. It's all on me. Doris told me about having family in Sierra Pines, and I came here to take out my anger on Florence. Doris didn't want that. She begged me to tell Florence how much she loved her."

"Oh, Dean." My voice choked.

"And I did. I told her earlier today when I was released. I think we're okay."

I wanted to hug him. He wasn't a bad guy. He was somebody who wanted a family after losing the one he had. "One more question. It's been bugging me since yesterday. What did you and Thaddeus argue about?"

"Oh, yeah. He heard me threatening Florence with blackmail. Guess he was one of the good guys. He warned me to leave Florence be or he'd take matters into his own hands. What he meant by that, I'm not sure. Anyway, I got angry and spouted off. I told him to mind his own business." Dean shrugged.

"There are classes for that." I smiled. When he looked clueless, I added, "For anger management."

"Ha. Yep. My agent tells me the same thing." He picked up his bag. "I should get going."

"Sure. Good luck with your show."

He grinned. It was genuine this time. "Thanks. My agent says the producer and network are willing to sign on for at least five more years. Funny how that worked out. Hollywood and racy gossip, you know. Ratings have been exploding through the ceiling."

"Yeah. Hollywood is a strange animal."

"But it's my home. You plan to stay in Sierra Pines?"

"Maybe." I shrugged. "Most likely." It was the first time I'd admitted it aloud, and the words sounded right to me.

With a final goodbye, he was out the door. As if on cue, Ollie shouted my name and limped from the kitchen into the foyer as quickly as he could travel. He carried Blackbeard's cage in one hand, which swung side to side with each uneven step he took. The bird squawked. I hadn't heard that much noise come out of his beak since I arrived. Then again, if I took a trip like his, jostled about as if riding an amusement park tilt awhirl, I'd squawk too.

"Ollie? What in the world?"

"Honest to say, I never could figure why Julia insisted I keep the blasted bird." He snickered. "She knew I'm not the best caregiver when it comes to pets. Feeding, remembering to clean the cage, and . . ."

"Ollie, please, is this conversation going somewhere important?"

"Oh, sure." His head bobbed. He set the cage on the floor next to him. Blackbeard quieted, ruffled his feathers, and tucked his head in his shoulder before closing his eyes. "Here. Take a look at what I found." He handed me a folded piece of paper.

I opened it. Familiar handwriting covered the entire page and a news article was paper-clipped to the bottom. After a quick scan of its contents, I gasped. "Ollie. This . . . do you know what this means?" I shook the paper at him. "Wherever did you find it?"

"On the bottom of Blackbeard's cage, or I should say the lower tray. The one you have to remove to clean." He cleared his throat and blushed. "Which I'm ashamed to say I hadn't since, well, since Julia passed. Anyway, I pulled the blasted tray out of the cage and stuck it in the stationery tub. The paper you're holding was wrapped in plastic and taped to the bottom side. Now, doesn't that sound like Julia to do such a thing? She was a clever gal." He faltered and wiped his eyes.

"Yeah, clever gal." I chewed on a fingernail while studying the notes once more. Julia's words described details of the Starlight scandal—the president who embezzled funds, along with his mysterious accomplice, Timothy O'Toole, who'd vanished and was never captured. A name scribbled at the bottom identified him as a Starlight employee. Underneath that was a phone number and a notation of interview dates. Maybe this was the source Julia mentioned on the sticky note.

The clipping was an article from the eighties, along with a photo, the same group photo displayed in Sebastian's trailer. I smiled. Only this one had names listed in the caption. Red ink circled one person in the group, and the name Sebastian Tubble was scribbled in the margin next to it.

I rocked back on my heels. "Well, I'll be. This is perfect. Julia discovered Tim O'Toole and Sebastian Tubble were the same man, and here's our proof."

"Enough to put away the filthy criminal for a long while, I'd say.

Thank you, Saint Genesius." Ollie slapped his knee, which startled Blackbeard, who began squawking again. Ollie removed the black cloth from his back pocket and dropped it over the cage. "So, what do we have?" Ollie ticked off the list of crimes on his fingers. "Murder, embezzling, evading authorities, false identity, oh and stealing money from the SPACA coffers."

"What?" My voice rose.

"Yep. Gladys and I have been going over the SPACA ledger, checking every entry. It's because of Minnie's claim. We had to see for ourselves if her suspicions were true. Discovered the error late last night."

"Minnie?" I puzzled over the person more than the discovery.

"Minnie is a sharp one. Notices all sorts of things. She takes care of finances when Sebastian's out of town on business, which rarely happens. Maybe once or twice a year. She found something in the ledger and commented to me how it didn't add up. Tubble has been stealing thousands, and I do mean thousands."

"How? The alliance isn't that big. How do you accumulate thousands?"

"That's where you're mistaken. We have the Christmas event, fundraisers, theater productions, and plenty of donations. The money adds up, all right. We build the funds and disperse them into the community programs we sponsor, like the children's home, and . . . Well, you've heard Julia talk about all that." Ollie settled on the foyer bench and rubbed his injured leg.

"You think Julia knew about Sebastian siphoning funds?"

"I think she did, and, most likely, it's what made her suspicious of him in the first place. Finding that article was pure luck. And as for the photo? Julia knew Sebastian since the day he arrived in Sierra Pines. Most folks around here do. Back then, he had a thick head of dark hair and was skinny as a bean pole. She'd have recognized him in that photo right off." Ollie nodded.

"Poor Julia. The only thing she didn't suspect was how dangerous Sebastian could be. I don't think she'd have confronted him if she knew what he was capable of doing when pushed too far."

"Not so sure about that. Julia had her spunky side. She believed she could take on the world and be the one who rights all the wrongs, if you get my meaning."

"Yeah, I guess I do." I stared at the article and Julia's notes. Even though it was foolish to confront him, she couldn't help it. Maybe she'd hoped, truly expected to convince Sebastian to turn himself in. That was another one of her qualities. Believing the best in people.

While Ollie carried Blackbeard in his cage to the atrium, I tucked Julia's notes and news clipping in my pocket and traveled upstairs. A tingle of excitement surged through me. Julia was right. Sebastian had been a thieving fraud for decades. Now, we were only one or two pieces of evidence away from putting Sebastian Tubble, aka Timothy O'Toole, in jail for the rest of his miserable life. Or so I hoped. The authorities would have to catch him first.

# CHAPTER EIGHTEEN

"ARE YOU SURE YOU WON'T COME with us?"

I shook my head. "I'll stick around in case Quint stops by later. I need to give him Julia's notes and the Starlight news clipping as soon as possible."

"Well, I'd much rather stay here and spend the evening with you, Alexis. Unfortunately, Florence is in one of her moods and claims it's urgent we meet." Gladys slipped her arms into a heavy wool winter coat she'd pulled out of the closet. The temperature had plummeted and a snowstorm was on its way to Sierra Pines. The first of the season.

"With her, it's always urgent," Ollie grumped and blew warm air on his hands. He'd been outside spreading salt on the icy sidewalk.

"This time she has a point. With Sebastian gone, we need someone to take over the acting classes for our youth," Gladys said.

She delivered a sly glance my way, and I held up my hands. "Nuh, uh. Not for me. You two are the acting professionals."

Gladys lifted her arms, palms facing up. "It's just as well. We can deal with Florence and her tantrums and demands. We're quite used to it."

"We'll see about that." Ollie waved his arm at the door. "Let's get a move on if we're going. The car's been idling for over ten minutes. Any longer, it'll run out of gas before we pull out of the drive."

"Have fun, you two. I'm heading up to my room to relax. Guess I can't keep up with your energy." I winked.

"Oh, pish posh. Don't be silly. You've plenty of energy. After all you've been through, and that distasteful confrontation with Sebastian, anyone would be exhausted. You get a good night's sleep, dear. We'll see you in the morning." Gladys waved as Ollie hustled her out the door.

I leaned against the stair railing and mulled over what she'd said. I had been through plenty these past twenty-four hours, but the ordeal was hardly over. Three hours had passed since I last spoke with Quint, which most likely meant Sebastian was still on the run. Thank goodness he'd been spotted a safe distance from Sierra Pines. I rested easier knowing that information. If circumstances were different, and even the slightest chance remained he was still in town, I'd have gone with the Bellwethers to the SPACA meeting. Until Sebastian was caught, they weren't safe. None of us were.

Ralph walked down the stairs. "Well, there you are. I assumed no one was at home but me."

I turned and smiled. "I'm your only audience. The Bellwethers left for a SPACA meeting. I believe Brooke is working late on set, not sure where Marianne went, and Dean had a flight to catch earlier this afternoon." I glanced at his carryon bag. "You're leaving as well."

"I'm needed back home. Owen called to say there's a snafu in a major order of ski pants and parkas. He's not quite as proficient with numbers and the business end of things, I'm afraid. Thank goodness he has such a cute face." Ralph winked.

I grinned. "Looks can make a difference."

"Though not the only difference. Seriously, when you meet him, you'll understand what makes me love him so much."

"I'll get to meet him? Does that mean . . .?"

"Yes." His eyes twinkled. "A new store's coming to Sierra Pines. He and I are returning here next week to go over the details. We hope to have a grand opening before Christmas. It's all planned. I've found the perfect store rental, right next to Bagels and Buns. Owen and I are thrilled. This will be such an adventure. And there's more." He clasped my arm and squeezed.

"More? How much more can I take?" I teased.

"Through Gladys, I met the most wonderful group of children at the orphanage. One of them is such a cutie. She's ten and the mirror image of Darla from *Spanky and Our Gang*. That's what Gladys says, and I have to agree. Dark curls, chubby cheeks, and adorable eyes. I pray Owen will love her as much as I do."

"You mean you want to adopt?"

"Absolutely. Owen and I have been considering it for years. Sierra Pines seems like the perfect town to raise a family. If things go well with the store, we'd like to stay here and hire employees to run the Squaw Valley location."

"That's wonderful, Ralph. I now have one more thing to look forward to during the holidays."

"It's official then? You're staying to run the B&B. That's wonderful. I know how much the Bellwethers were hoping you would."

"It took me awhile, but I have to say the B&B, the town, the people, everything here has touched my heart." It was true. I had lots to learn, but, in the meantime, I felt at home. Much more than I ever had in New York.

"Fantastic. Say, I forgot to mention my talk with Lenny Taylor."

"Oh?" I sat on the foyer bench and patted the space next to me. I had a hunch this would turn into a longer conversation.

"Lenny and I have been chatting quite a bit the past few days. Wise to know your neighbors, both at home and at your business. Right? I finally worked up the courage to ask Lenny about his quarrel with Sebastian. You'll never guess. He explained how Julia warned him not to do business with Sebastian because he was a thief and a scoundrel and how she'd discovered some disturbing news about him." His eyes brightened.

"So that's who Lenny was talking about the day we overheard their conversation."

"Lenny claims she planned to present her news about Sebastian at the town council meeting. Their talk happened the week before she passed."

"She never had the chance. Poor Aunt Julia." My voice hitched.

"He wanted to thank her, but then it was too late. So, he figured out another way."

I puzzled over his words for only a moment. "The rosy teacup dogwood?"

Ralph smiled and nodded. "He wanted to make the gesture anonymous so there'd be no fuss. That's the kind of man he is, I guess."

"He must have cared for Julia very much," I said.

"Seems most everyone in Sierra Pines did. Oh, I almost forgot. I was supposed to deliver a message." He tapped his chin with one finger. "Lenny said to tell you he hopes his note helped. Does that make sense?"

"Ha. What do you know?" I explained the warning message slipped into my pocket. "I've been puzzling over it for days." I chuckled. "Lenny Taylor is sure full of surprises."

The doorbell rang. "Must be my ride to the airport." His hand squeezed mine. "You should relax, Ali. Sheriff Sterling will find Sebastian, and all your investigating will help put that heel behind bars, where he belongs."

"Thanks, Ralph. I think we all helped. Anyway, have a safe trip home." I hugged him. Once he stepped outside, I locked the door before heading upstairs. Ralph's news and the unresolved search for Sebastian stirred my emotions. I couldn't sleep, but I could finish what Gladys and I had started by cleaning Julia's room.

The busy, but rather mindless task of sorting and packing her clothes into boxes left me time to sift through my thoughts. It was quiet in the house, other than the shrill whistling of wind outside and the rattling of window panes when it gusted.

The decision I'd made to stay in Sierra Pines and run the B&B hadn't quite sunk in. Maybe not a permanent commitment, but I'd allow myself plenty of time to figure out what I wanted to do with my life. If Quint Sterling figured into my plans, so much the better. I had feelings for him. As far as how strong those feelings might be was something I'd take time to explore. I smiled. Exploring would be fun. I had a hunch he shared my point of view.

My first task would be to make an appointment with the lawyer, Mr. Fenworthy. Next, I'd call my parents and let them down gently. Tell them I'd give managing the B&B a trial run because I enjoyed living here with the Bellwethers and all the wonderful people of Sierra Pines. Maybe I'd hint at a potential romance. Oh, they'd love that part. Most all parents wanted to see their children get married. Not that I was planning marriage. I shivered. I was a long, long way from such a step.

I stacked several boxes in the corner and brushed dust off my jeans. I viewed the dozens of books Julia had kept for herself rather than shelve them in the library. Most were nonfiction titles. Lots of biographies or autobiographies on celebrities. I trailed my finger along the titles and the familiar names. Cary Grant, William Holden, Greta Garbo, Errol Flynn, Jimmy Stewart, Katherine Hepburn, Bogart, Fonda, and the list went on. She'd spent time with them all. Her life had been full and more exciting than most anyone could ever hope to have.

I sniffed then wiped my eyes with the sleeve of my dusty shirt. Backing away from the shelf, I sat on Julia's bed. I'd leave those books where they belonged. Her treasured possessions. No guest would be staying in this room, at least for a while. I'd insist on it.

One idea I promised myself to make a reality, one Julia would love most of all, was getting her journal published. In a way, I had Sebastian to thank. His comment about a contact in publishing being interested in her work might have been a lie, but I was inspired to find out. I'd add emailing publishers to my agenda.

I shuffled a list of to-do items in my head then grabbed my phone to makes notes when a loud crash and what sounded like the shattering of glass came from downstairs. I dropped the phone and clutched my throat. "Good grief." I hiccupped and a nervous titter escaped my mouth.

With those strong winds, I'd worried all day there'd be damage. The windows were decades old, the frames cracked, and they needed replaced. I'd add that to my already overwhelming list. If one of them had broken, there'd be a nasty mess to clean.

As I reached the second floor, the lights flickered. I cursed under my breath. As if the house answered, the flickering popped and crackled like a grand finale of fireworks then faded. "Crap." I glared at the dark.

I waved my arm out to the side, feeling for the wall. When my hand touched, I took slow steps backward until I reached the hall closet. I remembered the flashlight stored on the middle shelf. I hadn't the slightest idea where the fuse box was located, though I assumed it was in the basement. No way I was going anywhere near the basement. Not while this felt like a true-to-life scene in Ollie's favorite scary movie, *Night of the Living Dead* or even Gladys's, *The Haunting*. Not a chance.

Gripping the railing in one hand, the flashlight in the other, I stepped slowly down the stairs. The cold winter chill shivered through me as I reached the foyer. The front door slammed against the wall, thrown wide open. Squalls of snow flew inside, leaving wet puddles on the floor as it melted. Sparkling pieces of broken glass lay scattered next to the table where a vase had stood.

I zigzagged a path around the glass to reach the door and shoved it closed. At least there were no broken windows, which, when I considered the situation, shouldn't be at the top of my list of worries. I'd locked the door. I was sure I had. Locked it because I was alone in the house.

Everything around me grew quiet, which made the sound of my heartbeat pound like an explosion of several cannons that would break through my chest any second. The bottom of my bare feet slid on wet flooring, and I slowed to catch my balance. I'd been in too much of a hurry to get downstairs and forgot my shoes. What if I touched a livewire and electrocuted myself? Moving toward the kitchen, I clutched the flashlight in both hands and pushed my mind to think of something else. *Mop the floor. Call Gladys. Find the fuse box. Fix the problem. You're a B&B owner, so toughen up, Winston.* My breath rattled.

I neared the kitchen. The utility closet was located to the left. I hoped the mop was stored in there. If Gladys and Ollie came home early, stepped into a darkened foyer, they might slip on the wet floor and fall. I couldn't allow that to happen. That was the practical me talking. The emotional me shouted to run and hide. My teeth chattered. *I know I locked the front door.* Those words poked at my brain and stuck in my head.

"Is anybody here? Gladys? Ollie?" I called out. If they were, wouldn't one of them have announced it or come to find me? At the very least I'd hear a noise, any noise.

The flashlight flickered. I shook it and the beam held steady once more. I stood outside the kitchen doorway and panned the room with my light to search for the closet. The shuffle of footsteps pattered on the floor and broke the silence. My arm froze. The footsteps sounded close, only several feet away. I twisted my hand and brought the beam of the flashlight front and center. It played off the back door leading out to the porch. The flashlight flickered again. I cursed and hit the casing against my hand until the light brightened and the beam focused on the person standing directly ahead.

# CHAPTER NINETEEN

I GASPED. "IT CAN'T BE." THE WORDS trembled from my lips as I steadied the flashlight.

"I was expecting no one would be at home." Sebastian sneered. He waved his arm, and his hand clutched a gun. "Of course, always come prepared for any scenario, I say. All the greats in the business know the tricks of improv. Your aunt certainly did." He stepped farther into the kitchen and closer to me.

Despite the tremors of fear, I held the flashlight steady. "You can't be here. Quint told me deputies spotted you in the next county." Why did I state the obvious? I moved one foot backward and followed with the other. Instinctive. Reflexive. Primal desperation to survive meant distancing myself, but it didn't matter. He was the one with the gun.

Sebastian used his free hand to shield his eyes and avoided answering my question. "Lower that flashlight, would you?"

"I don't think so. What I suggest is for you to turn around and leave. The Bellwethers will be home any minute now, and Sheriff Sterling is stopping by for a visit." An edginess tempered my voice.

Sebastian let go of an easy chuckle. "I doubt that. I know all the guests are away from the house. You see, I leave nothing to chance. I'm much too smart to make mistakes. As for the Bellwethers, I passed them on my way here. And Sheriff Sterling? I'm sure he's too busy coordinating my capture. He hardly has time this evening for a casual visit." He shifted his gaze back and forth across the kitchen.

He searched for something, and I had a strong hunch what that something might be. "Why come back here? You had every chance of getting away. Returning to Sierra Pines makes no sense." With any luck, as long as I kept the light on him, he couldn't see me. I traced my fingers along the wall until I touched the closet door. If I moved slowly, maybe he wouldn't notice. I dropped my hand from the knob, remembering how the hinges squeaked. Ollie had promised to oil them soon. I'd be taking a risk, not knowing if he'd done the job. I had to move on to plan B, or was it C? My head exploded, desperate to think of ways out of this. Turn off the flashlight, run back to my room, lock the door, and call Quint. That was if I didn't stumble, trip on the stairs, or run into a wall. This power outage was both a blessing and a curse.

Sebastian moved closer to the cupboards. He kept the gun aimed at me while opening and closing cabinet doors. "I underestimated your aunt. If it wasn't for that babbling idiot Beale, I might have never known. He bragged how clever Julia was, how my criminal deed would be broadcasted all over YouTube. Of course, I thought his comment was nonsense, but then the thought occurred to me journals don't end up on YouTube." He turned to face me and waved the gun. "I pressed, told him it was in his best interest to cooperate, but the fool refused to hand over the video or the journal. Why do people keep making things difficult for me? You had to get in my way. If I'd had more time to search her room and the rest of the house . . ." He narrowed his eyes. "Yes, I drove nearly two hours then circled back to Sierra Pines. I doubt those morons with badges noticed. They're probably halfway to Mexico by now. Anyway, I can't leave without that video."

I rubbed the top of my head as if the wound hadn't healed. "The video isn't here. Quint has it." I trembled as he narrowed his eyes into angry slits, but I kept going. "Too bad. Right? I'm sure you would've liked to destroy the evidence. Then there'd be no proof you intended to kill my aunt." I threw back my shoulders and clenched my jaw. I was furious and full of contempt, which powered my confidence. "I'll say it again. Leave. Maybe if you're lucky, you can still outrun the authorities."

"Oh, I'll outrun them." He wagged the gun at me. "I'll make sure of it. Still, I do like to stack the odds in my favor. Leaving no witnesses behind seems like a wise decision. Don't you think?"

I shivered, and my finger hovered near the flashlight's power switch. It had come down to plan B, C, or whichever. Lights out and run for my life. Literally. I waited until he raised his arm and pointed. I squeezed my eyes shut for a second then flipped the flashlight switch, blanketing the kitchen and hallway in darkness. I pivoted on both heels and tried for a zigzag path down the hall, expecting bullets to fly, only they didn't. No pop of a gunshot. No wiz of bullets. The sound I heard came as more of a thud, followed by a moan, which pulled me to a halt. Maybe not wise to do, but I stopped halfway to the staircase and listened.

"Ali, are you all right?"

My knees weakened, and I gripped the wall to steady myself. "Ollie? Oh, thank goodness." I powered on the flashlight and aimed the beam toward the kitchen. As if fate lent a hand, the house lights flickered on. I blinked until my eyes adjusted. "Oh, my word." I rolled back on my heels.

Sebastian lay sprawled out on the floor. Standing next to him was Ollie with the garden shovel in his hands.

"Ollie?" Guess he'd gotten his pound of flesh after all. With an unsteady gait, I walked to the kitchen.

Gladys suddenly appeared in the doorway with her phone slapped to one ear. "Yes. That's right. Sierra Pines B&B." She looked down and cast a vicious smile at the unconscious Sebastian. "And you better send the EMTs. Thank you." She hung up, the scary grin still in place. "Though why anyone would want to help that despicable creature is beyond me." In the next second, she ran over and grabbed me in a bear hug, her head tucked nicely under my chin. "Oh, Alexis. We were so frightened for you. I told Ollie it was Sebastian's car we passed. He didn't believe me at first."

"Then I figured, why take a chance?" Ollie chimed in. "So, I turned the car around and came back. Have to say, I'm sure glad we did." His fingers thumped the handle of his shovel and peered at Sebastian. "Sure glad."

I cringed at the smile on his face. Like a sinister carving on a jack-o-lantern, the expression hinted at evil thoughts. Not that Ollie was evil. However, he was the eye-for-an-eye kind of man.

"Well, I'm extremely grateful you did." I patted Gladys on the shoulders and sniffed. A misty layer covered my eyes.

Ollie glared at the unconscious Sebastian. "He came back for the video, didn't he?"

My jaw dropped. "Yes, but how did you know?" I relayed what I learned from my conversation with Sebastian. "He was the one who broke into the B&B and Julia's room and then knocked me out." I winced and rubbed my head again.

"We figured Julia told Thaddeus she planned to film her meeting with Sebastian. After all, she shared most everything with the man. God rest her soul. It makes total sense." Ollie leaned the shovel against the table before taking a seat. "Gladys and I have been piecing this together ever since you told us about Sebastian's confession to Beale's murder."

"It's quite simple, Alexis." Gladys chimed in. "Sebastian needed a better reason to silence Thaddeus. He could skate by the evidence of his shady past and wiggle out of it somehow. Maybe he counted on that bit of luck. But this video? This dealt with murder. Or the intention of committing one."

"The evidence in Julia's video must have been what pushed him. Sebastian couldn't let that get into the sheriff's hands. When Thaddeus refused to cooperate, I guess that was enough to send Tubble over the edge. So, he killed the poor man," Ollie said.

I shuddered. *Leave no witnesses.*

"At this point, none of it matters," Ollie added and nodded at Sebastian. "He tried to kill you, and we're your witnesses."

The high-pitched wail of sirens blasted out front and then cut off. At once, footsteps pounded up the walk and the front door broke open. I moved aside as two EMTs carrying a gurney rushed by me. I stared in silence while one checked for a pulse. Once they'd locked Sebastian's head in a brace, they laid him on the gurney and carried him outside. Quint passed them as he rushed into the house. One glimpse at me and he smiled.

My breath quivered as my body shook from top to toe. Whether from shock or relief, I wasn't sure, but I took a seat in the closest chair before I passed out. Even though the ordeal was over, I'd exhausted all my energy because of it, and the sharp image of Sebastian pointing that gun at me didn't help.

Quint sat next to me and covered my hands with his. "I'm sure glad you're okay. Wouldn't want anything to happen to you because . . ."

"Because you're getting used to having me around and you'd miss all of our arguments and insults?" I teased.

"*Your* insults, and yes, exactly that." He tweaked my nose.

I squeezed his hand and held on to it. "Thank you. Now, you can take care of business and arrest Sebastian, right?"

He nodded. "Yes. Now, I can. The coroner faxed over his report to my office this evening. Sebastian might believe he covered his tracks, but you've got to love forensic science."

I smiled. "He found evidence it was Sebastian, didn't he?"

"Lots of evidence. Traces of blood matching both Thaddeus's and Sebastian's DNA."

I blinked. "You'd need a DNA sample from both. How did that happen?"

"Oh, a certain lady had the wisdom to deliver Sebastian's water glass to us." He pointed at Gladys.

"Not so difficult to do when the person is unsuspecting." Gladys winked.

I laughed. "I think you missed your calling, Gladys Bellwether. You and Ollie both should've opened your own detective agency."

"Hardly. This has been tiring and much too stressful." Gladys turned to Ollie. "Isn't that right, Ollie?"

Ollie stuck his head in the fridge and pulled out a platter of sandwiches. "Oh, I don't know. I sure enjoyed clobbering that rascal over the head with the shovel. Quite the adrenaline rush."

"Well, I'm just glad you're here with me, helping to run this place."

"You mean?" Gladys rounded her eyes.

"Yes, I'll be staying." My glance lingered on Quint. "For a while at least. I'll give this place a chance and see how I like running a B&B."

"And the people?" Quint's voice softened. "Will you give them a chance?"

"Yes, and the people." I smiled and winked.

The house phone rang. Gladys jumped out of her seat. "I wonder who'd be calling this late." She hurried out to the parlor, calling over her shoulder, "Julia must be full of happiness to hear you're staying. Now she can finally rest in heavenly peace."

My brows lifted.

"Don't you worry. Gladys is as sane as the rest of us," Ollie said.

"I have another bit of news." Quint chuckled.

"What's that?" I propped one elbow on the table and cradled my chin in the palm of my hand.

"Brooke Seale. Turns out she trashed the production building."

"Brooke? Why?" I sat up straight.

"She refused to say but get this. O'Neil announced he won't press charges. Says it's bad P.R. for the movie. What do you make of that?"

"Well, I don't know." I paused to consider an explanation. "Maybe . . . nah. I haven't a clue." But I did. Sort of. The story involved three key players: Nina, Brooke, and Tom O'Neil. However, that was as much as I wanted to think about it.

Gladys rushed back into the kitchen, her face flushed with the effort. "That was Mr. Dunleavy. He and his wife managed to catch another flight after theirs was cancelled, and they'll be here within the hour." She twirled back and forth. "Oh dear. We weren't expecting them until tomorrow afternoon. I need to put fresh linens and towels in their room." She walked down the hall. "Scented soap. Lavender is what Mr. Dunleavy told me his wife likes. Oh, and the chocolates. I can't forget the chocolates. The box is in the pantry." She retraced her steps to the kitchen. "Ollie? Why are you still sitting there? We have work to do. Go sweep the porch. Put down salt if it's needed. We can't have our guests slipping on icy pavement, can we?" She grabbed the box of chocolates and left.

I laughed and shook my head. "Maybe I should go and help her."

"Sit still. Gladys is in her element. There'll be plenty of opportunity to help, now that you're staying on." Ollie stood. "Well, guess I'd better hurry along and sweep that walk. You two have a, eh em, pleasant conversation." Ollie blushed and limped out of the kitchen.

I tipped my head to one side. "What in the world has gotten into that man, blushing like that?"

"Isn't it obvious?" Quint leaned closer to me.

"Obvious? What are you . . .?" I never had the chance to finish.

His lips touched mine and lingered while his hands stroked my arms. That warm glow I'd been craving spread from top to bottom and left me tingling with excitement.

When he drew away, he smiled. "Let's say this is me making an effort to help."

I grinned. "Me giving you a chance?"

"Yes, exactly that. Is it working?" He snuggled closer.

"Oh, I'd say you're making great progress. And I'm totally enjoying it." I laughed and tweaked his nose this time.

"Alexis," Gladys called from the foyer. "Do you know where I put the new shipment of scented soaps? I can't find them anywhere upstairs."

I shrugged. "Guess I'm needed after all."

Quint stood. "And I have an arrest to make. Dinner tomorrow?"

"I'll call you." I raised on tiptoes and planted a kiss on his cheek. After a lingering glance at Quint, I turned toward the hall. A sense of purpose warmed my heart. I belonged here. I'd never been more at home. Looking up, I smiled. "Don't worry, Aunt Julia. I'll take good care of the B&B. I'll make you proud."

# EPILOGUE

*The Hollywood Star Gossip*

*IT DOESN'T TAKE MUCH TO STIR the pot when it comes to Hollywood gossip, but listen to this, faithful readers. I have something for you that involves no gossip, no hearsay, only the truth. A mystery has been solved. Some of you older fans might remember a small movie company from the eighties called Starlight. Its president and owner was Albert Reynard. And perhaps you'll recall the scandal in which Reynard stole hundreds of thousands from the company and its investors. Well, Reynard had an accomplice. His assistant, Timothy O'Toole, turned out to be an even worse "tool" than Reynard. He helped himself to plenty of the dough and then vanished by the time authorities got wind of his involvement. The search was on, but he was never found. Until recently, that is. O'Toole, better known these days as Sebastian Tubble, has been living in the quaint town of Sierra Pines, nestled in the Sierra Nevada Mountains, enjoying his high-standing role in the community. Oh, and he owns a successful ski resort. How nice for him. Right?*

*However, that's all changed. Tubble, aka O'Toole, sits in jail and awaits sentencing for his crime of embezzlement. Hold on. There's more. And this, my friends, has all the drama of a Hollywood thriller. Trust me. Tubble is also charged with murder. Yes, I said murder. Turns out he was very serious about keeping his identity a secret. Someone confronted Tubble about his scandalous past. We know how tragically the story ended. I have a reliable source from LAPD who claims Tubble shows no remorse and often comments the guy got what he deserved. Well, Sebastian Tubble, we think you'll get what YOU deserve. Next month, Tubble will be delivered to Sierra Pines where he'll stand trial for murder.*

*In other gossip news, camerawoman Brooke Seale has her eye on more than movie scenes. It's rumored Director Thomas O'Neil and Brooke are cast in a more personal and ongoing role, which is surprising since O'Neil has a reputation as a ladies' man. Watch out, Brooke. Time will tell and so will I.*

*Join me tomorrow when I'll be writing about another celeb with ties to Sierra Pines. Dean Thornton, star of daytime soap* The Young and Beautiful*, has plenty to spill about the Tubble murder case and his plan to collaborate with O'Neil and turn the story into a movie, starring—you guessed it—Dean Thornton. In the meantime, Dean has another juicy announcement to make. But let me stop there before I spoil the surprise.*

*Tune in to my web mag tomorrow and learn more about what Dean has to say. Until then . . . see you in the stars.*

*—Tiffany Bertram, the voice of Hollywood*

RETIRED TEACHER, KATHRYN LONG now spends her days plotting and writing mysteries. Her most recent credits are romantic suspense novel *A Deadly Deed Grows,* mystery *Buried In Sin*, and contemporary romance *When I Choose.* She's actively involved in the writing and publishing worlds with social media platforms, including her author website, blog, twitter account, and Facebook page. She's a member of Sisters in Crime as well as of International Thriller Writers. Kathryn also writes mysteries under the pseudonym Bailee Abbott. She lives with her husband and furry friend Max in the quiet suburbs of Green, Ohio. www.kathrynlongauthor.com

CPSIA information can be obtained
at www.ICGtesting.com
Printed in the USA
BVHW072345010321
601387BV00004B/133